Sinking
Sand

Prequel to *Sweet Sanctuary*

Sinking Sand

Kim Vogel
A NOVEL
Sawyer

Wings of Hope

Est. 2013

Published by Wings of Hope Publishing Group
Established 2013
www.WingsofHopePublishing.com
Find us on Facebook: Search "Wings of Hope Publishing"

Printed in the United States of America

Library of Congress Cataloging-in-Publication Data

Sawyer, Kim Vogel
Sweet Sanctuary/Kim Vogel Sawyer
Wings of Hope Publishing Group
ISBN-13: 978-1-944309-23-7
ISBN-10: 1-944309-23-3

Cover artwork by Kim Vogel Sawyer.
Typesetting by Vogel Design in Hillsboro, Kansas.

In memory of my aunties

Lois and Vivian,
who wanted the best for those they loved...
which included me

*"…He set my feet on a rock
and gave me a firm place to stand."*

Psalm 61:2 (KJV)

1

Callie Myers

"God, You sure outdid Yourself when You created this corner of the world." Calliope Myers stood on a wide expanse of white sand and gazed across the vast Pacific Ocean. The water of brilliant aqua seemed to stretch forever before meeting the azure blue sky at the horizon line. Cottony puffs of white drifted overhead but were ineffective in obscuring the late afternoon sun, which felt wonderful on her wind-tossed hair. Unable to remain quiet, she laughed. "February, and warm as toast. What a heavenly climate!"

She turned a slow circle, her eyes drinking in every unique feature. Several yards out, rocky outcroppings formed a perfect roost for sea birds who complained noisily and flapped their wings in apparent disgruntlement as the sea sent its spray across their feathers. The sparkling beach gently curved, inviting Callie to explore what would be found around the bend. Beyond the sandy beach, a profusion of foliage began—emerald and jade and deep hunter blending into a breathtaking array of greens with bright splashes of red poinsettias giving the island a Christmassy appearance.

Far upland the Waianae Mountains were covered with thick forests of what she had been told were kukui nut trees. She squinted into the sun, tempted to shield her eyes yet afraid of missing something. Her heart thrilled at the natural beauty, and she laughed again for the sheer pleasure of it.

How lucky she was to be in Hawaii. How fortunate that the opening had come just as she'd finished her nursing training and had been approved for Army service. Providential? Oh, yes. She had thanked God repeatedly since she received notice of her assignment to this idyllic, tropical island, but she figured He wouldn't mind a reiteration of her gratefulness. Throwing her arms wide she aimed her smile at the clouds floating on the expanse of blue. "Thank You, thank You, thank You!"

The answer came in the rolling thunder of the waves as they crashed across the sandy beach and washed back again. Desire to enjoy the water more fully rolled through her. After looking surreptitiously in both directions to be sure she wasn't being observed, she leaned over and tied her skirt in a knot at mid-thigh. Then she splashed into the surf until the waves hit her knees. The force of the water was surprisingly strong, and she braced herself against it, celebrating when she won the battle by remaining upright.

After three strong waves had attempted to push her ashore, propriety beckoned—someone could come along. She should lower her skirt to its more decent level of two inches below her knees. Reluctantly she backed away from the surf, untangled the knot of fabric, and let it fall. The cotton skirt was hopelessly wrinkled, something of which her Aunt Viola and Aunt Vivian would disapprove, but she shrugged, unconcerned about such things when surrounded by God's awesome creation.

Callie smiled as another wave seemed to chase her, washing away her footprints and coursing across her bare feet with a rush of warm foam. The ocean was toying with her. She scampered away from the next rolling wave and managed to escape getting so much as a toe wet. She waved at the receding rush. "Ha-ha! You missed me!"

Still chuckling, she began ambling along the beach, making careful note of her surroundings. Oahu wasn't a large island, but it wouldn't do to become disoriented and thus unable to locate her borrowed Hudson touring car. Around a gentle curve in the shoreline, she discovered a huge fallen tree. It had a skeletal appearance, as stark white as the sand, completely bare of bark. Nothing remotely like it grew anywhere on the island. Where had it come from? It must have washed in from miles away.

Maybe it fell off a Viking ship that had been sent to gather wood to take back to Greenland. She laughed at her own inventiveness. What a ridiculous yet thrilling thought. She sprinted across the sand and clambered up on the log. Smooth as bone and warm from the sun, it felt like satin beneath her bare feet. Once on top, she curled her toes to hold her balance. She turned toward the ocean and raised her arms, welcoming the breeze. She sucked in as much air as she could through her nose, reveling in the scent of crisp salt air, then released the breath with a long, happy sigh.

The joy of the moment spilled over. Her arms still over her head, she posed like a ballerina she had seen on the stage in San Francisco the evening before boarding the ship that brought her to this island. She began dipping and swaying as she hummed, caught up in the pleasure of moving her body. Far up shore, giant philodendrons swayed their elephants' ears in graceful accompaniment to her improvised recital.

Gaining confidence, she attempted a one-toe pirouette. Her foot slipped.

"Oh, no!" She scrambled to regain her footing, arms and legs flailed wildly, but it was no use. She tumbled backwards, sailing through the air for what seemed a lifetime before she landed on her rump and then slammed her head against the ground. Stars exploded in her vision.

Instinctively her legs coiled as the air whooshed from her lungs. She had no more than curled up like an armadillo when someone—or some*thing*—leaped over the log and knelt beside her. Strong hands grabbed her ankles and forced her legs back down. The grabber of her ankles was equipped with arms, legs, and a head, but beyond that she was uncertain of its origin. Its hair stood up wildly and its face and clothing were coated with some sort of black, powdery-looking substance. Whatever it was, she didn't want it touching her. She tried to pull away. A strangled moan left her throat.

"Don't talk. Straighten out your legs. And stop thrashing around."

The voice's timbre indicated it was a man, but what kind of man? She gestured weakly with her arms, her jaw flapping uselessly as she tried to tell the bossy, unrecognizable person to leave her alone. Would she die in front of this thing?

"Relax." One grubby hand pushed at her knees and the other pressed on her shoulder.

She really had no choice but to obey. She couldn't escape those strong arms. Even through the fabric of his dirty shirt, muscles bulged. She forced her body to stop fighting against his restraining hands and slowly the blessed air crept back into her lungs. She might live after all.

He must have sensed her life returning, because he relaxed his hold and sat back on his heels. His gaze roved from head to foot in patent detachment, leaving Callie feeling as if she'd been thoroughly examined and found wanting. Unnerved, she tried to roll away.

"Huh-uh, don't move." The man clamped that strong hand on her shoulder once more. "Keep your arms at your sides. I'm going to roll you onto your left side. Don't try to help me. Let me do the moving." He placed her arms along her sides. Strange how tender his touch when he used such a gruff tone. He rolled her from her back onto her left side, facing away from him. He kept one hand under her jaw to support her head. "Lie still." His nimble fingers explored the back of her head impersonally but expertly. "Does this hurt?"

Callie was able to see him if she turned her eyes sharply to the right. "Only when you touch it."

He frowned. At least, she thought he frowned. The black powder across his broad forehead shifted slightly. "Don't be a smart aleck. I can't help you if you won't cooperate." His fingers slowly shifted in increments from the base of her skull toward her shoulder blades, working their way along her spine the way a person might work the keys of a piano. "How old are you?"

It really wasn't any of his business, but she sensed he was a person who brooked no nonsense. She didn't dare to cross him. "Twenty-three."

"I would never have guessed you a day over twelve the way you were prancing across that log." He continued his perusal with his fingertips. "Do you have any common sense at all?"

He was now exploring the small of her back and his touch left her feeling tingly. To combat the uneasy feelings, she said tartly. "It had nothing to do with common sense. I was happy and I felt like dancing, so I danced. How old are you? You must be at least ninety because I've heard that very old people become quite cranky, and I've never met anyone as cranky as you."

He stopped his examination and leaned forward to look directly into her eyes. His eyes were snapping but the muscles in his cheeks twitched. Was he preparing to explode with laughter or anger? Completely defenseless and at the mercy of whatever he would choose to do, her heart began to pound in sudden trepidation. She had spunk, but seeing his eyes flash with restrained emotion, her courage wavered.

"Cranky? Well, perhaps I am." His stern gaze held her captive. "But I'm only cranky"—the sparkle in his dark eyes led her to believe he was forcing a severity into his tone that he didn't really mean—"when I'm required to stop my own work to take care of silly little girls who go dancing across unsafe surfaces and end up falling on their heads."

Callie decided he wasn't as dangerous as his fierce appearance originally suggested. "I am not a little girl, and I didn't fall on my head. I landed on my bottom, and if you want to know the truth, that's where it really hurts."

Now it appeared he was biting the inside of his cheeks. So it was humor he was hiding, not anger. The thought pleased her.

His Adam's apple visibly bobbed with a swallow. "Well." He cleared his throat. "At least you used good judgment there. Your...bottom...is a much safer spot on which to land."

"Easy for you to say." She wasn't about to tell this filthy stranger, but her tailbone was throbbing. She would probably have to sleep on her stomach tonight.

"I don't believe you've damaged yourself seriously. Let's get you on your feet." His tone had lost its rough edge. He rose and took hold of her arm as he spoke. Placing his other arm around her back, he slowly drew her to her feet.

Dizziness struck her, and she grabbed his dingy shirt front for support. She gasped as she felt something tear, and she knew if she pulled her hand away she'd be holding one of his buttons. Her face heated, but she kept her fist coiled tightly around the fabric and pretended she hadn't noticed anything unusual.

His stabilizing arm remained around her waist as he helped her find her balance. "Are you steady enough to walk?"

She put a shaky hand to her head. "I must have bounced my noggin harder than I thought. I do feel a bit muddled." Was the knock on the head or the present company causing her lightheadedness? Was this disorienting feeling what aunties Viv and Vi had warned her about?

He scanned the beach in both directions. "How did you get down here?"

"I borrowed a car from a friend. I left it…over there." She waved in the general northward direction. When he turned to look, she quickly tucked his button in her skirt pocket.

He swiveled his gaze back to peer down at her from his impressive height. "I'll help you return to your vehicle, and if necessary I will drive you to your lodgings so you can rest."

Callie shook her head. "Not to be rude, but I don't want you anywhere near my lodgings or the vehicle I borrowed." Smudges of the black dust that coated him now decorated her white cotton dress. "Why on earth are you so filthy? Have you been digging for diamonds?"

"I would imagine that would be a waste of time." He gave himself a quick perusal and frowned. "I do see your point." He bit the inside of his upper lip, his brow puckering. "If you prove to me as we walk that you are capable of driving yourself, I won't put a foot inside your vehicle, but I would feel safer if I escorted you to it. You don't seem completely steady on your feet."

She wanted to protest, but she knew he was right. "Oh, all right." She made no attempt to curb her churlish tone. "I drove my friend's Hudson through the Kolekole Pass and left it at the end of the road."

He nodded as if he knew exactly where she meant. They began moving in that direction. He sent her a speculative look. "You walked quite a distance on your bare feet."

She shrugged, offering a self-conscious smile. "The sand looked so inviting I had to feel it between my toes. So I left my shoes in the car."

"The sand may look inviting, but there are sharp rocks and broken shells. It isn't safe to go so far on bare feet. I'll trust you to use more wisdom in the future."

Wasn't he the bossy one? She swallowed a sharp retort. They continued walking, her steps stilted partly due to a dull ache in her lower back and partly due to embarrassment. She made a vow to never again emulate ballerinas on washed up logs.

After a lengthy silence he cleared his throat. "Where are you staying on the island?"

Would he find fault with her lodgings, too? "I'm sharing an apartment in Grant Hall."

He stopped abruptly, forcing her to stop, too. "You're staying in the nurses' quarters at Schofield?" His question made her feel as if she was part of an inquisition. Did he think she was a German spy?

"Well, yes, they allow that if you're a nurse." She intentionally chose a tone one would use with a rather dull-witted child.

"You are a nurse?"

His incredulity undid her. She plunked her fist on her hip. "Yes, as a matter of fact, I am. Why do you seem so surprised?"

He released a derisive snort as he started them in motion once more. "I assume a nurse would have more sense than what you exhibited by your lengthy barefoot stroll and that impromptu performance on a slippery log."

Now it was her turn to stop. He'd been watching her? To

cover her embarrassment, she drew on anger. "You know, I've had just about enough of your references to my lack of sense. Just because you've never felt the urge to throw caution to the wind and give vent to the enjoyment of God's beautiful creation doesn't mean—"

He held up both hands as if under arrest. "Okay, okay, Miss Joyful, I won't criticize you again."

She raised her right eyebrow, crossed her arms, and pursed her lips.

"Scout's honor."

She *humphed.* "You probably never even were a Boy Scout."

He tucked his arm behind her back and nudged, getting them moving again. "Why would you think a terrible thing like that?" He placed a filthy hand against his shirt front and peered down at her with his brows furrowed.

She ignored his pretense of being wounded. "Because a Boy Scout would have more sense than to cover himself from head to toe in soot." She peeked at him out of the corner of her eyes. "That is soot covering you, isn't it?"

He shrugged and sent her a lopsided grin that made her heart flop. "Okay, you're right. I never was a Boy Scout, and this is soot on my clothes."

"And your face," Callie informed him with relish.

"Well, of course. It needs to be everywhere."

Curiosity got the best of her. "What on earth for?"

"Mosquitoes. They're terrible here, but they won't bite through soot."

She laughed. "I can see why. They probably can't even tell that you're human. I was left wondering about it myself."

He didn't laugh, but she was sure she saw amusement spark in his eyes. They were incredible eyes, too, she noticed now that he was losing his crustiness. Deep navy blue around the outer rim of the irises turning a bright sapphire in the center, surrounded by thick, coal black lashes. The ebony of his pupils only served to showcase the intensity of his irises. What did the rest of his face look like? She couldn't make out his features under the coating of powder, yet for the moment it was enough to gaze into the endless depths of those breathtakingly charming eyes.

They reached the Hudson she'd borrowed from her roommate—the walk back had seemed much longer than the walk to the shore, thanks to her aching head and backside—and he gallantly opened the driver's door for her. She slid in and adjusted her skirt to cover her knees.

His forehead pinched. "Will you be all right to drive?"

His obvious concern touched Callie. "Yes. And thank you for your help."

"You're welcome." He backed away from the car by inches. "When you get to your apartment, put some ice on the bump on your head, and"—she was sure he was battling laughter—"perhaps sit on some as well."

Heat crept up her neck.

"If you experience any more dizziness, or if you feel tingling in your limbs, make sure you see one of the base doctors."

Giving orders again. She saluted. "Yes, sir."

One more quick flash of a smile in his eyes, and then without another word he turned and began trotting back down the beach. He'd gone about twenty yards when she suddenly realized something. She cupped her hands beside her mouth. "Wait!"

He continued jogging in place as he turned.

"I forgot to ask… What's your name?"

He lifted a hand in farewell, then turned and dashed away.

Disappointed, she slammed the door of the Hudson and

released a sigh. She reached into her pocket and withdrew the button. There were some strange scratchings on it. She lifted it, tilting it toward the light, and made out the initials *M.H.*

A clue. She would do some investigating. He was obviously a doctor—his expertise in caring for her had given him away. And he was obviously military. Someone that bossy had to have been through army training. On a base of Schofield's size, surely she'd be able to find the doctor whose initials were M.H. When she located him, she'd find out his name, and somehow she'd find an opportunity to spend more time gazing into those eyes. Because she was very interested in knowing this mystery man much better.

2

Holden continued jogging until he reached the tiny shack situated well above the beach on the east slope of the Waianae Range. Surrounded by ferns and palms and an assortment of other lush tropical foliage, it was a perfect vantage point. He could see everything happening below, but he was nearly invisible to anyone standing on the beach looking upward. He chuckled as he replayed the scene of the girl dancing on the log. How free and uninhibited she had looked in her graceful exhibition. And—he released an amused snort—how ridiculous when falling. Like an octopus rolling downhill. At least she hadn't seriously injured herself. She'd be stiff tomorrow, no doubt, but not too much the worse for wear.

He stepped into the murky depths of the small, square, ramshackle shelter built long ago by some unknown islander. When he had stumbled upon the sad-looking hovel with the weather-eaten thatch roof a few weeks ago, he'd bypassed it, not wanting to intrude into someone's private retreat. However, over time he had realized that whoever built it had obviously abandoned it, and he decided to adopt it as his own secret hideaway. Filthy, windowless, full of spider webs and dust, smelling like neglect, it would take elbow grease and a considerable amount of time to make it a pleasant place to use, but what else did he have but time? The rare illnesses that required his attention were few and far between at this peaceful island paradise. He needed something mind-consuming and physically taxing to fill the aimless hours. Restructuring the shack was a perfect outlet for his restless energy.

He returned to the task he had begun before the joy-filled laughter had intruded into his privacy. The vent pipe for the rusty iron stove still hung crazily from the ceiling, just as he'd left it when he'd gone to investigate the happy ruckus from down on the beach. Of course, now he could put his eye to it like a telescope and see blue sky overhead. The trapped soot had exploded all over his face and clothing when he'd foolishly tapped on it earlier. But the goal had been to clean it out, and he had accomplished that.

Holden wedged the pieces of pipe together again. It was too warm for a fire, but the only way to find out if the stove functioned properly was to try it. So he headed outside and scrounged for dried grass, leaves, and twigs with which to build a small fire. Straightening with his hands full of tinder, he let his gaze skitter down the beach to the sun-bleached log where the girl had danced. His mind's eye replayed the red glint of her curls under the sun and the lithe movements of her trim body.

The memory of her green eyes blazing with indignation appeared. If she was one of the base nurses, why hadn't he noticed her before? He shook his head in private amusement, recalling her reaction as he had bounded over that log. He hadn't known eyes could grow so wide—almost as big as saucers. And her feistiness in spite of her obvious fear impressed him. No shrinking violet, that one.

Twenty-three, she'd said she was. She appeared younger, especially compared to his thirty-one years. From a distance she'd had the appearance of a child who'd been hard at play all afternoon. But when he'd put his arm around her to assist her to her feet, he'd been left with no doubt that she was definitely a woman under that rumpled, dirt-streaked dress. An incredibly attractive woman, at that. Where had she been hiding herself? And why was he woolgathering?

He snapped himself to attention and stalked into the shack. Squatting on the balls of his feet, he thrust his handfuls of tinder into the belly of the old stove and then reached into his shirt pocket for a small packet of matches. Striking one, he recoiled as the match flared, sending out the sharp odor of sulfur. He placed his free hand over his nose to shield himself from the acrid smell and the unhappy memories the scent summoned as he tossed the match into the stove. He peered in. The match missed the pile of tinder and landed harmlessly on the rusted bottom of the stove where it fizzled and died.

Grunting with displeasure, he removed a second match and swished it across the rough side of the box. A quick flash of fire and another strong whiff of sulfur. He gritted his teeth and made himself carefully place the burning match on the pile of grass and twigs. This time it took, the flame licking across the surface of the grass first and then catching the leaves and twigs until a small but steady flame grew.

Holden remained on his haunches, watching the dancing yellow and orange tongues of fire greedily consume the small pile of twigs. Smoke snaked out from the open door, filling his nostrils and throat. Then, like firecrackers exploding, memories burst free. A cloud of smoke... Shooting flames from the roof of a house... From his house... And in the crackling of the tiny blaze he thought he heard the echoes of the frantic cries of his wife and son...

Wham!

He slammed the iron door of the stove with such force it bounced against the body and sprang open again. The stove vibrated briefly, the iron ringing, hurting his ears. But the memory had been scared away. His hand shook as he made himself take hold of the door gently and hook its rusty latch. He concealed the fire from his vision, but he hadn't trapped the smoke. White-gray wisps of it seeped from around the edges of the door.

He waved his hands at the coiling wisps. Then he remembered the flue. He rose and turned the lever on the stove's pipe. To his relief, the amount of smoke creeping from the edges lessened. He ran his hand through his soot-covered hair. Maybe starting a fire wasn't such a good idea, but he had to see if the stove would draw. If he planned to cook out here, he'd need a functional stove.

He took a few deep breaths, bringing his racing heartbeat under control. He examined the vent pipe. No smoke sneaked from the seams. Stepping outside, he observed the thin trail of smoke heading skyward from the protruding end of the pipe. All seemed to work perfectly. In that case, the fire was no longer needed.

He hurried inside and scanned the shack for something with which to carry water. An old tin can lay in one corner. He snatched it up. Rust had eaten a small hole in the bottom, but he'd be able to dam that with a finger. Can in hand, he trotted down the hill to the beach where he filled it with water from the rising tide, then climbed back up more slowly to avoid spilling. Once inside the shack, he used his shirt tail to protect his fingers and gingerly opened the door of the stove. Crouching before the opening, he threw the contents of the can on the small flame. The fire sizzled and then sputtered and died, sending forth a thin coil of smoke that went straight up the vent pipe. He imagined it floating harmlessly away over the roof of the shack. He sighed. He'd put it out.

If only the memories would float away and dissipate as thoroughly as the veil of smoke from a dying blaze.

His head dropped low as sorrow weighed him down once more. It had been over four years since he'd lost Lorna and Timothy. Four years of moving from hospital to hospital, searching for a place where he could finally erase the remembrances of his time as a husband and father. Yet there were moments when the pain of remembrance stabbed as fiercely as the day of his loss. How long would it take before time healed this wound?

Lorna had been so beautiful—the ideal wife. Small and graceful and ever so gracious. She possessed the ability to light up a room simply by entering it. Men always stared in admiration at her when she walked by, and women peered down their noses in envy until her infectious friendliness won them over. He'd been so proud to walk beside her, to hear people greet her as Mrs. Winters. Their happiness together was made more complete with the arrival of little Timothy. The baby seemed to be born with his mother's sunny disposition. He'd looked like her, too, with his blonde hair that curled in little ringlets behind his perfect ears and huge blue eyes that never missed anything. Lorna predicted that Timmy would be the second generation doctor in the family.

He could close his eyes and picture them so clearly—Lorna and Timmy, his wife and son—standing in the open doorway of their home, waiting for him when he returned from his rounds at the Chicago hospital. Lorna always in her pearls and heels, her dress perfectly pressed. When he teased her about her formal attire, she said his coming home was a cause for celebration. In her arms would be Timmy with his dimpled hands reaching for his daddy while he grinned his two-tooth smile and chortled with glee.

Unconsciously Holden put out his hands, his face relaxed into a smile of coming-home-again, reaching toward the memory of his son in his wife's arms…

"Holden?"

The voice jarred him rudely back to reality. He dropped his arms as his eyes popped open, and he cursed under his breath as Lorna and Timothy slipped away. He stepped into the slanting shadows outside the shack.

"Hey, buddy, where are you?"

Holden recognized the caller—his friend Micah, down on the beach, obviously wondering why Holden hadn't returned from his jog. He glanced at the watch on his wrist and muttered another mild oath. He'd completely lost track of time. Between the fire and that girl…

Keeping low, Holden circled behind the shack and ran east along the slope about ten yards. He came down through the foliage and onto the shore where Micah could easily spot him. He waved, and Micah's face broke into a smile of relief.

"There you are." Micah smacked the back of Holden's shoulder as he came to a stop beside him. "When you didn't meet me at the car, I wondered if a snake had gotten you."

"Snake?" Holden grinned, pretending to pant to keep up the pretense of a long jog. "You know snakes aren't indigenous to this island."

Micah shrugged. "Neither were mosquitoes, but somehow they found their way here." As if to prove his words, one of the pesky insects in question landed brazenly on Micah's arm and received a firm swat for its trouble. Micah circled a finger against his thumb and flicked the dead bug from his forearm as the two men turned toward Kolekole Pass. Micah always parked there when meeting Holden after one of his jogs along the beach.

"So…" Micah looked Holden up and down as they walked side by side, leaving sets of footprints in the moist sand, "You going to tell me how you managed to get so dirty jogging?"

Holden groaned inwardly. He'd forgotten about the soot.

"Yep, must've been a rough jog." Micah pointed at Holden's shirt front. "Not only are you dirtier than I've ever seen you, you're missing a button."

He was? Holden pulled his shirt away from his chest and gawked at the tear. When had that happened?

"If I didn't know better, I'd say you attended some sort of *wild luau*"—Micah drawled out the words in an exaggerated Texas twang—"and rolled through the fire pit instead of jogging today."

Holden laughed. Micah's sense of humor was one of the things he admired most. Although the two men had only become acquainted in the past year and a half, they'd developed a brotherly kinship. On more than one occasion, they'd been mistaken for brothers with their similar coloring and stature. However, they were far different in temperament. Holden tended to be serious where Micah was always looking for a reason to laugh, but they complimented one another well and had an excellent work rapport, which they needed since they shared leadership at the Schofield Station Hospital.

Micah arched his brow, waiting for an answer. Holden shook his head. "I'm sorry to disappoint you, my friend, but I found no *wyald loo-ows*." He imitated Micah's southern drawl. "But I do intend to hunt up a shower when we get back."

"Mmm-hmm." Micah gave Holden a sideways look that said he wasn't thrilled about having his question go unanswered. "Sounds like a good plan." They reached Micah's beloved '36 Ford Coupe which had been shipped over especially for Micah's use a little over three months ago. Micah held out his hand as Holden reached for the door handle. "Whoa there, buddy. Before you get in, brush yourself off good."

Holden remembered the girl's reluctance to allow him to touch her vehicle, and a grin tugged at his lips. He stepped a few feet away from the coupe, bent forward at the waist, and rapidly swished his hands through his hair. Amazing how much soot drifted out. Then he took off his shirt and banged it against a rock a few times. He held it at arm's length. Still pretty dingy. He turned it inside-out and put it on. He turned to Micah and held out his arms in silent query.

Micah scowled, but he nodded, and both men climbed into the car. Micah made an expert three-corner turn-around and headed toward the officers' quarters which housed the medical staff. Holden rolled down the window and allowed the breeze to ruffle his hair, his mind running idly over things he would need to do to make the shack habitable. Wash down the walls, repair the roof, sweep the floor and board up any holes around the foundation…

Micah nudged Holden's shoulder. "Home, buddy. Hop out."

Holden reached for the latch, but then he remembered something. "Hey, Micah, did we get some new nurses in the past couple days?"

Micah grinned. "Why, Holden Winters, I didn't know you cared."

Holden swung the door wide and slid out. "Sorry I asked."

Micah's amused chuckle erupted, which Holden chose to ignore as he slammed the door and headed toward his bungalow. Micah dashed out and moved into Holden's pathway, forcing him to stop. He glowered at his friend.

"Now, don't get your dander up." A slanted grin creased Micah's face. "You asked about nurses…" He scratched his chin. "Yeah, as a matter of fact, I think I did hear that a boatload arrived this morning on the SS *Washington*. A dozen or so, although I think we only got two or three here at Schofield. Why?"

"Oh, no reason, really." Holden offered a too-casual shrug and mumbled, "Just thought I saw someone new on the beach earlier today."

Micah's eyes lit. "By someone, you mean a *she*-someone?"

Holden frowned. "Don't get any wild ideas. It was just an idle question."

"Yeah, yeah." Micah thrust out his lower jaw and gazed at Holden through narrowed lids. "The impenetrable Holden Winters wouldn't go beyond idle questions. Might prove that he's human after all."

"Knock it off, Hatcher."

Someone else might have been cowed by the gruff warning, but not Micah. Holden alternately admired and bemoaned the fact that Micah didn't back down from his growls. Micah grinned. "Sure, buddy, I'll knock it off. But I think it's a great sign that you're asking about someone you saw on the beach today, even if it is just an idle question."

Holden read the sympathy hiding behind Micah's impudence. In a moment of weakness he'd divulged the loss of his wife and son. Micah had encouraged him to get on with living and build a new family, but it wasn't that simple. Holden hadn't told Micah everything, nor did he intend to. There were some things he'd never confess. And he'd never put himself in the position of losing someone he cared so deeply about—not ever again.

Micah gave him another companionable sock on the shoulder, then looked at his hand in mock dismay. "Buddy, you really need that shower. And now so do I. What say we meet at the mess hall in an hour or so and get some grub? Maybe take a gander at the new arrivals."

His grin was so ornery, despite himself Holden released a brief snort of laughter. "Micah, you are incorrigible."

"Yep, I know. So are we on?"

Holden's earlier irritation melted in light of Micah's unconquerable good humor. "We're on. See you in an hour."

Micah turned with a cheerful wave of his broad hand. Holden hurried on to his bungalow to wash away the remnants of soot and let the steaming spray of water clear his mind of the memories of the afternoon. But as he stood within that swirling fog of steam, the image of the girl dancing with such carefree abandonment on the beach appeared again.

3

CALLIE

"Callie, are you ready to find some supper?"

Callie had been penning a letter at the small writing desk in the corner of the room she shared with Lydia Eldredge, but at her roommate's query, she shifted and looked over her shoulder. She broke into a grin at the image of Lydia reflected in the sizable unframed mirror above the wide dresser on the opposite side of the room. Lydia's mouth stretched wide, her lips curled back from her teeth, and she seemed to be giving herself a dental exam.

Callie suppressed a laugh. "What are you doing?"

Lydia's dark eyes barely flickered in Callie's direction. "Checking for lipstick. I hate it when I smile with pink teeth."

Callie shook her head, still chuckling. She'd never met anyone as concerned about her appearance as Lydia seemed to be. They'd been assigned the same cabin on the *SS Washington*, the ship that had transported them to Oahu from California. Despite the differences in their backgrounds the girls had managed to make a connection and decided to continue sharing a room in the nurses' quarters.

Lydia was a beauty, Callie acknowledged without a hint of rancor. Her hair was as black and shiny as a raven's wing, cut short around her ears but longer on top so it poufed attractively over her neatly plucked eyebrows. She had wide-set eyes of velvety brown and incredibly thick lashes tinged in gold. Despite her dark hair and eyes, her skin was as creamy white and unblemished as new fallen snow. Yes, Lydia was unbelievably beautiful. If she had pink teeth, Callie doubted anyone would even notice.

"You would be breathtaking with *green* teeth, Lydia."

"Really?" Lydia acted as if she'd never heard anything remotely like this before.

Callie rolled her eyes. She hoped this roommate of hers wouldn't be one who constantly sought compliments. That would become tiresome. "Yes, really, so stop making faces at yourself."

Lydia turned away from the mirror and crossed to Callie, peeking over Callie's shoulder to the unlined paper on the desk. "Writing a letter to your folks?"

Callie nodded, nibbling the eraser on the pencil thoughtfully, not bothering to explain that her folks were two maiden aunts who had raised her since she was seven.

"Going to tell them about why you're sitting on that pillow?" Lydia's voice took on a teasing note.

Callie had placed her bed pillow on the wooden desk chair before sitting, but if she wiggled she still felt the effects of her clumsy tumble from the log earlier that afternoon.

Lydia had giggled uncontrollably when Callie had come hobbling in about an hour ago and explained the reason for her awkward gait. Perhaps someday Callie would see humor in it, but the discomfort was still too real to find anything laughable about her unexpected spill. She sent Lydia a sharp look. "I'll never get this done—and we'll never get to supper—

if you don't leave me alone and let me finish."

Lydia shrugged and turned away on a trim heel. "Okay. I'll sit over here and let you write. But hurry, huh? I'm hungry."

Callie turned back to her letter. She'd had no trouble briefly describing her journey over and her visit to the beach. She wanted to mention the arrival of her rescuer, but she wasn't sure how to put the mysterious man into words that would meet with her aunts' approval. They were so straitlaced and protective of her.

It had taken some real effort to convince them to allow her to follow through on her conviction to become a part of the Army Nurse Corps. The plan had been set in motion way back in September of '39, when the war in Europe prompted a State of Limited Emergency. Her aunts had balked at the idea, but by October of 1940 she was officially approved through the American Red Cross Training Service. Her best present for Christmas of that year was the notice that she would be working at the Station Hospital on Schofield Barracks on the island of Oahu. Her letter must assure her aunts that she had made the right decision by coming here.

She reread what she'd written so far.

> *Dear Aunties Vi and Viv,*
>
> *After six days at sea I am finally at Schofield Bar-racks. The SS Washington is one of the nicest ships available and we were given first-class accommoda-tions so I have no complaints there. It was rather cold on deck, and at times the water was quite choppy which made me nervous, but I kept praying that we would get here in one piece, and we did.*
>
> *The island of Oahu is beautiful! The base is situ-ated in a basin between two mountain ranges—I ha-ven't learned to spell their names yet, but I will—and*

*there are so many green growing things. It reminds
me of a rain forest. Auntie Viv, poinsettias grow wild
here and are blooming in profusion—I know you
would love to see that. Perhaps I will buy a Brownie
camera at the Post Exchange, or PX as they call it,
and send you some pictures soon.*

*This afternoon I took a long walk along the
beach. The view of the ocean makes one feel terribly
small and yet terribly full all at the same time. I kept
thinking what a marvelous job God did in creating it.
While I was there, I met a man who—*

And that's where she'd stopped. With a scowl she realized
there wasn't anything she could add that would make any
sense at all. Besides, she remembered the promise she had
made to them when the letter informing her of her assignment
to Oahu had arrived.

Should she mention the man at all? What could she say—
she met a man who helped her? She couldn't describe his
appearance, other than dirty with blue eyes. Or give his name,
except for his initials. She pinched up the button from its spot
on the corner of the desk. Examining it once more, her eyes
focused on the scratching of letters. *I met a man whose initials
are M.H. and I pulled off one of his buttons.* She finished the
sentence in her mind, then stifled a giggle as she imagined the
horrified looks on her aunts' faces as they read it.

With a sigh she put the button down again, carefully
erased a few words, and continued the letter.

*While I was there, I even did a little ballet dance
on a fallen log and behaved perfectly childishly, the
way you're always telling me not to, but it was fun.*

I will write again soon, when I've acquainted my-

self a bit more with the hospital and my surroundings. Until then, know that my loving thoughts are with you both.

Your niece, Calliope Jane Myers

She folded the pages in half, tucked them into a waiting envelope, and wrote her aunts' address in neat block letters on the outside of the envelope. She started to write the return address, but realized with a start she wasn't sure how to properly record it. It would have to wait. She stood, cringing as a pain shot across her lower back at the sudden movement, and slid the envelope into the pocket of her dress.

She turned to Lydia who was gazing out the window. "I'm ready."

Lydia turned with a smile of readiness on her face, but then her expression turned disbelieving as she looked Callie up and down. "Aren't you going to change your dress?"

Callie glanced at herself. She still had on the white cotton sundress she'd worn for her dancing walk along the beach. The skirt was shamefully wrinkled from having been tied in knots and then rolled on when the unknown doctor had turned her onto her side. There were dirt smudges along her hip, and Callie was sure there must be more on the back. "I suppose I should quickly change."

Lydia nodded. "Yes, you should." She followed Callie to their shared closet, where Callie removed a clean blouse and pleated skirt. "Do you realize that the male to female ratio here is about 100 to one?"

Callie flashed Lydia a quick smile as she fastened her skirt. "Good odds for you, huh?"

"I'd say so! For both of us. We will probably be pursued by every eligible male on the island. I don't plan to settle for anything less than the best." She aimed her finger warningly in Callie's direction. "You shouldn't either."

Callie frowned. She wasn't eager to be "pursued," as Lydia had put it, but she didn't like the insinuation that she would be easily caught. "Why would I?"

Lydia's perfectly arched brows raised high as she looked pointedly at the crumpled sundress lying across the end of Callie's bed where she'd carelessly tossed it. "What do you think you would have attracted, attending supper in that?"

Callie crossed to the mirror to check her reflection. She fastened the last button on her crisp white blouse, and as she did her mind wandered to the button on her desk. If she hadn't changed her clothes, would she have attracted the owner of that button? She froze for a moment, gazing at her reflection in the mirror. "Lydia, do you want to be married someday?"

Lydia came up behind her and locked eyes with her in the mirror. "That's a silly question. Of course, I do."

"What kind of man do you want to marry?"

"Rich." She spoke with the confidence of someone who'd given the subject much thought. "With manners. And handsome. No big ears or clumsy feet. A man who will give me fine-looking, strapping sons that my father will be proud to call his grandsons."

Callie turned and looked into Lydia's eyes, surprised to see a hint of insecurity lurking there. Lydia apparently realized she'd let her guard down, too, because she released a brittle laugh. "Yes, Callie, grandsons. I'm the only child, and I made the mistake of being born a girl. My dear father has never recovered. The only way I'll redeem myself is to bring forth a passel of grandsons for him to bounce on his knee and to take fishing and to teach his new sport, golfing. Then he'll approve of me."

Sympathy coiled through Callie's chest. "Lydia, your father must approve of you. Why, look at the wonderful going-away gift he gave you!" Among Lydia's belongings was the Hudson touring car, something that was outside of the realm of reality for Callie's family. "Why would he do that if he disapproved of you?"

"To help me catch that rich, handsome husband." Lydia's lips twisted wryly. "A rich man won't chase after a poor girl. It just isn't acceptable." She leaned toward the mirror to check her lipstick again.

A rich man wouldn't chase after a poor girl? Callie hadn't thought about that. Of course, she'd never really considered wealth a necessary attribute for her future husband. She wanted to be a wife someday, unlike Aunties Viv and Vi who were spinsters and often the ridicule of their small town. But all Callie really wanted was to be the wife of a Christian man—a man who would be the spiritual leader in their home, like her own father had been.

But to look for him here was foolish, despite the good odds. Her aunts had extracted a promise from her to return to her hometown as a nurse, and Callie knew that's what she would do. However, there was nothing in Shyler's Point to offer a man. The tiny community could barely support those already living there. It was pointless to pursue a relationship while here. This fascination with her unknown rescuer should not be encouraged, yet it plagued her.

Was the owner of the button a Christian? How would she find out if she never found him? Callie replayed the ministrations she'd received from the mysterious man. His hands had been strong yet gentle, his tone initially gruff, but he had softened and even seemed teasing by the end of their walk together. He'd been concerned for her, and the concern had touched her despite her irritation that he saw her behavior as childish. In retrospect, perhaps she deserved his reprimands. She had behaved foolishly and could have really hurt herself. She should, at least, thank him for his assistance.

Maybe she should put the dirty dress back on to be recognizable to the man, whoever he was. Then she remembered his comment about her irresponsible actions and she shook her head, making her unruly curls bounce. No, she'd find him, but she'd impress him with her neat, mature appearance. There'd be no question about her womanhood on their second meeting. In fact…

She caught Lydia's elbow. "Can you wait just one more minute?" Lydia huffed but nodded, so Callie plopped on the edge of her mattress and reached for her feet. It hurt her back to lean forward that way, but she popped off her tan and black saddle shoes and white cotton anklets and dropped them beside the bed. She crossed to the dresser and retrieved a pair of silk nylons, which she smoothed over her legs. Finally, she slipped her nylon-covered feet into a pair of beige and cream low-heeled spectator pumps. Then she smiled at Lydia. "Now I'm ready."

Lydia gave Callie a slow look from toes to head. "No, my dear innocent friend, you are not."

Callie examined herself in the mirror. Her brown and beige pleated skirt was unmussed and fit her trim hips perfectly, the white blouse bore no smudges and was neatly tucked in. She twisted to check the backs of her legs. No runs in her stockings, and her shoes were even on the right feet. She held out her hands. "What's wrong now?"

Lydia snatched her own hairbrush from the dresser and gave Callie a not-so-gentle push onto the edge of the bed. Callie yelped as her bottom collided with the mattress. Lydia snickered. "Sorry, I forgot your sitter was tender. Sit still and let me brush your hair, then we're going to put some lipstick on you."

"Oh, but Lydia, I never—"

"I'm sure you *never*, but it's high time you did."

Callie's face heated, but she allowed her new friend to

run the stiff bristles of the brush through her hair. She closed her eyes, the heavenly sweep of the brush taking her back to childhood, when her mother had brushed her natural curls into neat ringlets before sending her out to play.

"There!" Lydia dropped the brush on the bed and took Callie by the shoulders, turning her toward the mirror. Lydia had managed to tame the locks into a neatly waved bob that framed Callie's face. Callie smoothed her hand over the strands, amazed by the transformation.

"Now for lipstick. Lydia grabbed her clutch purse and removed a silver tube. "Pooch out your lips, like this." Lydia demonstrated. She looked like a fish gulping for air, and Callie burst out laughing. Lydia scowled. "Callie, cooperate, please."

Her words reminded Callie of the man at the beach. Would he be impressed if he saw her wearing lipstick? She stifled her giggles and imitated Lydia's poochy-lipped face. Lydia bent forward, her forehead wrinkled in concentration, and something smoothed over Callie's lips. Then she stood and smiled down at Callie, nodding. "Just as I thought. You really are a knock-out." She stepped aside and gestured to the mirror. "Look."

Callie looked. And she gaped. The gorgeous woman in the mirror was her? How could a simple splash of color give her skin a glow? Then she leaned closer to the mirror and noticed something else. "Oops." She turned to Lydia and pointed to her mouth. "Pink teeth."

Lydia plucked a tissue from a box on the dresser. "Blot."

Callie folded the tissue in half and bit down on it with her lips, as she'd seen Lydia do earlier. Then she carefully wiped the leftover lipstick from her front teeth. One more smile at the mirror revealed only white teeth.

Lydia winked. "Let's go wow 'em."

Nervousness danced through Callie's middle. She'd have to find him first.

4

HOLDEN

Holden was lifting his steaming coffee mug to his lips when an elbow applied sharply to his upper arm caused him to jerk. Coffee sloshed out into his aluminum tray, dousing his green beans with the strong, black brew. "Micah, be careful. Look what you did."

Micah looked, but Holden didn't see much of an apology in his expression. Instead, a boyish sparkle lit his face. "Oh, sorry, didn't mean to spill anything." His gentle Texas twang offered a hint of remorse. "But look over there." With a barely discernible jerk of his head he gestured to the wide doorway of the dining area.

Holden's gaze followed the path of Micah's vision, and he had to admit the two women framed in the doorway were worthy of admiring glances. The taller one had shiny black hair and dark eyes. She stood with a graceful ease—weight settled more heavily on her right hip, a small clutch purse pressed against her thigh, her chin angled confidently as she perused the area. She gave off an aura that intimated she was someone of importance. Her cream colored blouse looked like silk and clung in all the right places. Her trim-fitting black skirt was obviously tailored and showed her slender frame to full effect. Lorna would have looked ravishing in the outfit. That thought brought him up short, and he turned his attention to the second woman.

The shorter one, with rather tousled auburn curls, stood slightly behind her friend. She held her clenched hands against her stomach and peered around the shoulder of the dark-haired girl, seemingly uncertain of whether she wanted to enter the dining hall or not. He released a small *hmmph*. Who could blame her the way nearly every man in the room was ogling the newly arrived pair? Some of the men—including Micah—acted as if they'd never seen women before.

Micah grinned. "We must've died and gone to Heaven, because those are the two most heavenly creatures Ah've ever had the pleasure of feastin' my eyes upon…"

Holden snorted under his breath. "Your drawl is becoming as obnoxious as a bad itch, and I believe you're beginning to drool."

Micah scooted back his chair and bounced up. "Stay here. I'll be right back."

"Where are you—"

Why had he bothered to ask? Micah was already halfway across the room, and there was no doubt where he was going. Holden watched with mild amusement as Micah greeted the two women, who smiled and nodded politely. Micah pointed to Holden, speaking animatedly, and both pairs of female eyes settled on him. Self-consciously, he lifted his hand in a brief wave. The taller girl gave a finger waggle in his direction and beamed, but the shorter one only nodded and offered a flash of a smile.

The shy smile caught him in the solar plexus. The girl from the beach. He hadn't recognized her at first without her bare toes and wind tossed dress, but that auburn hair and green eyes… It had to be her. His heart seemed to lodge in his throat.

The trio headed in his direction, and he ordered his racing pulse to calm. He stood when the two women reached the table. "Good evening."

"Hello," they chorused. The dark-haired girl's gaze swept over Holden, making no pretense of her admiration. The girl from the beach didn't seem to know where to look—her gaze flitted back and forth between Micah and Holden like that of a nervous canary watching a pair of tomcats.

"Ladies, Ah'd like you to meet my friend, Dr. Winters. Holden, this is Miss Lydia Eldredge and Miss Callie Myers. They're new to Schofield—just got off the ship at Pearl Harbor this mornin'." Holden hid a smile at his friend's exaggerated Texas drawl. Micah tended to pull out that Texas twang whenever he was trying to impress someone, usually of the female persuasion.

"It's very nice to meet both of you." Holden settled his gaze on the one named Callie second so it could linger a bit. She was cuter with bare feet and wind-tossed hair.

"And Ah"—Micah placed his broad hand against his chest while raising his eyebrows and tipping his chin downward—"am Dr. Hatcher, as I already told you. But y'all just call me Micah."

The auburn-haired girl—Callie—snapped her head in Micah's direction and her gaze narrowed. She seemed to dissect Micah with her appraisal. Micah must have been aware of her attention, because he gave her a broad wink. A rush of color climbed her cheeks, and she turned away.

"Ah'm goin' to escort these lovely ladies through the chow line, Holden, an' then we'll return to join you." Micah turned to the women and held out both elbows. "Ladies?"

With a feminine giggle Lydia immediately placed her hand in the crook of his arm. Callie hesitated, but then she too took hold, and the three made their way between the tables to the food line. As they departed, sometimes crunching together to make it through the cramped spaces, Holden noted Callie's stiff stride. He bit the insides of his cheeks to keep from laughing, just as he'd done on the beach earlier. Twenty-three, huh? Merely a child… He lifted his coffee cup and took a sip. But then, Lorna had been twenty-three when Timmy was born, and he hadn't seen her as a child.

He thumped his cup onto the tray. This Callie was nothing like his Lorna. He couldn't even begin to compare the two. Low wolf whistles and muttered complimentary comments, some on the ribald side, jarred him from his thoughts. All across the room, the attention of hungry soldiers transferred from dinner trays to the young women passing by. The almost synchronized movements reminded Holden of the reverse of falling dominoes.

He gritted his teeth. Lydia Eldredge probably had the self-confidence to handle a roomful of lusty soldiers, but Callie… Despite the feistiness she'd exhibited earlier that afternoon, he got the impression she wasn't accustomed to fending off the attention of dozens of men. She might need some protection. But he'd let Micah handle it. Micah was capable and certainly willing. Holden didn't have the time—or the desire—to be anyone's protector.

The women, trays in hand, wove their way back through the crowded room, Micah bringing up the rear. Lydia's gaze roved over the assembled faces, and she offered flirtatious smiles in most directions which were returned one hundred percent. Callie kept her eyes straight ahead, and a slight blush touched her cheeks. Refreshing… Micah pulled out metal folding chairs for them with a courtly flourish, and Holden stood until they were seated.

Callie lowered her head, closed her eyes, and her lips moved slightly as she obviously offered a prayer of thankfulness for her meal. Holden's chest went tight. She might as well be talking to the chicken breast on her plate for all the good those prayers would do her. Yes, this one was best left to Micah.

As soon as she raised her head, Micah leaned in, his boyish grin intact. "So you ladies arrived this mornin', huh? Where are ya'all from?"

Lydia touched her lips with her napkin. "My family lives in San Francisco. Callie here, however, is from an incredibly tiny town in the hills of Arkansas. What was the name of your town, Callie?"

Callie swallowed the potatoes she was chewing. "Shyler's Point."

"Shyler's Point," Micah drawled, "in the hills of Arkansas, you say? Bet it's real pretty."

"There was nearly a foot of snow on the ground when I left. Quite different from here." Callie forked two green beans and carried them to her mouth.

Micah shifted his attention to Lydia. "Miss Eldredge—"

"Please call me Lydia. Miss Eldredge sounds like an old-maid schoolteacher." She smiled prettily and Holden choked back a chuckle. What a consummate flirt. How did she and Callie get together? The two didn't seem to fit.

Micah laughed. "Lydia. What a pretty name…"

Lydia released a light laugh. "If I may be so bold, I believe I'm the only one at the table with a normal name." Her gaze drifted around the party as she named them off. "Micah, Holden, and Calliope… Where did your mothers come up with these unique monikers?" She fluttered her lashes at Micah. "Are you named for a rock?"

Micah blasted out an over-enthusiastic guffaw. "No, I'm

not mica the rock, I'm Micah the doom-and-gloom prophet. Don't you read the Bible?" With his drawl, the word came out *Bah*-ble.

Callie's head snapped up and her eyes shone. "Do you read the Bible?"

Micah shrugged. "Sure do. My daddy was a Baptist preacher in Arlington—a real Bible-thumper. He ingrained in me and my brothers early the importance of hidin' God's Word in our hearts. I got it firmly right here." He settled his hand on his chest, right over his heart. When Callie smiled in approval, Holden wanted to thump Micah upside the noggin, preferably with the big black Book that rested on Micah's nightstand. It might knock some sense into Micah—and the dust from the Bible cover at the same time.

"What's your favorite passage?" Callie pinned her green eyes on Micah's blue ones with an intensity Holden found irritating.

Micah stroked his chin. "Well, now, it's kind of hard to choose just one—there are so many that have meanin'. I guess I'd have to say a passage from the last chapter of Micah. Let's see if I can remember it all the way through…" He pursed his lips for a moment, gaze rolling ceilingward, while Callie's green-eyed gaze remained riveted on him. Holden fought the desire to get up and leave.

At last Micah spoke. "'Who is a God like unto thee, that pardons iniquity and passes by the transgression of the remnant of his heritage? He retains not his anger forever, because He delights in mercy. He will turn again, He will have compassion upon us; He will subdue our iniquities; and wilt cast all our sins into the depths of the sea.'" He gave Callie a bright smile. "I always found that comfortin' when I was a boy—'thou wilt cast all our sins into the depths of the sea'—because I was a little on the ornery side and had lots of sin to be castin'."

By now Micah was twanging like old mattress springs. Callie, however, seemed completely taken by Micah's monologue. That rankled for some reason Holden couldn't understand.

Lydia tapped Holden on the wrist, pulling his attention to her. "Now we know the origin of Micah's name. What's yours, Dr. Winters? I don't believe I've ever heard the name Holden before."

Holden folded his napkin and placed it next to his half-empty tray. "There are actually two stories about how I acquired the named Holden. I'm the youngest of six children, the only boy. My father says that my mother was so delighted to finally have given birth to a son, she was reluctant to relinquish me at any time, thus she was constantly *holdin'* me, and I was named in that honor."

He sensed his listener's uncertainty as to whether to take him seriously or not. He shrugged, adopting an intentionally droll tone. "A second, more likely explanation is that my maternal grandmother's maiden name was Holden. She passed away two months before I was born, so my mother gave me the name as a remembrance."

Lydia chuckled. "The first story is much more whimsical, but I agree that the second is more believable."

"Because you can't imagine my mother *holdin'* me constantly?" Holden couldn't resist needling the girl a bit.

Lydia's perfectly arched brows came down slightly, but then she relaxed her face and gave a smile. "Of course not." Her voice dripped with manufactured sweetness. "Every mother is anxious to hold her baby. But I prefer the idea of a family name being passed down from generation to generation. It speaks of roots." She shot him one quick dagger of irritation before turning to Callie. "Callie, is Calliope a family name?"

Callie dipped her head in a brief, seemingly self-conscious

gesture. "Oh, no. Nothing remotely like that."

Micah said, "Then what?"

Callie glanced from Lydia to Micah to Holden, then down at her tray again. Holden got the distinct impression she'd rather not divulge the meaning behind her name. Should he come to her rescue by changing the subject? Before he could distract Micah or Lydia, she lifted her head and pinned her gaze on him.

"My parents met at the county fair in Benton. My father asked my mother if he could buy her an ice cream cone. There was a calliope playing in the background, and Mama said it was a sweet, heart-lifting tune, something that angels might hum. Forever after, whenever she had ice cream, she'd remember the tune from the calliope and my father's smile."

Holden couldn't turn away, even though he tried. He felt as though they were the only two people in the room.

"The day I was born, my father asked my mother if there was anything he could get her to help ease the pain, and she said she wanted ice cream. My father then asked, 'And do you want a calliope, too?' My mother laughed and said yes. So Daddy named me Calliope."

Callie continued to hold Holden captive with her unwavering gaze. His heart pounded somewhere in the top of his head. Was she trying to send him a secret message? For some inexplicable reason, he experienced an urge to lean across the table and place a kiss on her innocent, ruby-painted lips.

"Why, that's about the sweetest, most romantic story Ah've ever heard." Micah's voice intruded, and to Holden's relief Callie finally turned her gaze away from him to Micah, breaking the spell her brief story had cast over him. His pulse returned to normal.

"Yes." Lydia's puckered her lips into a pout. "It makes

having a normal name like Lydia feel very bland."

Micah gave Lydia one of his best smiles. "Now, there's nothin' bland about you, darlin.'"

Lydia flashed a brilliant smile coupled with more eyelash flutters.

Micah's annoying Texas hospitality, Lydia's too-practiced coquettishness, and Callie's seeking innocence... Holden didn't want to deal with any of them. He stood, taking hold of his tray and nodding to the ladies. "If you'll excuse me, I have the early shift tomorrow, so I'm going to bid you a good night. It was nice meeting you both."

"You, too," Lydia said, but Holden got the impression she was only giving lip service.

Callie fixed him with another penetrating, wistful gaze. "Thank you, Dr. Winters. Good night."

Micah sent Holden a smirking wink. "I believe I'll walk these ladies home." Holden hesitated. Should he play escort, too? But then he hardened his heart, reminding himself that these girls—specifically Callie—were not his responsibility.

"Good night, then." Holden strode to the kitchen doorway, handed his tray to one of the kitchen crew, and stalked outside without a glance in the direction of Micah's table. But he had the sneaking suspicion that if he turned and looked, he would discover he was being watched by a pair of jade green eyes.

5

CALLIE

"Good morning, ladies. I'm pleased to see that you are dressed and ready to begin your duties."

Callie and Lydia stood before their new supervisor, Miss Myrtle Torkelson. Callie didn't think the matronly nurse looked pleased. Deep furrows carved paths across her forehead and from nose to chin, creating a permanent scowl of displeasure.

"Here at Schofield Station Hospital we pride ourselves on a neat appearance at all times, so a crisply starched uniform is an absolute necessity." Miss Torkelson pinched the ruffle attached to the shoulder of Callie's tan and white striped pinafore. The furrows deepened. "More starch next time, Miss"—she consulted her clipboard—"Myers. Now, follow me and I will describe your duties."

Lydia and Callie exchanged glances and fell into formation behind their new supervisor. Miss Torkelson stopped frequently to fix them with her stern expression and deliver instructions. Callie tried to pay attention, but the adjusting of creases across the older nurse's face as she talked distracted her. Or maybe tiredness kept her from focusing.

Miss Torkelson's droning, almost monotone voice reminded Callie of the overhead fan which Lydia had insisted must run all night because she couldn't sleep without air moving. Callie was accustomed to wind through the cedar trees and the occasional hoot of an owl lulling her to sleep. She missed those familiar, soothing sounds. Instead, she was forced to listen to the ceiling fan's out-of-balance wicker paddles creating a rhythmic, low-pitched squawk.

The unfamiliar noise of the fan, added to lying in a unfamiliar bed in a unfamiliar apartment in an unfamiliar position, kept her awake long into the night. She hadn't been able to get comfortable sprawled on her stomach with her face twisted to the side. But she had no choice if she wanted to avoid putting pressure on the goose egg on her head and the bruises on her other end. How much of her sleeplessness was due to not being able to shut down her thoughts? The fan even seemed to squeak a repetitive message. *M.H.... M.H.... M.H....*

M.H.... Micah Hatcher. The button had to belong to him. But something didn't fit. His eyes were blue. Not the intense blue she had envisioned, but maybe the absence of all that black soot on his face had changed the appearance of his eyes. Or maybe it was her own knock on the head that had made the eyes seem so deeply blue on the beach.

But it wasn't only his eyes. The timbre of the voice hadn't matched. Dr. Winters had possessed a voice closer to the one of her memory, but on the beach she'd detected a hint of suppressed humor behind the gruffness. In the dining hall, all she could read was cynicism, aloofness, and an underlying sadness. Dr. Hatcher had been the humorous one.

A sharp jab with an elbow jarred Callie back to the hallway. Both Lydia and Miss Torkelson were staring at her,

Lydia clearly worried and Miss Torkelson clearly displeased. Callie had obviously missed something, but she had no idea what.

Lydia hissed through clenched teeth, "Answer the question."

Question? What question? Callie's mind raced. All she could do was take the plunge. She had a fifty-fifty chance of answering correctly. "Um...yes."

Lydia's quick intake of breath and the deepened scowl on the head nurse's face told Callie she'd guessed incorrectly. She hoped she wouldn't be quizzed further on what had transpired in the past several minutes.

Miss Torkelson rolled her eyes and Callie straightened her shoulders, determined to pay attention before she permanently stained her reputation.

"The duty roster will be posted each Monday on the bulletin board in the lobby of Grant Hall, but if you will remember this simple format you should have little need to wait until Monday morning to determine your shift. *A-B-C.* That's correct, ladies. The alphabet."

Was she trying to be funny? From her expression, Callie was sure she was not, yet there was something amusing about this somber woman reciting her ABCs, and Callie bit her tongue to keep the giggles inside.

"*A* is the first shift, *B* the second, and *C* the third. Always in that order. You will serve each shift for one week, then advance to the next shift. *C* is the longest, 10:00 P.M. until 8:00 A.M., which is why we alternate so one person is not on ten-hour duty each week. Are there any questions?"

How would Miss Torkelson react if Callie asked if she knew of a blue-eyed doctor with the initial M.H.? She cleared her throat. "No, ma'am."

Lydia echoed Callie's words.

"Very well then." Miss Torkelson tucked her head low, creating a crepe-like fold of skin beneath her chin. "I shall leave you to your duties. As there are no patients on the floor this morning, you are on cleaning detail. Mops, buckets, and rags are in the supply closet. I trust I will have no need to instruct you on how to mop floors and wash windows."

Both Lydia and Callie shook their heads.

Without another word Miss Torkelson turned on a rather flat heel and disappeared around the bend in the hallway. Lydia stepped forward several feet, tipping at the waist and peering after the retreating figure. After a full minute had passed she spun back to Callie. "What a sourpuss! Do you think she's forgotten how to smile?"

"I think she doesn't want to let her guard down until she knows us better." Callie paused, looking both ways down the long hallway. "Do you remember where the supply closet was?"

Lydia huffed. "I knew you weren't listening. And by the way, when you said 'yes,' Miss Torkelson had asked how long it had been since you got your Red Cross training."

Callie groaned. "I was daydreaming."

"Obviously!" Lydia took Callie by the arm and led her to the supply closet. "You were like this when we walked back to the apartment with Micah last night. He kept trying to talk to you, but you acted as if you were lost in another world. What's going on?"

Callie thought she detected more concern than irritation in Lydia's tone. She sighed. "Lydia, remember I told you about falling off that log on the beach?" Lydia's smirk provided the answer. "What I didn't tell you is that when I fell, someone came to assist me. I know he was a doctor by the way he acted—"

Lydia's eyes grew round

"—but I couldn't make out his face because for some reason he was coated with soot—"

Lydia's mouth dropped into an astonished O.

"—and when he helped me up, I pulled off one of his buttons."

"You did what?" Lydia's face mirrored her amazement.

"I pulled off one of his shirt buttons," Callie repeated, placing a finger against her lips to quiet Lydia even though there were no patients to disturb.

"How on earth did you do that?" Lydia sounded aghast, but Callie saw laughter sparkling in her eyes.

Callie flipped her hands outward in a gesture of bewilderment. "I grabbed his shirt front to help steady myself—I had hit my head, you know—and when I pulled my hand away, the button was in it."

"And he didn't know it?"

"Apparently not. I have the button on the desk in our room." Callie paused. Should she should trust Lydia with the rest of it? She poked her head from the closet and sent a furtive glance up and down the hallway. Empty. She turned to Lydia. "It looks as if there are initials scratched on it, and I think the initials are *M.H.*"

"Micah Hatcher." Lydia spoke the words like a mantra, and she covered her lips with two fingers, her eyes wide.

Callie nodded. "I think so. But last night, I kept looking at him, trying to decide if he was the one who helped me. His eyes are blue like the man's on the beach, but—" She stopped, unable to find the words to put her befuddlement into order. On the beach, walking beside him, feeling his arm around her waist, looking into his incredibly intense blue eyes, she had felt...electrified from within. She'd experienced nothing of that last night while walking side-by-side with Micah. Was it because he wasn't the same man, was it because Lydia had been with them, or was it—

Footsteps coming from around the corner intruded. Lydia and Callie scrambled for mops and buckets. They accidentally banged things together, creating a discordant clamor. Miss Torkelson stepped into the doorway of the supply closet, blocking the light from the hallway. She looked even less pleased than before.

"Have you not started cleaning?" The lines around her chin became more pronounced as she drew the corners of her pursed lips down sharply. "It is obvious to me that you two should not be placed on duty at the same time. I will allow you to finish this week both as *A*s. But starting Monday, Miss Myers will go on to *C* duty, while Miss Eldredge will go to *B* duty."

Her chin nearly disappeared within the folds of the next ferocious scowl. "And in the future, Miss Myers and Miss Eldredge, when you are given instructions, I expect you to follow them immediately. You are not in the States at a social event." She crossed her arms over her ample chest and tapped a thick foot impatiently. "This is a military hospital, and there will be times when your immediate action will mean the difference between life and death. Have I made myself clear?"

Callie nodded, her face hot.

Miss Torkelson looked from Callie to Lydia, her glare as sharp as a sword. "Carry on, ladies." She disappeared once more.

Lydia released a huge sigh of relief. "She is really tough. I didn't know we were going to be considered part of the army. It makes me wonder if I did the right thing by coming here."

Callie snatched up a bucket to go with her mop and headed for the hallway. "Well, I for one am going to get busy. I don't think I want her mad at me for long."

A few minutes later, as Callie pushed the stringy mop head

across a floor that didn't need to be cleaned, her thoughts once again returned to the button. Was it Micah Hatcher's? There was one way to find out. She could ask him. Although her heart pounded in nervousness even considering doing such a bold thing, it would bring the mystery to a close. Unless, of course, it wasn't his. Then the mystery would only begin.

Would 3:00 never come? Callie and Lydia mopped every floor of the 250-bed hospital, washed all of the windows on the north side, reorganized the storage closets, and restacked the jumble of bedpans Lydia accidentally knocked over with the handle of her mop. The clatter of the final mishap had apparently provided more than enough excitement for Miss Torkelson. She seemed relieved to send them out the door at the end of their shift. Callie glanced back and caught the portly nurse shaking her head at their retreating figures, obviously wondering what she was going to do with them tomorrow.

The giggles that Callie had squelched earlier in the day returned, but now in the freedom of walking below the pleasant afternoon sun, she let them flow.

Lydia looked at her. "What's funny?"

"Miss Torkelson." Callie hunched her shoulders. "I know I shouldn't make fun of people, but didn't she rather look like a Christmas pudding that's been left out until it dries and cracks?"

Lydia laughed. "Yes! And from behind, I could swear there were two bed pillows shoved up underneath her skirt."

"She probably thinks my head is stuffed with feathers after that foolish answer I gave to her question."

Caught up in their merriment, Callie missed the two soldiers standing in their pathway until she'd nearly stepped on the closest one's feet. Her laughter died.

"Well, hello, ladies." The taller of the pair looked them up and down, his perusal making Callie's skin crawl. "Off duty for the day?"

Callie didn't want to answer, but Lydia drew herself up and looked him boldly in the eye. "Yes."

"That's good. That's good." The taller one appeared to be the spokesman. The shorter one stood to the side and grinned stupidly. "That means you're free now for some fun."

"We were having fun," Lydia said, "until you came along. Now if you would kindly step aside, my friend and I are in a hurry."

The man moved a few inches closer, and his buddy also stepped forward, blocking the walkway. Their faces were friendly, but their presence felt menacing to Callie. She caught hold of Lydia's arm.

Lydia gave her hand an assuring pat before addressing the men again. "Listen, fellas, Callie and I—"

"Callie, huh?" The tall one smiled directly into Callie's face. He tipped his cloth, olive green cap. "Nice to meet you, miss." He turned back to Lydia. "And your name is…?"

Lydia took a deep breath, as if trying to gain control of her irritation. "Callie and I were on our way to rest. We've had a rather stressful day, and—"

"What's going on here?"

A stern male voice intruded. The two men glanced over their shoulders, then wheeled and came to attention, their right elbows bending into a crisp salute. Dr. Holden Winters strode up to them. Attired in his military uniform, he was so handsome that Callie's heart turned upside-down in her chest. He sent a concerned glance at the girls before turning his hard, unsmiling gaze on the men. He saluted briskly and both of the other men dropped their arms.

"I asked a question." His narrowed gaze pinned one man, then the other.

"We were just offering the ladies here some entertainment, sir." The tall one answered while the short one gulped, his ears flaming red.

"It appears to me the ladies aren't interested in being entertained." The doctor's tone became even sharper. "Have you two been drinking?"

The shorter one dropped his head, but the taller one stuck out his chin. "Only a little, sir." Callie gaped at him, shocked by his boldness.

Holden took in a deep breath through his nose, his nostrils flaring. "Apparently a reminder is needed of the rule, *Fun after sundown.* I want the two of you to return to your barracks for the remainder of the afternoon. At 5:00 we will meet with your first sergeant for instruction on appropriate times to be consuming alcohol and the appropriate way of 'offering entertainment.'" He paused, his eyes harsh. "Dismiss."

Both soldiers scuttled for the barracks.

Dr. Winters turned to Callie and Lydia, and his expression softened. "I'm sorry if those two frightened you. I'm sure they didn't mean any harm, but I'll make sure they leave you alone from now on."

Lydia reached for his hand. "Thank you."

"You're welcome." Dr. Winters let Lydia hold his hand, but he focused on Callie. "Are you all right?" The concern in the tone was reminiscent of the man from the beach. Callie's heart pounded so hard it stole her ability to speak. After a few seconds, Dr. Winters drew in a breath that raised his shoulders and released his hand from Lydia's grip. "You are safe now. You may proceed to your apartment." He started to step around them.

Callie finally found her voice. "Dr. Winters?"

He stopped and fixed her with that concentrated look. The blue of his irises appeared sapphire in the sun. "Yes?"

"I…" She swallowed. "I thank you for your kindness." *Was it you who was kind to me yesterday at the beach?*

"You're welcome." He shifted as if to take a step.

"Dr. Winters?"

She detected a hint of impatience in his eyes, but she bravely formed a question anyway. "Do you share an apartment with…anyone?"

His brows came down, and Lydia gave her a puzzled look, but Callie kept her face aimed toward the doctor.

"No." His lips twitched. "I do not."

"Then…do you ever…borrow clothes from anyone?" Callie knew how absurd she must sound, and heat climbed her cheeks, but she didn't waver in her gaze as she held her breath and awaited the answer that might help her solve her mystery.

One side of his lips tipped upward for just a moment before he resumed his firm countenance. "No, I am not in that practice."

Disappointment struck, and Callie released the breath she was holding in a *whoosh.* Her shoulders drooped as she deflated. "Oh."

"Why do you ask?"

Her head snapped back up. The heat in her face increased. She began fanning herself, hoping he'd think the sun created her discomfort. "Oh, no reason. Just…curious."

He nodded, but that slight grin appeared again briefly, proving he didn't believe her. "Are there any other questions, Miss Myers, or am I permitted to return to the hospital now?"

Now he was teasing her, but she was too embarrassed to play along. She waved a hand at him. "Oh, no—no more questions. Good-bye, Dr. Winters."

The minute he was out of earshot, Lydia grabbed Callie's arm. "What on earth were you doing?" Her tone made it clear she thought Callie had lost her mind. "First it seemed like you were probing to find out if he was married, then it almost sounded as if you wanted to lend him some clothes!"

Callie yanked her arm away. "I was trying to find out if he borrowed one of Micah's shirts."

Lydia's eyes widened. "You think he's the one."

"I'm not sure. His eyes, and something in the tone of his voice…" She had looked deeply into his eyes when relating the reason for her unusual name in the mess hall last night, trying to determine if he'd been the one on the beach. He'd returned her steadfast look, yet offered no clues. She still wasn't sure.

Lydia gave Callie a speculative, sideways look. "Do you hope it's him?"

"I—I don't know."

Lydia nibbled her lower lip for a moment. "If you hope it's him, does that mean you're not interested in Micah?"

Micah had proclaimed to be a Christian, his initials matched the button, and his sparkling eyes spoke of a fun-loving spirit. Callie was certain he would be an easy man to like. Even so, she felt no such longings toward Micah. She sighed. "I'm not interested in him that way."

"Good!" She giggled and leaned close. "I like Micah. And he's a doctor, which means there's a chance for being very wealthy when he's no longer serving on an army base."

Callie scowled. Lydia was so sure of what she wanted. Why couldn't it be so easy for Callie?

Lydia set off on the sidewalk and Callie automatically matched her stride. "If Dr. Winters is the one you met on the beach, don't count on him becoming a permanent fixture in your life. There's ice water running through that man's veins."

Callie shot Lydia a sharp look. Ice water? Well, yes, he

did present a cool demeanor. But Callie was sure there was something more, something beneath the surface he was trying to hide. She wanted to dig deeper until she revealed the real Dr. Holden Winters. Surely that was a man worth knowing well.

6

CALLIE

"Callie! Callie!"

Callie sat bolt upright in her bed where she had been soundly sleeping. Lydia burst into the room and jumped, landing on her knees in the bed next to Callie's hip and nearly bouncing Callie out the opposite side. Lydia grabbed Callie's arm. "Guess what?"

"What?" Callie's voice emerged croaky from sleep.

Lydia shook Callie's arm. "Oh, wake up! You've been sleeping for hours. I just ran into Dr. Hatcher." She giggled. "I mean *Micah*, and he invited us to dinner. Not dinner in the mess hall, either. He'd like to take us to Haleiwa, to an outdoor café on the beach where they have Hawaiian musicians and dancing. Of course I accepted! So come on, get up and get dressed." Lydia bounced up and began flinging off her nurse uniform.

Callie yawned. "Dinner? Haleiwa? But that must be hours away."

Lydia paused, her arms over her head with her dress caught tightly across her elbows. "Of course it is, silly, that's why we have to get moving."

Callie remained on the bed. After the week she'd put in, she didn't have the energy for a long drive, even for a meal at an outdoor, oceanside café. The nursing duties weren't taxing—on the contrary, most of her duties had been janitorial rather than medicinal. All of the mopping was wearing her out.

Only once had her services as a nurse been required, and that was to help hold down a drunken sailor who required several stitches in his arm. The man had accidentally ended up at Schofield when he fell asleep on the Pineapple Limited, a train that had once been used to cart pineapples to market but now provided transportation from Schofield to Honolulu. When he awakened and found himself in unfamiliar surroundings, he'd shoved his fist through a train window. Dr. Winters had handled the actual stitching, and it had been all Callie could do to keep her focus on the patient instead of the doctor. What was it about him that captured her attention so thoroughly?

Lydia spun around, hands on hips, wearing nothing but her under things. "Callie, please, if you don't hurry, he'll leave without us."

"What time is it?" Callie squinted at the small wind-up clock sitting on the dresser.

"Just after three."

Callie flopped against her pillows. "Then I'm on duty in seven more hours. I'm a *C* this week, remember?"

"Wrong. You *were* a *C*. This is Saturday, Callie. Tomorrow is Sunday, your day off. No duty tonight for you. Miss Torkelson has it covered."

"It's Saturday?"

"Saturday. So come on!"

"Are you sure he asked both of us, not just you?"

Lydia groaned. "Callie, for goodness sake, yes! He asked both of us. Now get out of that bed and get dressed, or I'll drag you out of here in your pajamas."

Callie smirked. "You would, wouldn't you?"

"For the chance to have a real dinner out under the stars and a handsome doctor to dance with, yes, I certainly would."

Lydia's good mood was infectious. Callie was catching on. "Do I have time for a shower?"

"No. It's outdoor, and we'll probably drive with the windows down. You'll be all mussed by the time we get there anyway." Lydia pawed through the hangers. She withdrew a bright, tropical dress with a flaring skirt, low scooped back, and wide fabric belt and held it against her front. Callie battled a wave of envy. She owned nothing that flashy.

Callie pushed herself out of the bed. "Lydia, do…do you have something I could wear?"

Lydia grinned. "Do I ever." She reached into the closet again and pulled out a simple white-on-white checked dress covered with deep green leaves and tiny red flowers. It was longer, mid-calf at least, with a full skirt. The fitted bodice was sleeveless and boasted a square neckline both front and back. The pattern reminded Callie of her first view of the beach—all that green foliage dotted with red poinsettias. She loved it immediately.

She took it in both hands and held it at arm's length. "Do you think it will fit?"

"You won't know until you try it on."

With a grin, Callie skimmed off her pajamas and slipped the dress over her head. It buttoned up the back with large, round buttons, and Lydia fastened her in. Then she stepped to the mirror, looked at herself, and gasped. "Oh, Lydia, I love it!" She twirled a circle, making the skirt flare out, laughing with pleasure. She stopped twirling and gave Lydia a worried look. "Is it too long?"

Lydia examined it with her brows pulled down. "No. Of

course, it's longer on you than it would be on me, but it's not too long. It looks wonderful, as if it was made for you. In fact..." She tapped her lips. "Why don't you just consider it yours?"

"Oh, but—"

Lydia jammed her palm in the air. "No arguments, Calliope Myers. I have more dresses than I can possibly wear, and that one looks so much better on you than it ever did on me. Please keep it."

It was the sweetly worded *please* that finalized it. Callie threw herself at Lydia and gave her an impulsive hug.

Lydia laughed, hugging her in return. "Okay, now, leave me alone so I can finish my lipstick." Lydia pushed away and turned toward the mirror. "I told Micah we'd meet him at his car at 3:45 sharp. So we've got to hurry."

HOLDEN

"Why Haleiwa tonight?"

Holden had answered the knock on his door to find Micah on his doorstep. Without so much as a greeting, Micah had informed him they'd be going to Haleiwa for supper that evening.

Micah shrugged a bit too nonchalantly. "Why not?"

Holden puckered his lips and peered at Micah through narrowed eyes. "You're up to something..."

Micah laughed, but Holden detected forced frivolity. Micah was never malicious, but he could be mildly devious.

Suspicious, Holden crossed his arms and waited. "Come on, Micah. Out with it."

Micah sighed as if persecuted. He held up both palms and shook his head. "Okay, okay. You got me. I do have an ulterior motive."

Holden cocked an eyebrow.

"I asked a couple of nurses to go, too."

Holden dropped his arms. "No." He turned and headed into his bungalow.

The screen door banged into place and Micah followed him through the porch into the living area. "Come on. It's harmless. Just a dinner. No strings, no commitments. What's the big deal?"

Holden swung around, scowling. "You know what the big deal is. I don't date."

Micah shrugged. "So don't think of it as a date. Think of it as…a night out that happens to include a female. It doesn't have to be a problem unless you make it one."

Holden let his head drop back and stared unseeingly at the ceiling for a moment, collecting his emotions. Without even asking, he knew which nurses Micah had invited. All Micah had talked about for the past two weeks was Callie Myers. Micah was too nervous to ask Callie for a date, which was completely out of character and told volumes about his feelings for the girl. Holden surmised that Micah worked his way around it by asking both Callie and her roommate to accompany him to dinner without making a solid commitment to either girl. But Micah would want to pair himself with Callie at the first opportunity. And there was the problem.

Holden wanted to pair himself with Callie, too.

Which of course was absolutely ridiculous.

What was his fascination with this tousle-haired slip of a girl who was nothing like his prim and cultured Lorna? The scene on the beach, her uninhibited dance of joy, replayed itself in his memory at will. When he reprimanded her for her foolishness, she accused him of never experiencing the urge to throw caution to the wind and give vent to the enjoyment of God's creation. Oh, to have that freedom… But he would never be that carefree again, and there was no use in pretending.

"So, Holden, yes or no?" Micah waited, his boyish face hopeful.

Holden sighed. It was foolhardy, reckless, and would lead to nothing but trouble in the future. He lowered his chin and examined his feet. "Yes."

Micah released a whoop. "Yes?"

Holden raised his chin and forced the word past his gritted teeth. "Yes."

Micah clapped Holden on the shoulder. "Great! We'll have a terrific time. I told the girls to meet me at my car at 3:45, so there's not much time. Slip into something comfortable, and I'll see you then." Micah slammed out the door.

Change into something comfortable... Khakis and a Hawaiian shirt, his mind dictated. But as he pulled the shirt from its hanger, he stopped mid-action. An evening with Callie? What did he think he was doing?

CALLIE

Micah was stewing—that was obvious—and Callie, cramped in the backseat of the Coupe with Lydia, knew why. Dr. Winters had plunked himself in the front passenger seat, leaving the girls no choice but to share the back. So she was given the privilege of staring at the back of the doctor's silent head the entire three-hour drive. Although Micah attempted jocularity for the first quarter of the journey to Haleiwa, it had seemed flat, and he gave up completely when Dr. Winters never responded. Besides, it quickly became clear he needed to focus on the road.

How did one converse while bouncing up and down as

if riding a kangaroo? Micah's knuckles glowed white as he gripped the steering wheel for dear life. Dr. Winters had one arm locked against the dashboard and the other on the ceiling to keep himself in place, and Callie and Lydia braced their arms against the ceiling to prevent bouncing into it with their heads. What little visiting was done took place quietly between the girls in the back while Micah seethed and Dr. Winters seemingly ignored all of them.

But at last they arrived, and when Callie spotted the quaint, oceanside outdoor setting, she decided instantly the uncomfortable drive had been worth it. Although her arms were aching, her legs were fully functional, and she bounded out of the car with a huge smile. "Oh, Lydia, look! It's wonderful!"

Lydia climbed out of the car, and the girls exchanged grins of pleasure. Rough-hewn tables were set up beneath a huge, open-air pavilion constructed from crude posts and covered with thatch. Colorful lanterns hanging from the pavilion cover and fat candles on each table provided muted lighting. Torches stabbed into the sand offered flares of light plus sent out a warning to mosquitoes to stay away. Callie pointed, delighted, at the cups formed from coconut shells.

Micah came up behind her and touched her shoulder. "Are you hungry?"

"Oh, yes. Since I slept most of the day away, I haven't eaten anything. My tummy has been growling for the past several miles."

"And all that bumping around didn't shake your appetite loose?"

She laughed, enjoying his humor. "Oh, no, that's not likely. My appetite is pretty well intact. And it's making itself known right now!" She placed her palms against her stomach and pretended to grimace. "Do you hear that? My stomach is demanding, 'Feed me!'"

"Then let's go feed it." He placed his hand at the small of her back and guided her forward. Her sandal-covered feet sank into the soft sand, and Micah grinned when she paused to shake her right foot, sending out a spray of minuscule particles.

While clutching Micah's firm forearm and hovering on one foot, Callie glanced back at Lydia and Dr. Winters. They hadn't moved away from the Coupe. Dr. Winters' eyes met hers briefly, then he turned to Lydia and raised his eyebrows in a silent question as he gestured with one hand toward the waiting tables. Without a word in reply, Lydia began following Micah and Callie with Dr. Winters close on her heels.

All at once Callie felt out of place. Hadn't Micah given the invitation to Lydia? Surely he intended to be Lydia's date for the evening. Yet after he seated Callie, pushing in her chair like a true gentleman, he placed himself on her left. Lydia and Dr. Winters seated themselves on the opposite sides with the doctor directly across from Callie. This positioned Lydia across from Micah. Lydia's dark eyes snapped, confirming that she was no more pleased with the seating arrangement than Callie was.

A bare-chested waiter approached their table. His teeth appeared snow white against his dusky skin as he smiled. "Good evening, and welcome to the Tahitian Terrace." His English was perfectly enunciated. He handed each of them a menu which was printed in bold black letters on a thickly textured sheet of brown paper. "May I offer you a drink or an appetizer while you are making your selections from the menu?"

"Yes," Micah said. "We'd each like a piña colada, and please bring us a fruit tray."

The waiter hurried off, and Callie's heart skipped a beat. What exactly was a piña colada? She tapped Micah's wrist.

"Um, Micah? I don't drink."

His eyes crinkled in the corners, and he took her hand. "Darlin', this place doesn't serve alcohol. That piña colada is coconut and pineapple juices blended together—real tasty. They serve it in one of these nifty coconut cups with a skewer of pineapple and cherries in it." He squeezed her hand, fixing her with a tender look. "You can trust me not lead you astray, Callie."

Heat filled her face, and she gently withdrew her hand. Behind her, music started. She turned sideways in her chair and searched for its source. Near the water, a small band of musicians played next to a wooden platform. The ukuleles, kettle drums, and some sort of flute-like instrument serenaded the diners with a sweet, uniquely Hawaiian tune that blended perfectly with the gentle whoosh of the waves.

Callie leaned toward Lydia, putting some distance between herself and Micah. "Isn't the music pretty?"

"Do you like to dance?" Micah drew her attention back to him. His eyes shone with such admiration it made her uneasy.

She offered a sheepish shrug. She'd never danced before, but she knew how it was done. The idea of being held in his arms sent a nervous tremor through her. She shifted her gaze again only to have it settle on Dr. Winters. His blue eyes were locked on hers, and something smoldered beneath the surface that was infinitely more disturbing than the prospect of being served alcohol or dancing in Micah's arms. A shiver slithered down her spine, and she dropped her gaze to her menu, but she knew he was watching her. Her pulse increased in tempo.

She snapped her menu to chase away the discombobulating feelings. "Lydia, do you know what this is? 'Ah-hee po-kee.'"

Lydia shrugged, one corner of her mouth pulling upward in a feeble smile. "Sounds fishy to me."

Micah grinned. "Oh, fishy it is, ladies. Ahi Poke is raw Ahi tuna."

Callie gaped at him. "Raw? They eat it *raw*?"

Micah burst out laughing, throwing back his head in amusement, and even Dr. Winters appeared to bite the insides of his cheeks.

Callie's cheeks flooded with heat. "I'm certainly not ordering *that*." She gave the menu a firm shake and held it up to hide her flaming cheeks. She peeked over the top of the menu. Dr. Winters was watching her again with the penetrating look that made her feel as if he was trying to see beneath her skin, but a hint of a smile hovered there as well. Her pulse throbbed wildly and she couldn't decide where to turn her eyes. Then stubbornness set in. Would she spend the whole evening trying to avoid his gaze? How silly. And pointless with him sitting directly across from her.

She met his gaze. "What do you suggest, Dr. Winters?"

His lips twitched, and he seemed to turn up the intensity in his eyes as if trying to make her avert her gaze. She mentally dug in with her heels and held the contact. It seemed a lifetime passed while they squared off, a silent battle of wills being waged across a planked table while the flickering flame of a fat candle in a green jar reflected in two pairs of eyes.

He cleared his throat. "I plan to order the pulehu steak, steamed mixed vegetables, sweet potato in coconut milk, fried rice, and for dessert guava cake and coffee." His gaze never wavered. He didn't even blink.

Callie's eyes were burning with the desire to blink. "Do you recommend each of these items?" She tried to maintain a businesslike tone but it was difficult with her heart lodged in her throat.

"Highly."

She recognized all but the first item he listed, and the list was lengthy enough her hunger should be satisfied even if she found the first item was something served raw. "Then I shall bow to your discretion and have the same." She smacked the menu onto the table.

His gaze darted toward the sound for only a second, and she hid her smile. She'd won. For the moment. Immediately his incredible blue-eyed gaze bounced up and fixed her with an expression Callie found more unnerving than any before. Heat blazed under her skin, and she prayed it didn't show.

How could gazing into Micah's eyes be uncomfortably disconcerting, yet gazing into Dr. Winters's eyes left her disconcerted yet longing for more? It made no sense. When Holden turned toward the musicians, her heart dropped because he no longer graced her with his attention.

She looked beyond him and gasped at what she had been missing by focusing only on his eyes. "Oh, Lydia, look. What a beautiful sunset." Lydia and Micah turned to look, and they both echoed Callie's announcement.

"The colors here are so much more vivid than home." Callie's awe came though in her tone. "I keep thinking what a marvelous job God did when He created this area. The beauty is so inviting, I want to hug it."

Micah took her hand again. "I wish I could inspire that reaction in you."

Dr. Winters swung around and his gaze lit on their loosely clasped hands. His gaze narrowed, and Callie surmised Micah's forwardness annoyed him. Or was he troubled by her acquiescence? She tried to free her hand, but Micah somehow laced his fingers with hers. She was caught.

Dr. Winters turned to Lydia, offered the most breathtaking smile Callie had ever seen, and held out his hand. "Miss Eldredge, would you care to dance?"

Lydia's brows came down in a quick, puzzled expression,

but then her face relaxed and she returned his smile. "Yes, thank you, Dr. Winters, I believe I would."

"Oh, please, call me Holden." He issued the invitation in a gentlemanly tone, and Callie heart's clutched with jealousy.

"Holden." Lydia fluttered her lashes. "And please remember to call me Lydia."

He nodded. "Lydia. Shall we?"

Lydia smiled her assent. The two of them stood and moved toward the dance floor with Holden's broad hand on Lydia's spine, and Callie set her jaw against the sting of tears.

7

"You know, we could dance, too."

Hope carried through in Micah's voice, and she knew she should acknowledge him, but she couldn't stop staring at the couple who moved with such ease together on that makeshift dance floor.

The doctor's lips were close to Lydia's ear as they turned a gentle circle, and he must have whispered something because Lydia pulled back, smiled, and nodded before settling her temple against his cheek. With effort Callie turned away from the image of Holden—if Lydia could call him Holden, then Callie could, too—and Lydia in what appeared to be an embrace as they moved slowly to the sweet melody wafting across the sand.

Callie sighed. "I don't know how to dance, and to be honest, I don't think I would be comfortable with it."

He smiled in a tender yet boyishly handsome way. "That's what I like about you, Callie Myers. You're a grown women, yet you've maintained your innocence. Don't ever change. Keep askin' for drinks that don't have alcohol, keep gettin' worked up at the prospect of eatin' raw fish, keep marvelin' at the beauty of sunsets, and keep enjoyin' music with your ears instead of your feet."

A laugh bubbled up without effort. "Enjoying music with my ears instead of my feet?"

"Why, sure." He tipped his head, resting his chin on one fist and giving her his full attention. "Listenin' from here, with that gorgeous sunset to peek at, is just as good or better than movin' around on those slabs of wood."

She shook her head, amused. "Your southwest twang is creeping in again. Do you draw that out at will?"

A grin lighting his eyes. "Yep. Do you *lahke* it?"

She laughed again. It was impossible not to. He was so relaxed with himself, how could anyone dislike him? She mentally counted the positive aspects of spending time with him. He was a Christian—or so he'd indicated. He was pleasant, polite, and attentive. He would be able to provide well for her should a relationship develop. And of course there was that button. *M.H.*, it said. She'd felt so drawn to the man on the beach. It had to be Micah Hatcher. Responding to his attentions would be a sensible thing to do, if she was going to respond to anyone's attentions...

But nothing felt sensible right now. In spite of all the reasons to give her heart to Micah, she knew she wouldn't do it. Someone as outgoing as Micah Hatcher would never be able to settle in a small town like Shyler's Point. And then there was that mysterious *something* pulling her toward Dr. Holden Winters, the man who held her with his eyes but held Lydia in his arms...

The waiter approached their table, a square wooden tray balanced on one palm above his left shoulder. He swung down the tray with a twist of his wrist and placed their drinks and the fruit tray on the table. Holden and Lydia returned, and everyone placed their dinner orders.

Callie took a hesitant sip of her piña colada, and she raised her eyebrows in pleased surprise. "You're right, Micah. This is very good." While he beamed at her and took up his cup to drink, she took another, longer drink. Then she removed the thin wooden skewer and nibbled off a chunk of pineapple, giggling when the juice ran down her chin.

Micah held the fruit tray for her. Pineapple wedges with the rinds still attached, and chunks of banana, mango, and papaya were artistically arranged in a fan design, dotted with huge red cherries.

Callie helped herself to some of each. "It's a shame to ruin such a pretty layout."

Lydia popped a piece of mango into her mouth. "It tastes too good to leave it alone."

Micah nodded. "Yep. Now o' course in Texas, we didn't have these tropical fruits, but we had grapefruit and oranges nearly every day. And in the backyard of our house grew the biggest ol' crabapple tree you ever did see. Not good for pickin' and eatin', but I tell you those little apples made the clearest, best-tastin' jelly." He laughed and leaned forward conspiratorially. "I'll tell ya'all a little secret if you promise not to hold it against me."

Lydia and Callie exchanged a quick look, then both nodded. Holden leaned back in his chair with his elbow on the table, one finger along his cheek. They all looked at Micah expectantly.

"Back in Arlington, we Hatcher boys weren't exactly known for bein' little angels despite Daddy's job as preacher. I suppose we acted up now and then just to prove we were just like everybody else." Micah gave Callie a wink. "Well, my oldest brother, Jonah, rigged a giant slingshot by attachin' a strip from an old inner tube to the branches of an oak sapling that hadn't survived. He cut away all of that tree except the trunk and two branches. It formed a 'Y'—a perfect slingshot tree."

He leaned on his elbows, his eyes sparkling with mischief. "Now, me and Jeremiah, bein' the youngest, were given the job of collectin' all the rotten apples from underneath that big crabapple tree. We'd make a pile of mushy apples next to the slingshot, and then Jonah and Amos and Joel would take turns firin' crabapples at cars or wagons that came by on the road in front of the house. Since that slingshot was situated in the middle of a whole cluster of scraggly oaks, it was pretty hard to see us in there. Amos was the best shot. He could time his release to hit a horse *smack* on the rump or an auto *smoosh* on the windshield as it passed by."

"Micah, shame on you!" Callie tried to scold, but her voice bubbled with laughter.

He gave her his best innocent look, placing a hand against his chest. "Now, I was just the collector. I didn't do the shootin', remember?" He grinned and went on. "Well, one day we hit the same horse three times. That must've been one time too many, 'cause the driver stopped his wagon, got out, and came runnin' to find us. 'Course, we boys scattered to the winds, but we all ended up huddlin' together in the barn loft. We stayed up there 'til Ma hollered it was suppertime. You never saw a sorrier mess of boys than my brothers and me that night, sittin' at the dinner table, waitin' for Pa to haul us all out to the woodshed."

He shook his head sorrowfully, then his expression brightened. "Only Pa never said a word about that man and his horse. And we boys went on up to bed figurin' that for some reason the man hadn't talked to Pa. We all fell on our knees for our bedtime prayers and thanked the Lord for bein' released from punishment." He sighed. "'Course, the punishment came in the mornin', but not the way we expected…"

Callie and Lydia each leaned in, eager for the rest of the story. Holden apparently had heard it before, because he tipped his chair back on two legs and smirked at them.

"Next day, when we headed out to the slingshot tree, we got an awful surprise. The rubber sling had disappeared, and our tree was cut up into kindlin' wood. It was all neatly stacked right next to the little stump of what had been our slingshot." He heaved a mournful sigh. "Never did get big enough to shoot from it before Pa hacked it to pieces. Always have regretted that."

Lydia and Callie laughed. Lydia teased, "You're lucky your father didn't cut that tree into a half dozen switches to tan your hides!"

Micah inhaled through his teeth and feigned fear, then he laughed. He looked at Callie. "I bet you never got into mischief like that, did you, Callie?"

Callie tipped her head. "I wasn't perfect—my folks were always after me to slow down and be more of a little lady. I suppose because there was no boy to traipse after him, Daddy didn't discourage me from tagging along, and I became a bit of a tomboy. But I never zinged crabapples at passing wagons."

Micah turned to Lydia. "What about you?"

"I never zinged crabapples either." They all shared another laugh.

Micah leaned back and sighed, angling his crinkled grin in Holden's direction. "And of course Holden never would have done somethin' so reckless and darin' in his youth. I bet you were born responsible and old beyond your years. Am I right, buddy?"

Callie thought she detected a bit of goading beneath Micah's question. Holden must have felt the undercurrent, too, because his brows came down slightly in a displeased frown as he looked into Micah's face. He waited several seconds before responding, and when he spoke his dry tone put an end to the topic.

"My youth was typical—boyish and full of pranks aimed at my older sisters, although I can attest that crabapple flinging was never an activity in which I participated. It wasn't until adulthood that I developed the penchant for being old beyond my years." He continued to pin Micah with his chastising glare for long seconds, until Micah's face flushed slightly, and only then did Holden turn his head. The corners of his lips tipped up slightly as he addressed the girls. "Of course, I may only appear much older when compared to Micah because he's a man who's never grown up."

Callie joined in when Lydia laughed at Holden's comment, but she wasn't sure he'd intended to be funny as much as hurtful. However, Micah threw back his head and laughed much harder than the girls as if to prove he hadn't been insulted. He might have made a response to Holden, but the waiter appeared with a larger tray than before. The young man delivered a steaming plate of food to each of them and promised to bring them another drink before hurrying off.

As was her custom, Callie lowered her head to pray. When she lifted her face she noticed that Micah, too, had bowed to pray for his meal. Lydia was waiting for them to finish, but Holden had already taken up his knife and fork and begun cutting into the sizable steak on his plate. She frowned. Even if Holden didn't thank God for His provision of food, didn't he at least have respect for those who did?

She didn't have a chance to ask him, because conversation turned to the delicious variety of food on their well-filled wooden trenchers. At first glance, Callie wondered if she would be able to eat even half of the ample serving, but she cleaned her plate of every bite, including the pulehu steak which turned out to be a grilled-to-perfection fillet.

When they'd finished dessert and were relaxing over cups of fragrant coffee, Callie looked heavenward and released a long sigh of pleasure. "I know you're probably getting tired of hearing me say it, but I just can't help marveling at the beauty of God's creation. Arkansas is a truly beautiful state with its mountains and evergreens and roaring streams, but it's a different kind of beauty than here. God is so creative! He made so many different ways of pleasuring our senses."

Holden placed his empty coffee mug in the center of the table and leaned on an elbow, pinching his chin between two fingers. "Callie, may I ask you a question?"

The solemnity of his tone raised her guard, but she nodded.

"Why do you keep giving a God credit for everything you see? What makes you so certain that one even exists?"

Was he needling her? She examined his expression. No hint of teasing in his eyes, only the cynicism she'd witnessed before, and perhaps a bit of unwilling curiosity. Her heart raced as she searched for the words to answer his question. "Well, the Bible tells us that God created the heavens and the earth, so it seems—"

"The Bible is just a book, like any other story book. That isn't proof."

"Just a storybook?" Callie tipped her head in disbelief. "Holden, the Bible is God's inspired word."

"Written by men."

"Yes, men who were instructed by God as to what to write."

Micah's and Lydia's gazes moved back and forth, following the conversation much as spectators might watch a tennis match.

Holden leaned back in his chair. "I'm not saying the Bible doesn't have some good stories in it—lots of drama and even some humor. I believe I heard tell of a talking donkey. That in itself should tell you it's fiction. Animals don't talk."

Fire blazed in Callie's face. "No, not to us, but with God all things are possible."

Holden shook his head. "Callie, you're no doubt a very intelligent woman—you'd have to be to pass all of the nurses' trainings—but you've been terribly duped if you've been taught to believe in the Bible and God as fact. Leave the fairy tales behind with your childhood. You'll be much better off."

Did he really mean what he'd said? She looked at Micah, hoping to see a sparkle of humor, but instead sympathy glimmered in his gaze. She glanced at Lydia, and her roommate's expression of *I told you so* finalized it. Callie hadn't misunderstood. Suddenly she was fighting tears again. What an evening of ups and downs it had been. She blinked rapidly to keep from giving way to the sadness washing over her, and suddenly she knew exactly what she wanted to say.

She looked Holden full in the face, her chin high. "Dr. Winters, I am not better off seeing God as only a figment of imagination and His Word as a book of fairy tales. God is alive and real, and His Spirit is living in my heart at this very moment." She touched her chest with a quivering hand and then gestured to the surrounding area. "His hand created all of the wonders my eyes and ears enjoy. Look at the twinkling stars—millions of them shining in the vastness of space! And those mighty ocean waves—see how they crash? Listen to the power as they roar across the beach, carried by winds that rush around the world and touch every person who lives on this planet. When that wind touches you, you're experiencing the reality of an awesome God, whether you choose to acknowledge Him or not."

She glared at him, daring him to contradict her. She was sure amusement glinted behind the cynicism in his blue eyes, and it both irritated and challenged her. "I see your pessimism, Dr. Winters, but I'll not be dragged down by it. On the contrary, be prepared, because somehow, in some way, I'll prove I'm right. Just wait and see."

Micah burst into applause, startling Callie. Wrapped up in her desire to penetrate the wall Holden had erected around himself, she'd forgotten about her audience.

"Hear, hear!" Micah's face was alight with pleasure. "Callie, remind me to never get in an argument with you. You'd win hands down."

Holden snorted, but his expression was far from harsh. "She's merely thrown down the gauntlet, Micah, she hasn't won any arguments yet. All I hear is her passion, no proof. I suppose time will tell on that. But there isn't time for it yet tonight. We need to head back to the base."

Callie's hackles rose at being discussed as if she wasn't present. She spoke more loudly than she'd intended. "I suspect you're afraid to continue this conversation with me because deep down you know there's a Higher Being, but for some reason you've decided to fight against Him. That in itself is proof of His existence, because you don't fight a nothing." She crossed her arms and gloated as if she'd achieved checkmate in a championship chess game.

Holden's mouth fixed itself in a stern line and his eyes darkened with anger. "The only thing I'm fighting, Miss Myers, is indigestion from too much food and too much unpalatable table conversation." He stood, pushed in his chair, and began stalking toward the car without a backward glance.

Callie watched after him, her chest-expanding elation now a rock of disappointment setting in her stomach.

Lydia sighed. "Callie, don't let him bother you. Remember what I told you before? Ice water. Pure ice water."

Callie shook her head. "I can't believe that, Lydia. There's something wrong—something he's battling that closes him off."

Micah placed his hand on Callie's arm. "Listen, I love Holden like a brother, but in this case, Lydia is right. Holden is cold, and he means to be." He closed his eyes for a moment, as if praying for guidance. When he looked at Callie again, she read regret in his expressive blue eyes. "I hope I'm not overstepping my boundaries here. We don't know each other all that well, but I think I see you getting attached." He glanced toward Holden's retreating figure, then turned back and spoke quietly. "Don't fall for him, Callie. You'll only get hurt." He gave her arm a quick pat before striding off to pay for their meals.

Callie and Lydia headed slowly across the sand toward Micah's Coupe, but Callie saw nothing of the beauty of Oahu's nightfall. Her senses were attuned to the solitary figure of Dr. Holden Winters standing beside the waiting vehicle with his back to them, his shoulders slumped and his hands thrust deep in his pockets. She read in his pose an overwhelming sadness, not a coldness no matter what Lydia and Micah would have her believe.

He needed God. Was that why God had sent her to Hawaii, to introduce Holden Winters to His love? Holden had accused her of issuing a challenge, and she accepted it. She wouldn't stop until she'd proven God's existence and Holden admitted his need for God in his life. Calliope Jane Myers never backed down from a challenge, so Dr. Ice Water better ready himself. He wouldn't know what had hit him by the time she was through.

8

Callie's determination to convince Dr. Winters of the reality of God became an obsession in the weeks that followed the dinner in Haleiwa. Each time their paths crossed, which wasn't as often as one would think given the size of the army base and their mutual hospital territory, she worked in some reference to God into their conversation. There was never time for a long, heartfelt talk, but she prayed every night for God to water the seeds she threw at Holden.

At first he met her proclamations of God's existence with distant coolness. But as time slipped by, Callie noticed a subtle softening. Oh, he was never openly accepting of her words, but instead of ignoring her or responding curtly, she began to sense a teasing undercurrent, as if he actually enjoyed the challenge. She took it as a dent in his armor, and she was determined to keep hammering away until she'd made a gaping hole.

Miss Torkelson discouraged fraternizing with the doctors while on duty, and Holden kept a professional distance that sometimes aggravated Callie. But somehow Micah always managed to locate Callie and spend a few minutes in conversation. Callie enjoyed his company. He was very charming and always made her laugh. But afterwards she'd find herself wishing she could have similar exchanges with Holden.

On a Thursday afternoon in late April, Callie was humming softly as she removed the sheets from a bed. She turned, her arms full, and found someone standing directly behind her. She shrieked and threw the whole wad of linens in the air. Once she'd caught her breath, she smacked her intruder on the arm. "Dr. Hatcher, you scared the life out of me!"

Micah laughed in his typical, unruffled way. "Well, you're in luck then, because my specialty is putting the life back into people."

Callie laughed, too, unable to stay irritated with him even though he had startled her beyond belief creeping up behind her that way. She gathered up the linens and headed for the laundry room.

Micah fell in step beside her. "So, Miss Myers, do you have any plans for your weekend?"

Callie shrugged and shifted her arms slightly to keep a corner of the sheet from slipping loose. "No, not really. Lydia and I had talked about possibly taking the Pineapple Limited into Honolulu now that the cat fever epidemic seems to be under control." How helpless she'd felt, watching the poor afflicted men battle for breath against the inflammation in their respiratory tracts. "We need a little lighthearted fun after the past three weeks. It was really hard to lose those two men."

"Yes." For once Micah lost his teasing tone. "We should be thankful it was only two. Considering how many men contracted catarrh, I'd say there could have been many more deaths. Holden said you did a great job caring for everyone."

Callie stopped and gaped at him. "Really? Holden said

that?" She wouldn't have guessed he even noticed her, he always appeared so focused when he was on duty.

"Yes, he did. And take it as a big compliment because Holden doesn't say positive things often."

"I've gathered that." Callie set her feet in motion.

"So what were you and Lydia planning to do in Honolulu?" Micah sauntered alongside her, his easy smile in place again.

She grinned. "Lydia wants to spend the night in the Royal Hawaiian Hotel and spy on the officers as they take their wives to the evening dance. But I don't know if the Limited would get us back in time for work on Sunday night. Lydia's on C duty next week." They reached the laundry, and Callie paused outside the door and looked up at Micah. "Why do you ask?"

A hint of pink tinged his ears. "There's a good movie playing at the base theatre, and I thought you might enjoy seeing it."

"Oh? What is it?"

"*It Happened One Night*, starring Clark Gable and Claudette Colbert. Did you see it when it came out?"

Callie wrinkled her nose. "Huh-uh. I've never been to a theatre."

Micah's eyes widened. "You've never been to a theatre? You've never seen a movie?"

"No."

"Silent films? Talkies? Nothing?"

Callie laughed. "Micah, you forget that I grew up in a very small town. There was no theatre nearby, and my folks didn't see it as something I needed to experience, so no effort was made to take me to one."

"And you're *how* old?"

Callie burst out laughing.

He grinned. "I forget how innocent you small-town Arkansas girls can be. Well, as I said, *It Happened One Night* is playing this weekend. It won some awards—in 1934 or 1935, I think—so it's not new, but I guess if you've never been to a theatre it will be new to you, huh? Would you like to see it?"

Callie smiled. "Sure. I'll check with Lydia, but I'm sure she'll be agreeable."

To her puzzlement, Micah's bright expression dimmed momentarily, but then he spoke in his usual, jovial way. "Sounds great, Callie. I'll let you know the details tomorrow before you get off work, okay?"

"Okay." As Micah turned to walk away, she called out, "Will Dr. Winters be accompanying us?"

Micah turned back. His face was a study. Callie couldn't quite decide what he was thinking."Probably not. Holden doesn't care much for movies." He sucked in his lips. "Would you like me to ask him?"

Callie gave her best smile as she shook her head. "If he doesn't care for movies, don't bother him. I'll talk to you tomorrow." She stepped into the laundry room and dumped her armful of sheets into the wash tub. As she straightened, she frowned. If she was going to get her point across to Holden, she needed time with him. Brief snatches caught on the hospital floor weren't enough. How could she spend time with him without appearing forward? If only she had more experience in dealing with men. Then she'd know how to deal with Holden and how to react to Micah.

Micah's expression had definitely changed when she mentioned checking with Lydia. Was it possible he hadn't intended to ask the two of them, but only Callie? Had she just been asked out on a date? She lifted her quivering fingers to her lips. She wasn't averse to spending time with Micah. He was fun, and she trusted him to be a gentleman. But Lydia had set her sights on him. How would Lydia react to Callie spending time alone with Micah? Callie didn't want to jeopardize her friendship with Lydia, but neither did she want to hurt Micah's feelings. He, too, was a friend.

"What a pickle." She turned the spigot and began filling the wash tub with water. Then, needing an in-depth talk with her Lord, she turned off the water and knelt beside the tub. "I need Your guidance, Lord. Help me know how to handle Micah's attention. Although I shouldn't, I feel my heart leap every time Holden is near. Surely that means something, doesn't it? I'm meant to return to Shyler's Point—the people there need me as a nurse—so please settle my heart and point me away from Holden. Help me focus in the direction You would have me to go." She remained on her knees for several more minutes, her mind quiet and her spirit in tune with her Maker. Then, feeling better, she rose and returned to her task.

Even though her spirit had calmed, her mind continued to wonder. Why was she continually drawn toward a man who had neither the desire to be with her or to recognize her God?

HOLDEN

Holden yanked open the heavy wooden door to the base hospital and nearly collided head-on with Micah who was coming out.

"Whoa, buddy!" Micah laughed, grasping Holden's upper arm. "Guess I'm destined to startle people today."

"Oh?" Holden pulled the door shut behind him and leaned against it. Micah was fairly twitching with excitement. He'd share the reason if given time. It didn't take long.

"Yep, I almost scared a handful of bed linens out of Callie's arms earlier, and while her defenses were down I took advantage and asked her out for tomorrow night." Micah waggled his eyebrows and his grin spread from ear to ear. He poked Holden with his elbow. "She said yes."

An image of Callie holding Micah's arm and smiling up at him in her sweet, attentive way, flitted through Holden's mind, and he stifled the urge to snarl. "Congratulations." He stepped forward to move around Micah.

Micah stopped him with a hand on his arm. "But there's a problem."

Holden waited, his head tipped in an impatient angle. "What can be the problem, Micah? You've talked for weeks of little else than asking the girl out. Now you've done it and she's agreeable. I see no problem in that." He heard the hard edge in his tone, but he couldn't control it. As much as he resisted his own growing interest in Callie, the idea of Callie with Micah hit a nerve.

Micah, as always, ignored Holden's grouchiness. "Callie—when I asked her—automatically assumed the invitation was for her and Lydia both. So I've got two dates."

Holden pulled away. "Nuh-uh." He made it two steps before Micah dove into his pathway.

"It wouldn't be so bad. We're going to a movie, so you won't have to talk, and Callie specifically asked if you would be going. Besides that, Lydia's gorgeous."

Holden's heart jumped at the mention of Callie asking about him, but he hardened himself against it. "Micah, I know I went last time, but—"

"You had fun with Lydia at Haleiwa—you know you did." Micah put his hands in his pockets and grinned. "So come on. How about it? Just one more time as a double?"

Holden looked past Micah's shoulder, his mouth set in a firm line. Yes, Lydia was a beautiful woman, and he had paid attention to her at Haleiwa. Mostly to keep himself from paying too much attention to Callie. But he had no desire to continue a charade of interest. His mother had preached to him firmly about the Golden Rule when he was growing up, and he wouldn't want someone using him as a barrier against someone else. He shook his head. "No, Micah."

"Oh, come on." Micah's joviality slipped a bit. "Why do you have to be so stubborn? It's not normal for a man to be alone. You can't spend the rest of your life as a hermit because Lorna died. You've got to start living again."

Holden's face grew hot, and he tightened his jaw to keep a rein on his temper. Micah had no right to speak of Holden's past. Micah couldn't begin to fathom the depth of pain Lorna's and Timmy's deaths had wrought. Did Micah expect him to blithely brush the hurt aside and pick up with someone else as though his years with Lorna had no meaning?

"I'm not in the habit of toying with women's affections." Holden growled the words in an effort to keep his tone low. "I will not play footsie with Lydia just to give you an opening with Callie."

"I'm not asking you to—"

"You're putting me in the position of keeping Lydia tidily out of the way to help clear the pathway for your pursuit of Callie." Holden raised his palm, a gesture meant to suppress any other protests. "It's dishonest. I may be a lot of things, but I am not dishonest. I will not play games with Lydia that make it easier for you to chase after Callie."

Micah's face flamed red and his forehead wore a series of deep creases. "Are you insinuating that I'm not honest?"

"I'm not insinuating anything, but may I remind you of your insinuation when you first met Callie, that your Bible is something you read on a daily basis? I happen to know that Bible hadn't been opened regularly. Maybe it was back when you were a boy, because you do have a knowledge of scripture, but you haven't actively pored over that Book since I've known you. Yet you intentionally led Callie to believe otherwise. If you truly care for the girl, then be honest with her."

Micah's jaw thrust out belligerently, but he didn't argue.

Holden continued speaking as if the words had been waiting for a chance to break through a gate. "Callie is obviously unschooled in the ways of flirtation. You, on the other hand, have had a great deal of practice. Now, it's none of my business if you choose to flirt with her, but I won't be a party to it. Leave me out of it."

"Seems to me you want to be right in the middle of it."

Micah's uncharacteristic sarcasm stirred Holden's anger. "What is that supposed to mean?"

Micah crossed his arms and peered at Holden through squinted eyes. "You're awfully protective. Are you sure you aren't interested in Callie, and you're trying to steer me away to keep her available for yourself?"

Holden balled his fists and counted to three. "Micah, if you weren't my friend, I'd punch you right in the mouth."

"And if you weren't my friend, I'd sock you right back."

"My interest in Callie is strictly platonic." Holden spoke firmly to convince himself as much as Micah. "She's innocent, and she has high values. We both know that. Don't try to compromise her values for your own personal pleasure."

Micah's mouth dropped open and his eyes widened. He placed his hand against his chest and jutted his chin forward. "You think I'd do that to Callie?"

"I don't know what to think." Holden's anger paled in light of Micah's reaction. "I've watched you flirt with every one of the base nurses, yet you've not made a commitment to any of them. Callie's new, so now you're going after her. How can I be sure you aren't going to cut her loose after playing with her for awhile?"

"Because Callie's different. She's the kind of girl who inspires you to be a better person than you were before. She's not the kind of girl you toy with. I don't want to hurt her, Holden. I think…" He looked aside, his jaw muscles twitching. Then he shrugged. "Aw, what do you care anyway?" He turned toward the door.

Holden stopped him. "You think…?"

Micah searched his eyes, as if trying to decide whether or not to trust Holden with his thoughts. Finally Micah sighed, and his shoulders slumped. "I think I might be falling in love with her."

Their long-standing friendship overcame the irritation Holden had felt earlier. "How can you think that? You don't really know her that well, Micah."

"I know I don't, because I can't ever get any time with her. At least not time of substance." His voice took on a fervency. "But she's everything I could ask for in a wife. She's a Christian, she's reserved yet somehow also spirited. Not to mention she's just as cute as can be with that unruly hair and eyes like emeralds. My parents would welcome her with open arms if I brought her home. How do I know God didn't send her to this island to become my helpmate?"

The old-fashioned term made Holden smile.

Micah's face twisted into a grimace of disgust. "Aw, I should've known not to trust you with this." He braced his hand on the door.

Holden sighed. "I'll go."

Micah froze in place, his eyes wide. "You mean it?"

Holden nodded. "It's against my better judgment, but I've never had a better friend than you. Just make sure both Callie and Lydia understand I'm not along as Lydia's date, I'm along to round out the foursome."

"You got it, buddy." Micah pounded Holden's shoulder, all smiles. "And you won't regret this. Thanks, Holden." He headed out the door, a spring in his step and a whistle on his lips.

With a sigh, Holden scuffed toward his office. Micah was better suited to Callie than he ever could be. He was too formal, too sad. Too faithless. Maybe if he encouraged a relationship between Micah and Callie to grow, he'd find peace from his own odd yearnings for her. While it seemed the wisest thing to do from an intellectual standpoint, his heart was harder to convince.

9

Saturday evening Holden walked with Micah to Grant Hall to pick up Callie and Lydia. Every step that brought him closer to Callie made his blood pressure climb, and by the time Micah opened the main door, Holden was gritting his teeth in self-reproach.

The girls waited in the large group room, and when Holden spotted Callie his palms began to sweat and his heart started thumping like the bass drum in a Sousa march. She wore a sweet red and white polka dot dress. He'd always heard redheads shouldn't wear red, but somehow this dress brought out the gold highlights in her auburn hair, and her green eyes seemed even larger and more luminous than before. He could hardly keep his eyes off her.

Micah whistled softly between his teeth. "Callie, darlin', you look good enough to eat—like a peppermint candy." His gaze swept toward Lydia who stood beside Callie with a practiced smile on her painted lips. "You too, Lydia. Too bad we'll be holed up in a dark movie theatre. You two need to be shown off on the town. You'll rival the movie starlets, I'm sure."

"Oh, Micah." Callie laughed, her cheeks flushing scarlet. She turned her smile on Holden. "Good evening, Dr. Winters."

Holden nodded in her direction, swallowing to dislodge the lump that filled his throat. "Good evening, Miss Myers. Miss Eldredge."

Micah rolled his eyes and gave Holden a friendly slap on the shoulder. "Now, come on, let's not all be so formal. We're going to a movie, not an opera. So can we drop all those titles and just stick to first names?"

Lydia shrugged with a feminine lifting of one shoulder, coquettishly batting her eyelashes in Micah's direction. "I'm all in favor of being familiar rather than formal, Micah." She stepped forward and slipped her hand through his elbow, smiling up at him.

Micah sent a helpless glance at Holden. "Well, then, are you ladies ready to go?"

Callie, too, seemed suddenly uncertain how to proceed. She looked from Micah to Holden to Micah again. Then with a self-conscious giggle she skipped forward two steps and took Micah's other arm, the way the girls had done at their first meeting in the mess hall. She peeked around Micah at Holden. "Dr. Winters? I mean, Holden. Catch hold of a spare elbow and we can go."

He couldn't keep the grin from twitching at his cheeks. She looked like a nymph with her tousled hair falling across her sweet forehead and those incredibly green eyes sparkling mischievously. He recognized her ploy, and although he would have dearly loved to step clear around the three of them and offer his arm to her, it made much more sense to simply present his elbow to Lydia. Callie had very gracefully saved all of them from an uncomfortable moment, and his admiration grew tremendously in the few seconds it took for him to follow her lead.

He held out his elbow in gentlemanly style. "Lydia?"

The girl immediately took hold, giving him her too-practiced smile. They moved as one, chuckling lightly as they kept their feet in perfect left-right-left formation. When they reached the door, Holden opened it with a slight bow. Since it was impossible for all four of them to pass through together, it would have been natural for him to guide Lydia through. But to his amazement, instead of stepping aside with him and allowing Micah and Callie to pass, Lydia removed her hand from his elbow. She kept a firm grip on Micah's arm and moved through the doorway, forcing Callie to release Micah's arm or be slammed into the doorframe.

Micah followed Lydia's lead, but he turned a perplexed grimace over his shoulder as Lydia guided him onto the sidewalk.

Holden and Callie were left in the doorway, looking into one another's uncertain eyes.

"Are you coming?" Lydia assumed the role of hostess, seemingly unaware—or uncaring—of everyone else's discomfort.

Holden couldn't decide if she was incredibly naïve or incredibly manipulative. Either way, it left him in an impossible situation. Should he escort Micah's date—the woman with whom Micah thought he was falling in love? Whose feelings should he spare, Micah's or Callie's?

Callie stood motionless, her eyebrows raised in silent query as she waited for him to make a move. Another glance at Micah confirmed his displeasure with the situation, but even Micah seemed unable to come up with a solution.

At last Holden shrugged and gestured for Callie to precede him. Once they were outside, he held out his elbow. After only a moment's hesitation, she placed her small hand through the crook of his arm. He detected a slight quivering, but he chose to ignore it. He hoped she would ignore his nervousness, as well.

Lydia and Micah led the way toward the base theatre with Holden and Callie following a few feet behind. Lydia kept up a steady stream of lighthearted conversation, intermittently looking over her shoulder to include the pair behind her, but for the most part directing her comments to Micah. Micah nodded, but it was obvious to Holden he was doing more listening than anything else. Holden didn't contribute, nor did Callie. Although she glanced up at him occasionally with a quick smile, her eyes were wide and she seemed skittish. He longed to put her at ease. How could he encourage the fiery, full-of-vinegar Callie to rear her regal head?

Ah. He knew. He only needed an opportunity.

They reached the end of the walkways protected by overhead balconies and stepped out to move across the open courtyard. His chance presented itself. He pointed skyward, and her gaze followed the direction of his guiding finger. "Looks like we might have a full moon tonight."

"'The sun has one kind of splendor, the moon another and the stars another; and star differs from star in splendor.'"

"Tennyson?" he questioned, tongue in cheek.

A quick shake of her head made her curls bounce.

"Lord Byron, then."

She gave him a slight tug on the arm along with a frown of mild rebuke. "No, silly, the apostle Paul."

"Oh, yes." He nodded sagely. "How could I be so foolish. Of course it would have been the apostle Paul."

"You're making fun of me again, Dr. Winters." Her reprimand held an undercurrent of amusement.

He assumed an affronted air. "Would I do that?"

"Only every chance you can get."

He laughed and tightened his elbow against his ribs to

hold her hand more securely. He glanced down to find her smiling up at him, much more relaxed. It set his foolish heart into fluttering again.

She tipped her head. "You know, Holden, you and the apostle Paul have a great deal in common."

He raised his eyebrows in a show of inquisitiveness, although he was reasonably certain he knew where she was heading.

"You see, before Paul was Paul, he was Saul, and he fought fiercely against Christians. It took a blinding light on a road to convince him of the reality of God, and once realization came, he became as zealous in his belief as he had been in his disbelief. You fight fiercely against anything that smacks of Christianity, but once you're convinced of God's presence, you'll be completely changed, too."

Holden peered down his nose at her. "Before Paul was Paul, he was Saul?" He meant to tease her, but she apparently took him seriously, because she nodded earnestly.

"Yes, originally Paul's name was Saul. He was on his way to Damascus to arrest as many believers as he could when a light from heaven blinded him, and the Lord Himself spoke to him. Then the Lord sent a man named Ananias to Saul to help him learn about God, and Saul became a believer. Later, as Paul, he became a great apostle, leading many people to believe in God."

"You definitely know your stories, Callie." Holden patted the hand that rested in the crook of his elbow. She'd gotten every detail correct. "Micah, are you familiar with Paul-who-once-was-Saul?"

Micah lobbed a grin over his shoulder. "Why, sure. He's was a real trouble-maker until he lost his sight on the Damascus road. When he got his sight back three days later, he could truly see. Became a great disciple."

Callie grinned up at Holden smugly. "See?"

"I see that you and Micah have been reading the same storybook." Holden stifled the urge to laugh aloud at Callie's indignant expression. She was extraordinarily cute when she pouted, but it was best not to point that out, just as he would keep to himself his previous knowledge of Saul's incredible transformation. There was no sense in opening himself up to too many questions.

"Dr. Winters, you are impossible."

"So I've heard it said." He hid his smile at her scowl. "But I believe I've also heard it said—by a rather small-of-stature red-headed nurse—that nothing is impossible with her God." He glanced at her out of the corner of his eyes. Sure enough—his words found their mark.

Her expression softened into one of apology, and her steps slowed. Her fingers pressed into his arm until he looked her fully in the face. The contrition in her green eyes was almost his undoing, but with effort he kept a solemn expression.

"I'm sorry. You're right. I won't call you impossible ever again."

This contrite, sincere Callie was very difficult to resist. He quickly sought a way to stir her ire once more so he could remain on safer footing. "Don't make promises you can't keep because I can try the patience of Job."

Callie gratified him by rising to the bait. "I just said I wouldn't call you *impossible*. That leaves you wide open for lots of other titles."

Holden threw back his head and laughed as he started them in motion again. "Ah, Miss Myers, I'm sure it does." Her sparkling eyes shone up at him, rivaling the brightness of the stars now appearing in the sky, and he turned his gaze away before he gave in to the urge to kiss her breathless.

"And here we are." Micah came to a halt in front of the

theatre. "Wait here while I get the tickets." He stepped up to the ticket window while Lydia, Holden, and Callie waited.

Holden's gaze roved across the assembled boisterous servicemen, and when a noisy group moved aside, his eyes found the advertising poster in the window of the theatre. He had an almost physical sensation of traveling backward in time, to a Saturday night with Lorna, her hand on his arm as they entered the Chicago Palace to see the debut of *It Happened One Night.* The memory was so strong he could smell Lorna's perfume, feel the gentle weight of her head against his shoulder, hear her soft sigh as the hero took the heroine into his arms.

The urge to run, to hide, to escape pummeled him. What was he doing here with another woman on his arm? He battled for breath.

Micah returned. "What say we trade partners for awhile, buddy? Give you an opportunity to visit with Lydia, and me with Callie?"

It took a few seconds for Micah's words to filter through Holden's brain and make sense. "Sure. Sure, that's fine." He transferred Callie's unresisting hand to Micah's extended arm. He didn't look at her. Despite his need to release her, for some reason he didn't want to see her willingness in being released.

Lydia expelled a small huff, and for a moment Holden wondered if she would refuse. But then she took his offered elbow. He drew a deep breath for fortitude, then escorted Lydia inside the theatre.

CALLIE

"I have a headache." Lydia voiced the complaint as she trailed Callie and Micah from the well-lighted lobby of the theatre and stepped onto the shadowed sidewalk.

Callie glanced at her in concern. Holden trailed Lydia instead of escorting her. Was his stand-offishness the source of Lydia's headache?

"I'm sorry." Callie released Micah's arm and took Lydia's hand. "Would you like me to help you back to the apartment and get you an aspirin?"

Micah touched Callie's arm. "I was hoping we could go to the mess hall for a cup of coffee."

Lydia pressed her fingertips to her temple. "I think I'd better return to my room. I haven't had a chance to read the letter I received from a friend from home, and I want to do that before my headache becomes worse."

Callie nodded. "All right, Lydia, I'll—"

"I'll walk you to your quarters."

Callie frowned at Holden's interruption. He'd been behaving peculiarly since she and Lydia had switched partners—aloof and almost angry. But aloof and angry was probably closer to normal for Holden than relaxed and humorous.

"That's kind of you." Lydia shot daggers at Micah. She clutched Holden's arm with both hands, holding it tightly against her ribs. "Thank you for your concern." They started up the sidewalk.

Callie called after them, "Will you be all right?"

Lydia didn't bother to turn around. "I'll be fine. Take your time, but be quiet when you come in."

Callie lifted her gaze to Micah. She shrugged, offering a weak smile. "I guess I'm all yours."

"Lucky me."

His husky comment created a fire in Callie's face. She looked aside and bit her lip.

He put his hand on her spine. "Are you interested in a cup of coffee?"

"Actually," she said, hoping he would appreciate her honesty, "I prefer not to drink coffee so close to bedtime. I think I'd rather take a walk. I can't get enough of the beauty of this island. There are so many unique flowers blooming. Do you mind?"

"Not at all." His cheerful tone proved she hadn't offended him. "We'll stroll around the outer periphery of the barracks as we head you home again. Lots of hibiscus and oleander growing along those walkways."

Micah linked fingers with Callie and gently swung their joined hands as they ambled toward Grant Hall. The contact took Callie by surprise—it was much more intimate than a formal arm-in-arm position of escort—but she didn't want to hurt his feelings by pulling away. For awhile they walked without speaking, but Callie labeled it an easy silence, one that spoke of friendship where there was no need to fill each moment with prattle. She sighed, enjoying the opportunity to walk under a canopy of stars while a gentle breeze ruffled her hair and Micah's warm hand offered security.

They paused beside a large bush, heavy with a profusion of delicate blooms, and Micah released her hand. He pinched free one fragrant red blossom and, his expression tender, tucked the bloom in her hair above her left ear. He then stepped back, openly appraised her, and smiled.

"That's perfect. You were meant to wear a flower of oleander in your hair." He took her hand again and led her along the walkway.

The gentle weight of the flower against her ear gave Callie a strange, fluttering feeling in her chest. The silence wasn't as comfortable as it had been moments before. As they walked beneath the arched opening to the courtyard between the barracks, Micah aimed a warm smile at her.

"So, Miss Calliope, did you enjoy your first movie?"

Relieved by his casual question, she nodded. "Oh, yes!"

They spent a spirited few minutes discussing the plot and characters. Micah claimed the whole thing was too far-fetched—what rich girl would intentionally leave all that behind her? But Callie insisted it proved that money wasn't everything. They argued fiercely, laughing much, and by the time they reached Grant Hall, Callie had forgotten her earlier discomfort and was fully enjoying herself again.

When they reached the doors of the hall, Micah leaned his shoulder against the stucco wall and tugged slightly on Callie's hand. She was drawn forward until her nose almost bumped against his chin. His arms crept around her shoulders and held her there. She looked up into his eyes, puzzled and a little unsettled by his assertiveness.

"You are very pretty in the moonlight, Calliope Myers." His eyelids drooped slightly, giving him a contented look.

"Thank you." She backward slightly in an attempt to put some distance between them.

"Actually..." His fingers began drawing circles on her shoulder blade. "You are pretty in the sunlight. In fact, I can honestly say I've never seen you look anything but pretty. How do you manage that— being pretty all the time?"

Callie swallowed a nervous titter. While Micah had never hidden the fact that he found her attractive, he'd never been so blatantly forward. How should she respond? "I—I guess it just comes naturally." Such a feeble attempt at humor, but Micah chuckled.

He pulled her briefly against his chest in a hug. His lips were near her ear, and his breath stirred the petals of the flower. "Ah, Callie, you are truly irresistible." Without warning, he took her by the upper arms, turned her, and tipped his face toward her.

Callie averted her face. His lips grazed her cheek.

He pulled back and looked into her eyes, then released another light laugh. "Did I surprise you?"

Surprise was an understatement. She closed her astounded mouth and blinked rapidly a few times to convince her eyelids that they needn't remain as wide as saucers. "Y-yes."

"Don't you like surprises?"

With a soft laugh, she slipped from his embrace. She removed the red oleander from its spot above her ear and shook it at him to cover her embarrassment. "Don't you know a gentleman asks permission before trying to kiss a lady?"

"But then he might not get the kiss after all." His eyes glittered with humor. "And think of all the fun they'd both be missing."

He reached for her, but she sidestepped, eluding his grasp. His hands lowered to his sides, his face creasing in perplexity. "What's the matter? Did I offend you? If so, I apologize."

Callie shook her head. "I'm not offended, Micah. I'm flattered that you find me attractive enough to want to kiss me."

He struck a gentlemanly pose, one hand on his heart, the other reaching, palm up, towards her. He lifted his chin and gave her his best serious expression. "Then may I kiss you, Miss Myers?"

She couldn't help it—she burst out laughing.

His shoulders drooped as if he'd been injured. "The lady scoffs at me. I may never recover."

"Oh, Micah." Callie giggled. "How can anyone take you seriously when you're such a clown?"

He gazed directly into her face, his expression serious. "Callie, I'm not playing a game. I truly would like to kiss you. May I?"

Callie prayed for the right words, then said very kindly, "No, Micah, you may not."

"Why not? You said I didn't offend you." Realization seemed to dawn across his boyish face. "Oh. You don't like me."

"No!" Callie scampered to him and grabbed his hand. "I do like you, Micah. It's just that…well…I don't *like* you."

He scratched his head. "You lost me."

How could she make him understand without hurting him? "I like you, Micah. Who wouldn't? You're handsome and funny and very charming. You're a wonderful friend. Of course, I like you. But, just then, when I knew you were going to kiss me…" She held her breath, gathering her courage.

"Yes…?"

She gulped and looked down. "Well, it was like being kissed…by a brother." She peeked at him from the corners of her eyes.

His lips twitched. He sniffed, rubbed his nose, and sniffed again. "It's pretty hard to argue with that."

"I'm sorry, Micah."

He gave one of his Micah grins—the left side of his lips tipped upward sweetly. But the grin didn't quite reach his eyes. "Hey, don't be sorry. You were honest with me, and I appreciate it. After the way I came on to you, you could have taken advantage of the situation and played me for a fool, but you didn't. You have nothing to apologize for."

Callie impulsively hugged him. "Thank you, Micah. You are such a nice man. I can see why Lydia likes you so much." Then she jumped back and clapped her hand over her mouth, her eyes wide. "Oh, my goodness, I wasn't supposed to tell you."

He chuckled. "Callie, darlin', you're not revealin' anything I didn't already know. Lydia isn't exactly subtle." The Texas twang was back, which meant the teasing Micah was in full swing. Suddenly his expression changed, and he reached for her hand. "Callie, you've been honest with me. May I be honest with you?"

She nodded slowly.

He guided her to a short bench at the edge of the walkway and sat, tugging her hand so she sat next to him. The overhead porch light bathed them in a soft, yellow glow, and Callie clearly read the concern in Micah's blue eyes as he draped his arm across the back of the bench and shifted sideways to face her. "Callie, just like it's been obvious that Lydia likes me, it's obvious that you feel something for Holden."

Her cheeks flamed, and she turned her face away.

He caught her chin with his fingers and made her look at him. "Now quit that blushin' and listen to your big brother."

She offered a small smile, her fingers toying with the bloom she still held, and met his gaze.

"There's something you don't know about Holden, but I'm not going to betray his confidence by sharing it with you. However, I will tell you this much—Holden is a man who has hardened his heart. He's hardened it toward God, he's hardened it toward loving, and he's working overtime to harden it toward you because you are such a tempting distraction." He paused for a moment, looking skyward as if seeking guidance, then he tipped his head and settled his gaze on her again. "Continue to pray for him, reach out to him with Christian caring, but don't give him your heart. I'm not telling you this to try to persuade you to love me. Please believe me. I'm telling you this because if you give your heart to Holden, he'll hurt you. I don't want to see that happen."

This was the second time Micah had warned her about being hurt by Holden. What had happened to make Holden shut his heart away? She sighed. "Micah, I appreciate your concern, and I don't question your motives. But you needn't worry. I'm not at all interested in developing any romantic relationships here." His expression remained dubious. She nodded. "It's true. When I've finished my stint here, I'll return to Shyler's Point. The only way my folks would agree to me getting the Red Cross Training was if I promised to use it in my own hometown. We have no doctor there, and the people desperately need some sort of medical care. I'll be it."

"That's very commendable, Callie, but I don't see how one relates to the other. Why can't you be a nurse in Shyler's Point and still pursue a relationship here?"

She laughed. "If you'd ever visited Shyler's Point, you'd know. There's not much there, no reason for anyone to want to move there. If I get involved with someone, I would be inclined to follow them wherever they wanted to go, just as Naomi promised Ruth. I can't imagine anyone choosing to go to Shyler's Point."

Micah grimaced. "People have to make a living. If there's no way to provide for a family, then you're probably right."

"So you see why I can't become romantically involved?" She needed him to understand. "I have a responsibility to my home and family."

"Yes, I understand." He lifted her hand and brushed his lips across her knuckles. "But I admit I wish it could be different."

She allowed him to hold her hand, and she blew out a noisy breath. "This boy-girl stuff is complicated. Makes you wonder how anybody ever gets together."

Micah laughed. "Oh, it's complicated, but it's worth it. And when the right two find each other—*shazam*! Things are never the same."

For Callie, things had been unsettled ever since she flew off the top of that log and yanked the button from the shirt front of her mysterious rescuer. She looked sharply at Micah. Here was her opportunity to ask. She turned her face toward the stars and pursed her lips pensively, gathering her courage.

"All right, what are you thinking?" Humor laced his tone. She looked at him, her eyebrows high.

He laughed. "You can't hide anything with those big green eyes, Miss Myers, so don't look so baffled. Come on, spill it. You can tell big brother Micah." His eyes twinkled merrily.

She ducked her head then peeked at him out of the corners of her eyes. He was waiting patiently, and the question was on her tongue, ready to be asked. But suddenly she didn't want to know if her unknown helper was Micah. Somehow it would spoil the mystery. She wanted to find out on her own, not through an open inquiry.

"It's nothing, really." She could tell by the look on his face he didn't believe her. She stood. "It's late, and there's church service tomorrow, so I better go in. Besides, Lydia is probably wondering what happened to me."

Micah nodded and rose. He placed her hand into the crook of his elbow and walked her to the door. As he opened it for her, he said, "Good night, Callie. Thank you for a very pleasant evening."

"Thank you. I had a very nice time." But as she walked inside, she lamented inwardly to her heavenly Father. *God, I wasn't quite honest with Micah when I said I wasn't interested in pursuing relationships here. I have complete peace about returning to Shyler's Point—I know that's where You want me, and I know I simply can't attach myself to anyone here. So why does my heart tug me toward Holden?*

10

"**B**ack so soon?"

The voice in the dark startled Callie. She dropped her shoes, which she had removed so she could enter the bedroom quietly. At the abrupt *thud-thud*, the bedside lamp came on. Lydia raised up on one elbow, her mouth set in a grim line.

"I'm sorry, I didn't mean to wake you." Callie sat on the edge of Lydia's bed. "How is your headache?"

"Fine." Lydia glanced at the wilting flower in Callie's hand, then she flumped back onto her pillows and crossed her arms over the covers. "Did you and Micah have a good time?" Her voice was caustic.

"I suppose so." Callie sighed. Lydia's anger was the result of jealousy. But how to fix it? Callie had never been actively pursued by a man before, and she had no idea how to handle being seen as competition for a man's attention.

"Well, I'm glad you had fun. That Holden is rude. He's stiff and uncommunicative, and I don't ever want to be dumped with him again."

"Lydia, I didn't dump you with—"

" 'I'm all yours,'" she sing-songed. "It's disgusting for you to hang all over Micah when you told me you didn't like him. You're leading him on."

"Lydia! I am not—"

"I don't want to discuss it, Callie. Good night!" Lydia rolled over, pulling the covers up to her ear. "Now that my headache is gone, I want the fan on. It's stuffy in here."

Callie stared at the back of Lydia's head. Honestly! She dropped the oleander bloom on the stand between the beds, rose, stomped to the center of the room, and pulled the fan's cord. The rhythmic squawks grew closer together as the blades picked up speed. Oh, how she hated that intrusive sound. She'd suffered enough angst tonight. She wouldn't listen to the squeaks. She gave the cord another mighty yank—so mighty that when she released it, it sprang back into the air and almost hooked over one of the blades. Then she marched to the window, disengaged the catch, and swung the window outward as far as it would go. If Lydia wanted air, then she could have air from the great outdoors for a change. No more of that noisy, irritating fan!

Callie stripped off her dress and tossed it carelessly at the foot of the bed. She snatched up her nightgown and threw it on with clumsy, angry motions. Then she turned off the lamp with a violent twist of her wrist, relishing the loud *click!* as she did so. She threw the covers back, flapping then unnecessarily, and flopped onto the mattress. The springs pinged as she bounced from her side to her back and to her side again.

Lydia sighed. A persecuted sigh.

Callie smiled. A smug smile.

But then her smile faded. What was she doing, bouncing around, intentionally trying to irritate Lydia? What purpose would it serve? Lessons from her childhood flitted through her

mind—*Love thy neighbor as thyself... Turn the other cheek...*
Lydia's behavior was wrong, but Callie's aunts had taught her
that two wrongs never made a right. She wouldn't be able to
sleep unless she made restitution for her churlishness.

With a sigh of defeat, she laid back the covers, slipped
carefully from the bed so the mattress wouldn't bounce,
and crossed on tiptoe to the window. In the dark, she nearly
tripped over her shoes, but she righted herself without falling
and went steadily on across the room.

She paused for a moment in front of the window, enjoying
the scent of the breeze as well as the muted sound of crickets
somewhere nearby. She wavered in her resolve, but then her
conscience pricked once more. She pulled the window shut,
latched it, then turned, sweeping her hand around in the air
until she located the fan cord. She gave it a gentle tug that set
the fan into motion. She cringed as the squawking began, but
she fixed her jaw and crawled back into bed, taking care not
to jostle the mattress.

There was no response from Lydia, save a slight adjusting
of the covers, but Callie felt better anyway for having done
the right thing. Lydia could deal with her own conscience for
her unreasonable behavior. She closed her eyes, whispered
her nighttime prayers, sending up an extra one for her
relationship with Lydia to be restored to its prior footing, and
she managed to drift off to sleep.

Callie awakened in the morning and found Lydia already
dressed and at the mirror, applying makeup. She yawned.
"Good morning. You're up early. Are you going to chapel with
me?"

"No, I decided to take the Pineapple Limited into

Honolulu. I want to find someone who can give me a decent haircut. I'm beginning to look like a sheepdog." Not a hint of humor colored her tone. Apparently Lydia was still angry.

Callie propped herself up on her elbows. "Do you think you'll be able to find someone open on Sunday?"

Lydia shrugged and dropped her lipstick tube into her purse. "If I can't, I'll just stay over and get it done tomorrow. I'm on C duty, so I don't need to be back until late anyway."

Callie worried her lip between her teeth. "But you'll be exhausted if you don't get any rest before a ten-hour shift, and it will be hard to stay awake for duty. Are you sure this is a good idea?"

"Stop acting like my mother."

"I'm not trying to—"

Lydia hooked her purse strap on her shoulder. "Has it not occurred to you that I might need a little time to myself? There's no privacy here anywhere, and I'd like to make a telephone call away from listening ears."

"There are more people in Honolulu than here on the base." Callie tossed her covers aside and sat up. "Why not stay here, and—"

Lydia gave Callie a scathing look. "I'll be fine." She headed out the door without another glance in Callie's direction.

Scowling, Callie hopped out of bed and headed to the shower. She tried not to worry about Lydia—after all, Lydia was incredibly independent. But was it safe to stay alone in Honolulu overnight? As she walked to the mess hall, where chapel was held each Sunday morning, she heard the whistle of the Pineapple Limited signaling its departure. She paused, looking toward the sound and wishing she'd been able to convince Lydia not to go.

"Good morning, Callie." Micah strode to her side. His handsome face wore a welcoming smile. At least he held no ill will about their evening ending in a disappointing manner.

"Good morning." The *chug-chug-chug* of an engine starting captured her attention again. A billow of steam rose above the roof of the Post Exchange. The train was departing. Callie released a sigh

Micah frowned. "Something wrong?"

Callie pointed in the direction of the train. "Lydia's on the train, heading into Honolulu by herself. She says she needs a haircut, but I think she's really just trying to get away from me for awhile. She's angry with me."

"Because of me?"

Callie shrugged, unwilling to make Micah feel bad. "It doesn't really matter—we'll work it out. But I'm worried about her being there by herself. She said she might spend the night and come back tomorrow."

Micah's brow creased. "That's not a good idea. A woman, alone? She could meet up with trouble."

"I tried to tell her that, but she wouldn't listen to me."

Micah scratched his chin. "Hmm, I was planning to go to chapel, but maybe I'll fire up the Coupe and take a drive into Honolulu instead."

Callie gawked at him. "You'd go after her?"

"Don't get the wrong idea." His lop-sided grin appeared. "It's only Christian concern. Mostly for you, because I know you won't rest until she's safely accounted for."

Callie offered a grateful look. "Thank you, Micah. You're really a very nice person, you know that?"

"So I've been told." He paused. "But I've also heard it said that nice guys finish last…"

She dropped her gaze briefly. She wished she felt differently toward him, but there was no sense in pretending. "I'm sorry, Micah…"

"Hey, don't let it bother you." His bright tone matched his

smile. "You can't win them all, right? Besides, I kind of like the idea of being big brother—no sisters at home, you know. Having a sister could really come in handy."

Callie shook her head, affection for this easy-going man touching her heart and cheering her spirit. He really was impossible to dislike, and she was finding out that he made a very dependable friend. "I think having a brother could come in handy, too."

"Take notes on the sermon," he said, inching backward, "and share them with me when I get back. I'll make sure Lydia is okay." He lifted his hand in a wave and trotted off toward the officers' quarters.

Callie continued on to the mess hall where chapel services were held. She took notes, as Micah had directed, but her thoughts kept drifting to Honolulu. She hoped Micah would find Lydia and everything would be all right.

Lydia hadn't returned by bedtime, so Callie left the bedside lamp burning for her. She awakened around three in the morning and scowled groggily at the clock, wondering why the light was on. Then, remembering, she sat bolt upright, wide awake and fully worried because Lydia still wasn't back. Had Micah found her? Was Lydia all right? She snuggled back under the covers, stared at the motionless fan overhead, and prayed again for Lydia's safe return. Eventually, despite the light in her eyes, she managed to fall back asleep.

When she awoke again, it was nearly seven thirty, and she was due at the hospital by eight. She leapt out of bed, threw on her nursing uniform, ran a brush through her tousled hair and another one over her teeth, and dashed to work without the benefit of breakfast. As she checked the clipboard for her assigned tasks, Holden came up the hallway.

Callie waylaid him. "Dr. Winters, I'm so glad to see you."

"Oh?" He rested one hand on the nurse's counter and fixed her with a flat look.

"Yes. Have you seen Micah—er, Dr. Hatcher—this morning?"

He didn't change expression. "No, Miss Myers. I have not."

Her shoulders drooped. "All right. Thank you." Crestfallen, she turned back to the clipboard.

"Is that all you wanted?" He sounded slightly miffed.

She glanced at him. Scowl lines creased his forehead. Bewildered by his stern countenance, she sought an explanation. "I'm a bit worried. He drove into Honolulu yesterday, looking for Lydia. She still isn't back. I was hoping he was so I could find out if she's okay."

The stern lines relaxed. "You worry too much. Lydia is a grown woman. I'm sure she is capable of caring for herself, even in Honolulu."

"But she's on C duty this week, and if she doesn't make it back—"

He pushed off from the counter. "Isn't there a verse in Matthew that says something about not worrying about tomorrow because each day has enough trouble of its own?" He cocked an arrogant eyebrow in her direction before presenting his back and moving on down the hallway.

She stared after him in amazement. "Dr. Winters!"

He stopped, paused for a moment, then slowly walked back to the counter and propped up his chin with his hand. "Yes, what now?"

"How did you know about that verse?"

He huffed a short laugh. "How could I not know several verses after spending time listening to you for the past few months? You spout little but. Good day, Miss Myers." He traveled the hallway with long, determined strides.

HOLDEN

Holden stepped into his office and shut the door, leaning against it until his heart rate returned to normal. How could he have been so foolish as to quote scripture to none other than the queen of biblical knowledge? He'd given himself away now. The look on her face—that wide-eyed expression of discovery—had said more clearly than words that he'd made a tremendous error in judgment.

He moved away from the door and sank down at the large, organized desk. He propped his elbows on the edge and ran his hands down his face. The other evening, walking to the movie theatre, he had slipped and made a reference to Job. To his relief she'd apparently missed it. But not this time. This time he'd been too brazen. He slammed a fist down on the desk top and flung himself back in his chair, leaning his head against the high headrest and staring at the ceiling.

Funny how, even after three years of studiously ignoring his Bible and refusing to attend any type of worship service, the knowledge was still hiding under the surface, waiting for an opportunity to present itself. *"I have hidden thy word in my heart, that I might not sin against thee."* He'd memorized the verse from Psalms, as well as countless others, as a boy.

He'd grown up listening to Bible stories—his mother read to him and his sisters daily from her black Book—and he had accepted the saving grace of Jesus as a tender child of ten. He'd leaned heavily on the promises from that Book when his mother died unexpectedly of a burst appendix when he was twelve. His earthly father had been a rather brusque man, not as much uncaring as distant, and Holden had clung to the idea of a loving Heavenly Father who was always there, always listening, always caring... Until the night of the fire when he'd stood on the sidewalk that freezing night, praying that his family would be spared. The God of his childhood, the God of miracles who had saved Shadrach, Meshach, and Abednego could save Lorna and Timmy.

But He hadn't.

And Holden's faith had turned to ashes that blew away in the harsh December wind.

As a doctor, Holden had seen plenty of evidence that there was no loving God in heaven. Daily, the broken, battered bodies had raised the question of a God who cared. But until he had stood helplessly as his wife and son perished, he had believed God would help him reach out to those in pain and make a difference. But how pointless it all had been. If there was a caring God, why did such horrible things like cancer and withered limbs and crushed spirits…and terrible house fires…happen?

This realization led to his two-year commitment as an army doctor for Schofield. He'd specifically chosen Schofield Station Hospital. At this peaceful island paradise, the illnesses were so few—a complete paradox from doctoring in a bustling city as he'd done for years. He wasn't having to face life and death situations with his human, limited knowledge. When his two years was up, in only another ten months, he would seek another career, something that wouldn't require such an awesome responsibility.

Because, despite the teachings of his youth, Holden now knew the truth. He was on his own. Helping people was an exercise in futility. Helping led to caring, and caring opened oneself up to loving. And loving had too many risks, too many opportunities for heartache.

"So, Callie Myers, stay away from me." He shook his fist at the empty room. "You and your God—you leave me alone!" Despite his urgent command, Callie's incredulous, wide-eyed image refused to disappear.

11

CALLIE

Callie looked up, her pulse leaping in anticipation, when she heard footsteps in the hospital corridor. One of the other nurses came around the corner, and Callie's shoulders drooped in disappointment Where was Lydia? She forced a welcoming smile to Trudy. "Your turn for the night shift, huh?"

Trudy shrugged and pulled a sour face as she glanced over the duty clipboard. "Clean, clean, and clean some more. When will there be something that requires nursing?"

Even though Callie had come to learn nursing—and one learned best from experience—she clicked her tongue on her teeth. "Be thankful. Remember the flu epidemic and the two men who died? I'd rather clean every day for the rest of my time here than risk losing any other souls to illness."

Trudy hung her head for a moment, but then she sighed. "At least it was something else to do—something we trained to do. Look at my hands!" She held them up. "They look like they belong to a scullery maid!"

"Stop bellyaching, Trudy." The sharp reprimand came

from behind Callie, and she spun around at the familiar voice. Joy filled her heart as Lydia stepped up to the nurses' station.

"Lydia!" Callie flew at her friend, feeling much like the father of the prodigal must have felt when his son returned home. She wrapped Lydia in a hug. "I was so worried!"

Lydia disengaged herself. "You worry too much. I can take care of myself. You know that."

Although Lydia stood with her customary, regal posture, Callie couldn't help thinking something wasn't quite right. Lydia's eyes looked bruised, as though she'd been crying recently—crying hard. And her hands trembled.

Callie frowned. "Lydia, what's wrong?"

Lydia pasted on a bright smile that didn't reach her eyes. Turning towards Trudy, she pretended to make a gallant introduction. "Callie—the world's biggest worry wart." Then she leaned forward and whispered sarcastically in Callie's ear, "I'm tired, Callie. It's been a long two days with little rest, and I'm worn out." She yawned. "As soon as I get the chance, I'm going to sneak into one of the empty rooms and take a well-needed nap. Trudy, you won't tell on me, will you?"

Trudy shook her head. "Nah. It only takes one person to push a mop." She ambled up the hallway toward the supply closet.

Lydia snatched up the clipboard and ruffled through the papers.

Callie leaned against the counter to put herself in Lydia's line of vision. "Did Micah find you?"

Lydia seemed to blanch for a moment. She kept her eyes on the clipboard. "Yes. He found me."

Callie waited, hoping for more information, but Lydia kept her lips pressed tight. Callie sighed and stepped away from the counter, lifting her hand in a gesture of farewell. "Well, have a good shift." Hesitantly, she added, "I'll see you in the morning, Lydia?"

Lydia barely raised her glance to acknowledge Callie, and Callie once again read something beneath the surface that troubled her. But then Lydia nodded and said, "Sure, Callie. See you in the morning." And she turned her back, shutting Callie away.

Callie left the hospital and, without considering the ramifications, did something her aunts would disapprove. She went to Micah's bungalow and knocked on the door.

Several minutes passed before the porch light came on, its harsh, yellow light forcing her to squint. Only when the door opened to reveal Micah in a bathrobe and with disheveled hair, Callie remembered the lateness of the hour.

"Oh! I'm so sorry!" she clapped her hands to her face. "I—I'll just go and—"

"Nonsense. Big brother Micah always has time for you." He caught her wrist and pulled her over the threshold where she hovered uncertainly. He allowed the screen door to shut behind her, but left the inside door open. He yawned widely. "You're curious about what happened with Lydia."

Callie nodded, staying as close to the screen door as possible. Standing in a darkened room with a man who wore only his sleeping clothes was completely disconcerting. She clasped her hands behind her back. "Did you have trouble finding her?"

Micah scratched his head and yawned again. "It wasn't as hard as you'd think, given the size of the town. I just went to hotels and asked until I located her." He pulled a wry face. "She wasn't overjoyed to see me, though."

Callie's heart rolled over in sympathy. "Did she give you the sharp side of her tongue?"

"And then some." He tugged the tie belt of his robe a bit tighter. "We had a bit of an argument. I'm not sure I did any good by going after her. I'm pretty sure she was trying to figure out a way to get on a ship for California. I couldn't talk her into coming back right away, so I stuck around and acted like a chaperone as best I could until she was ready to come to her senses and return to the base. Of course, that wasn't until late this afternoon. Neither of us got much rest."

Callie got the distinct impression there was something Micah was withholding.

His mouth stretched with another yawn. "Can't tell you much more than that. Guess you'll have to ask Lydia."

Callie's curiosity had not been satisfied, but being caught in Micah's bungalow would look unseemly. So she pushed the screen door open and stepped onto the porch. "All right, I'll ask her. Thanks for going after her." She turned and headed down the steps, nearly colliding headlong with someone on the dimly-lit sidewalk in front of Micah's bungalow. A pair of hands grabbed her shoulders, preventing her from barreling any further.

"I'm so sorry." She squinted, trying to make out the features of the person who'd caught hold of her. "I wasn't looking where I was going."

"Somehow I don't find that to be a surprising admission, Miss Myers."

Callie stifled a groan. She'd practically plowed over Holden Winters. "D-Dr. Winters, what are you doing here?"

"I'm walking home." His face was so shadowed she couldn't see his face, but his feelings were easily read by his tone. "It's on my way. What are you doing here?"

Callie licked her lips. "I—I wanted to ask Micah about Lydia, but—"

"Callie?" Micah called from the porch. "Let me walk you back to your apartment. It's dark, and you shouldn't be wandering around the base alone."

Callie giggled nervously, on edge with Holden so near. "But you shouldn't be wandering around the base in your pajamas."

"Give me one minute to change, okay? Then I'll walk you home."

"Never mind, Micah." Holden apparently decided it was time to let Micah know of his presence. "You're ready for bed. I'll walk Miss Myers back to her apartment."

Aggravation stirred in Callie's chest. Why did he talk about her as if she wasn't standing right next to him? "I can walk myself back," she said, her voice too loud.

Micah called out, "Let Holden walk you home, Callie. You really shouldn't be wandering around the base at night alone."

Callie gave a quick look down the street, becoming aware of nightfall's shadows. A shiver wiggled down her spine. Although she hated to admit it, she was apprehensive about walking home by herself. She sighed and turned toward the bungalow. "Good-night, Micah. Thank you again for going after Lydia."

"No problem. G'night." The door closed, the porch light snapped off, and Callie and Holden were left standing in the middle of the sidewalk. How must it have looked, her running out of Micah's home and Micah standing in the doorway in his nightclothes? Callie felt guilty even though she'd done nothing to feel guilty about. She crossed her arms. "Dr. Winters, I only came to ask Micah—"

"You don't owe me any explanations, Miss Myers."

No, she didn't, but she wanted to give one anyway. "I wanted to know—"

"I am well aware of your overwhelming curiosity." His dry tone made her grit her teeth. "I presume you got the answers to your questions?"

She scowled. "No, not really."

"Have you considered that it really isn't any of your business?"

She released a frustrated huff. He could make her hackles rise faster than anyone else she knew. "You know, Dr. Winters, maybe it would be very good if we didn't talk."

A long, pained silence fell. Holden cleared his throat. "Well…"

"Well…" Callie repeated, feeling guilty again for no good reason. She flipped her palm in the direction of Grant Hall. "I guess we'd better get moving, hmm?"

"That seems wise." They turned and plodded along, their footsteps hollow against the walkway. They'd only taken about twenty steps when Holden spoke again. "Do you generally wander alone around the base at night?"

Why hadn't she let Micah get dressed and walk her home? Micah wouldn't lecture her. "No." They reached the area where tall lamp posts sent out a soft glow. She could finally see her feet, so she picked up her pace. "Usually Betsy and I walk from the hospital to the dorm together, but tonight I waited for Lydia, and Betsy went on without me."

"I suggest you don't ever do this again."

Callie rolled her eyes. "Don't preach, stay out of other people's business, don't walk alone at night…"

"What are you blabbering about?"

She huffed. "These are all commands you've given me. Do you have any idea how bossy you are?" She thought his cheek muscles twitched, but it was hard to tell in the muted light.

"And grumpy," he said. "Don't forget grumpy."

"Oh, yes—and grumpy." Saying it out loud made it sound humorous, but she didn't want to laugh. "Why are you always telling me what to do?"

"Because you're always doing something you shouldn't." He took her hand and placed it in the crook of his arm. "Callie, about wandering around the base at night… Most of the men here have enough respect for a lady not to pull anything, but there are some who indulge in drinking when they're off duty. When a man is drunk, he doesn't always behave appropriately. You need to remember that, Miss Small-town Girl."

His concern chased away her aggravation. Callie nodded. "I'll be careful. I was just so worried about Lydia, I wasn't thinking clearly."

He patted her hand. "You're a good friend to Lydia. She's lucky to have you."

Callie started to reply, but the roar of engines intruded. Callie and Holden stopped, looking skyward as six American B-17 bombers flew over in perfect formation, their shining silver bellies visible. Callie's heart pounded at the impressive sight, somehow all the more powerful against the dark backdrop of the night sky. The reverberation made her stomach tremble, and even the soles of her feet tingled. When the planes had circled away from the base, she sighed. "You know, it's so peaceful here that I sometimes forget a war is waging elsewhere in the world until something like that reminds me. Do you think America will get involved in the war eventually?"

Holden's brows pulled down. He gave a little tug on her hand that set her feet in motion again. "I don't know how we'll avoid it, if it continues much longer. We're allies with England and France. Their involvement will have to pull us in. The last newspaper I read said that America has already begun shipping food to Britain to assist the country—some kind of 'Lend-Lease' program." He looked down at her and must have read the worry in her mind, because he smiled. "But even if it comes to sending men rather than food items, the battles won't take place on American soil. No country would be so brazen as to attack America."

"Hawaii is considered America, so we're safe here?" Trepidation raised her voice higher than normal.

"Very." He spoke so staunchly, she believed him. "Why else would this island have been chosen to house so many military bases? We've got everything on this island—Army, Army Air Corps, Navy... Think of all the building going on at Pearl right now, with Battleship Row expanding to become the strongest American naval base in existence. The leaders in Washington would never spend all that money if they thought there was a chance of those ships being attacked. They know we're in a perfect position to launch attacks, but also we're very protected here. You don't need to worry."

She squeezed his arm. "I'm really not worried. I think the anxiety about Lydia, and then the walk through the dark, got me spooked. But really, I'm okay."

"Good." He pointed straight ahead to Grant Hall. "And you're safely home again." He stepped up to the door and opened it for her. "Now go in, read your Bible—I prescribe something in Psalms—and I guarantee a peaceful night of rest without a hint of worry."

She tipped her head. "Did you really prescribe Psalms?"

"I always prescribe what will be best for the patient, and I know you well enough to know that Psalms is a perfect choice."

She nodded slowly, recalling his reference to the verse in Matthew earlier that day. "You know your Bible better than you'd like me to believe."

"Don't presume, Callie." The stuffy Holden presented himself again. "I believe the word psalm refers to a song generally sung to a harp, which in essence would be soothing. One who is worried is in need of soothing, thus my suggestion to go to the Psalms. Nothing more was being intimated."

"Okay, whatever you say." She shook her finger. "But I still don't believe you."

"I'm not surprised, but neither am I willing to stand here in the dark and debate with you further. Good-night, Miss Myers."

Callie laughed, then impulsively stood on tiptoe and planted a quick kiss on Holden's cheek. "Thank you for walking me home." Oh, his expression! She laughed again and entered the dormitory. After changing into her night clothes, she picked up her worn, leather-bound Bible and turned to the Psalms, as Holden had unexpectedly suggested. She flipped pages, skimming, until she came to Psalm 121. Then she read word-for-word, relaxing as the message flowed over her heart like a healing balm. When she came to the end of the chapter she read aloud, "'The Lord will keep you from all harm—He will watch over your life; the Lord will watch over your coming and going both now and forevermore.'"

She set the Book aside and closed her eyes. "Thank you, Lord Jesus. Watch over me, Holden, Micah, and Lydia here at Oahu, and Aunt Vi and Aunt Viv until we're together again. Thank you for Your care. Amen."

Even though the prayer was much shorter than her usual night-time chat with her heavenly Father, Callie was ready to rest. She slipped between the sheets of her bed and fell immediately into a peaceful sleep.

Callie cranked the agitator on the old washing machine in the hospital laundry room with viciousness. She was out of sorts, and the inanimate machine seemed a good place to vent her irritation.

For the past several days, she'd repeatedly sought the comforting words from Psalm 121, reminding herself that the

Lord was watching over her and all those she held dear. Yet she constantly fought the urge to wallow in worry.

As she swished uniforms in soapy water, sending out a frothy spray to dot the front of her apron, she reviewed all the reasons she had for sprouting gray hair before she was even twenty-five years old. She had received a letter from Aunt Vivian telling her that Aunt Viola was ill, running a fever and coughing. Pneumonia possibly, but there was no way to know for sure. She had written back, giving a list of instructions for proper care, but it took so long to get news back and forth, she had no way of knowing whether Aunt Vivian would receive her instructions in time to do any good. How she wished they had a telephone so she could speak to them directly!

And she worried about Holden. Although she sensed he was softening, and she took advantage of every opportunity to witness—or, as he put it, preach—to him, she still hadn't gotten through to his soul. There were moments when he seemed light-hearted, teasing with her, but teasing wasn't what she wanted. There was something damming up his emotions, but she hadn't discovered what it was. Until she did, she wouldn't be able to find a way to reach him. A constant, stubborn prayer whispered in the back of her mind as she sought a way to finally get through to him and win his heart for God.

If Aunt Vi's illness and Holden's obstinacy wasn't enough to keep her up nights worrying, something was wrong with Lydia. She had lost her sparkle. Callie was overwhelmed with guilt, fearful that her going out on a date with Micah had created a permanent rift between herself and her roommate. She tried to make it up to Lydia, but Lydia refused to acknowledge her efforts. In desperation, Callie had resorted to starting an argument by accusing Lydia of pouting because Micah hadn't fallen for her. All she'd managed to do was rile her roommate.

She transferred the soapy clothing from the washer into a tub of rinse water, wincing as Lydia's scathing words roared through her memory. *"I am not pouting, Callie Myers! Yes, I was attracted to Micah, but he isn't the only fish in the sea. I can live without him. And I can live without your sanctimonious, holier-than-thou spouting that makes everyone around you feel like a second class citizen. You and your Bible reading and scripture quoting... Why can't you leave people alone? You make everyone uncomfortable when you prance around like Little Miss Perfect."*

Being called sanctimonious stung even in remembrance. Did she truly come across as holier-than-thou? She'd never intentionally treat someone as if they were inferior. Lydia's aloof, prickly treatment was a mystery to add to her other mysteries. Who did the button belong to? Why was Holden so full of cynicism? What was bothering Lydia?

Callie sloshed the pinafores up and down in the rinse water before sending them through the wringer. As she turned the handle, watching the clothing spurt water from one side of the roller bars and emerge flat as a pancake from the other side, she continued to ponder Lydia's odd behavior. The strong-willed girl who'd seemed able to conquer the world now seemed defeated, and Callie feared she was the one who had broken her spirit.

"Lord," she murmured as she cranked the handle and fed clothing through the wringers, "I'm at a loss. I can't seem to do anything right these days..." As if to substantiate her words, she fed the tips of her fingers between the roller bars.

She yelped and released the handle, yanking her fingers free. She shook her hand, trying to shake away the pain, and danced around the little room as if she walked on hot coals. "Ow, ow, ow, ow!"

Miss Torkelson, with Holden on her heels, bustled into

the room. "Miss Myers, what on earth is the matter?"

Callie ceased her dance and cradled her hand against the bib of her pinafore, wincing in pain. Apparently she'd made more noise than she had realized. Her face flooded with heat, but she was in too much discomfort to focus on her embarrassment. She hissed, "I caught my fingers in the wringer."

"Let me see." Holden stepped past Miss Torkelson to and took Callie's hand. He gently pressed each fingertip. "Does this hurt?"

"Yes, it hurts a lot!" Callie hollered, trying to pull away.

His lips twitched.

"This isn't funny!" She glowered at him, and he swallowed hard, obviously trying to curb his humor.

Miss Torkelson crossed her arms. "Your injury is not funny, Miss Myers, but your childish reaction to it certainly inspires amusement."

Callie clenched her teeth as Holden continued to pinch her fingers and bend them in directions she didn't want them to go. Miss Torkelson stood guard, a scowl marring her pudgy face. Callie gulped. "I'm sorry if I behaved inappropriately, but—" Her voice grew louder with each press against the tips of her sore fingers. "—that really hurts!"

Holden turned to Miss Torkelson. "She hasn't broken anything, but there is some slight swelling. I suggest soaking her fingers in ice water for several minutes, then wrap the tips with some gauze and tape to offer protection. She'll be fine in a few days."

Whose fingers were these, anyway? Couldn't he address her directly? Callie yanked her hand from his light hold. "I can take care of my own fingers."

He raised his eyebrows. "Oh, yes, you've certainly proven that."

Heat rushed from her neck to her hairline. All of the fretting and worry of the past weeks rose to the surface and came spewing out. "You are most irritating, insufferable, exasperating individual I have ever met. Stop pinching my fingers, stop talking about me like I'm not here, and stop looking at me like I just sprouted purple ears and a tail."

"*Miss Myers!*" Miss Torkelson's shocked, venomous tone robbed Callie of every bit of indignation.

"Yes, ma'am?"

"You have been unspeakably rude to your superior. You will apologize immediately, and then you will return to your apartment while I consider an appropriate consequence for such outlandish behavior."

Callie's chin quivered. She turned her gaze from Miss Torkelson's anger-blotched face to Holden's, which seemed devoid of any emotion. She licked her lips. "Dr. Winters, I—"

"Don't apologize, Miss Myers. I provoked you, and although the extent of your attack was perhaps unwarranted, I'm willing to credit it to the tenderness in your fingers." He turned to Miss Torkelson and the warmth of his smile raised at least twenty degrees. "Miss Torkelson, I would ask that Miss Myers not be placed on report for her behavior. I am not offended, and it seems"— he sent a quick, smirking glance in Callie's direction— "that all of her shouting has managed to take her attention off her fingers, which I'm willing to concede is good medicine."

Miss Torkelson pursed her face. "I don't know..."

"I do know. That was her sore fingers talking, not Miss Myers." At last he bestowed a congenial look in Callie's direction. "Soak your fingers in ice water, Miss Myers, before the swelling becomes more acute. If you need assistance in wrapping them, I'll be in my office." He turned and left the room.

Miss Torkelson waved a plump hand at Callie. "You hear the doctor. Do as he said. Then return to your duties."

Callie started toward the door.

"But, Miss Myers, don't ever speak to one of our doctors in such a manner again, regardless of pain or provocation. It will not be tolerated a second time."

Callie nodded without looking at her. "Yes, ma'am." She hurried out in search of ice and a bowl. She would have to get her worries under control. It wouldn't do to explode like that ever again. She thought of her log at the beach— the peacefulness of listening to the waves crash against the shore and the birds calling while the trees whispered a lullaby behind her. As soon as possible, she'd borrow Lydia's car and drive there. At her log, in solitude with God, she should be able to put some of these concerns to rest.

12

"Ooph." Holden grunted as he dropped the heavy burlap sack onto the floor of the hut. Dust rose, and he waved his hand at the cloud then sneezed mightily. He'd driven Micah's Coupe clear onto the beach, as close to the base of the mountain as possible, but carrying his load made the walk seem much longer. He placed his hands on the small of his back and arched backward, relieving the kink. Then he rotated his aching shoulders as he glanced around the small space to reacquaint himself. Other than a few more spider webs, not much had changed.

He knelt on the dirt floor and began removing the items from his bag. He'd meant to have this hut usable by now, but it had been more difficult than he'd first imagined to find time to spend up here. Not that he hadn't tried, but things kept getting in the way. He chuckled ruefully. Well, things and one *somebody* kept getting in the way.

Only that morning, as he prepared to leave, she'd managed to temporarily distract him by standing in the gentle mist so common in Oahu, her face raised toward the east. Most people shielded themselves with an umbrella, but not Callie. She stood bareheaded, mist beading on her tousled hair, smiling upward. He'd called out, unable to resist goading her a bit, "Don't you have sense to come in out of the rain?"

She pointed to a huge rainbow that seemed to hover over the entire island. "Look at that, Holden Winters!" Her lilting voice held triumphant. "See the evidence of God's presence?"

Looking upward, he nodded. "Look at nature's evidence that the sun is connecting with raindrops and forming a mighty prism." Even from the distance separating them, he saw her lips purse, and he hid his smile.

"Dr. Winters, *God* sent the rainbow as a sign to His people that He would never again flood the earth. It says so in Genesis, the first chapter of the Bible."

He shook his finger at her. "You're telling me stories again." He'd turned his back and tossed his bag into the trunk of Micah's Coupe, and he hadn't needed to look to know she had her fists on those slim hips of hers in a saucy stance. He'd seen the pose a lot in the past two weeks since he'd helped bind her pinched fingers.

He chuckled again, recalling her obstinate insistence. He'd accused her of throwing down the gauntlet and she'd gallantly risen to the challenge. She was nothing if not tenacious. And since he'd slipped with a Bible verse in lecturing her, it seemed as if she waited for him to slip again. However, he'd fully erected his guard, so she wouldn't catch him quoting scriptures again. Truthfully, he enjoyed their little repartees. As long as they were sparring, he could keep himself emotionally distant. That is, if he quit thinking about her.

His bag contained cleaning rags, a variety of tools, a box of nails, a small straw broom, work gloves, a canteen of drinking water, packets of crackers and cheese, and a bucket. He removed everything except the food items. Using the hammer and a nail, he created a makeshift hook on one of the support beams and tied the sack to it. Then he turned his attention to the mess around him. Where to begin?

Snatching up the broom, he began whacking down spider webs and swatting dust out of corners where it had been accumulating for years. He snuffled and sneezed, and on more than one occasion stepped outside for a breath of fresh air. He glanced down at his shirt front, noticed the coating of dust, and released a brief, derisive snort. The last time he'd been here, he'd covered himself with soot. Today, dust.

"Well, no one said cleaning was a clean job," he said, surprising himself with his own voice. "Besides, the shirt is ruined anyway." He'd chosen this shirt since it still bore light gray stains on the shoulders, leftover from the shower of soot he'd received on his previous cleaning excursion. Between the stains and its missing button, it wasn't suitable for anything but a work shirt anymore.

He stood on the patch of ground outside the door, enjoying the clean air and pleasant sounds that surrounded him. The leaves of the palms overhead rustled with the wind that came in off the ocean, creating a hushed *whish-whish* that couldn't compete with the crash and roar of the waves across the shore. Even this far upland, the power of the surf was impossible to ignore. Sea birds squawked, and a bird call he thought sounded like a door hinge in need of oiling carried from somewhere in the trees.

"It's peaceful up here." He shook his head, chuckling becuase he'd spoken aloud again.

Normally he didn't talk to himself. He left that to Callie. Of course, she wasn't always talking to herself, but rather talking aloud to her constant imaginary companion. Again, she would argue the imaginary part with him. To her, God was very real. In a way, he pitied her. Someday she'd trust God to be there and He wouldn't show. On that day, the realization of God's absence would likely shatter her, the way it had him.

Even if he didn't believe God created it, he did concede that Oahu contained more than its fair share of wonders to titillate the senses. No matter what direction he sent his gaze, he witnessed beauty from the massive palm fronds overhead to the magnificent bushes of poinsettias still in full bloom. Flashes of the scarlet, orange-red, or yellow plumage of birds flitting through the foliage awed him with their vivid colors. Even the sky was a different blue—clearer, more vibrant— than in Chicago, thanks partly to no factories belching out their smoke to obscure the view. Then of course, the expanse of sea stretched before him until it seemed to reach eternity.

Oh, yes, much beauty existed. But Holden knew all too well there was also much ugliness. If you were going to give a God credit for the good, then God needed to be prepared to take credit for the ugly, as well. That was his main argument with Callie, but she wouldn't listen to reason.

He drew another chest expanding breath before turning back into the murkiness of his hut. It took a moment for his eyes to adjust, and he muttered, "I need to figure out a way to put some windows in here." Light would make a big improvement to the appearance of the inside—even more so when he finally had it clean. Which would only happen if he quit woolgathering and got to work.

He spent a good half hour using the sorry excuse for a broom to swipe as much dust as possible from the underside of the thatch without knocking holes in his ceiling. Then he brushed from ceiling height to floor level on each of the walls. Amazing how much dust he stirred up. The tiny particles swirled in the air and probably half of it settled right back where it had been originally. But how else could he get it cleaned?

The floor still needed to be swept, but the small broom he'd brought would only meet the floor if he doubled over or crawled. Neither process appealed to him. He scowled at the floor, hands on his hips, the way Callie so often stood. He chuckled. She plunked those little fists on her hips as often as a seasoned gunslinger hovered in readiness above his pistols. And she was just as ready to fire, the way had last week when he'd spotted her emerging from the supply closet.

He'd goaded, "Curious... Do you give your God the credit for all the dirt you mopped up today?"

Her pert chin came up and her green eyes snapped. "No, Dr. Winters. However, I do give Him credit for these two arms which are growing stronger by the day thanks to all of the mop-pushing they've been doing." She posed like a muscle man, elbows bent and fists curled at shoulder height.

He'd quickly turned away to hide his amusement. How silly she looked in the tough-guy stance while wearing her striped, ruffled pinafore and saddle shoes. Besides, she might think she had muscles, but he hadn't seen much evidence of it. When he headed up the hallway, the light clap of her soles against the tile floor followed him.

"And have you ever considered the marvel of muscle, Dr. Winters? Our entire bodies are a miracle in and of themselves. Humans are wonderfully and fearfully made. Is there anything more intricate than the human body?"

Holden had paused and looked down at her with what he hoped was disdain. He found her green eyes beneath that constantly-mussed auburn hair increasingly difficult to resist. "The human body is a machine, Miss Myers. Each part is likened to the cog or piston of an engine—but miraculous? Hardly. The same 'machinery' is seen everywhere in nature. It happens." He started moving again, only to have her continue to trot along beside him. She never seemed able to keep her adorable mouth silent.

"It happens? All by itself? Then please explain how the reasoning of the brain 'happens' only in humans." He started to answer, but she went on. "I can tell you. It's because God made man in His own image, and He gave us dominion over the beasts of the field and the birds of the air. He gave us a reasoning brain so we can choose to believe in Him."

"Or we can reasonably choose not to believe, hmm?" He'd meant to be funny, but her face fell and her shoulders deflated.

"Well, you can, because it's your choice, but..." Tears glistened in the corner of her eyes. "I don't know how I would have gotten this far in life without Him. I don't know why you want to."

Her sorrow had made his chest twist with regret, an emotion he didn't want to explore. So he'd set off again for his office, hoping she wouldn't follow. "Miss Myers, this has all been very interesting, but I have paperwork to complete and you have windows to wash. If you get the panes clean enough, perhaps we can argue later about who is responsible for providing us with the landscape outside the window."

Funny how disappointed he'd been when she'd let him go without further recourse. He blew out a breath and reached for his bucket. "Time to wash down these walls." He followed a narrow path down the mountainside to the beach. As he passed a gap in the trees, he glanced toward the weather-worn tree trunk where he'd first seen Callie. He stopped, his feet sliding. Was Callie perched on the log? Surely he imagined it. She'd been sneaking into his thoughts, so he only thought he saw her. He rubbed his eyes then looked again.

Not his imagination after all. She was sitting on the log with her back to him, her arms straight beside her, holding herself erect. He stood for a moment, admiring the glints of red in her hair and the way the breeze gently ruffled the strands. She looked so peaceful, so at ease with herself and her surroundings. The way he never felt.

He bit back a groan. He'd be right in her line of vision when he stepped out of the foliage at the base of the mountain. Why did she have to disrupt his plans? So what now? He scowled, contemplating his choices. He could go back to the hut and do some repair work instead of washing walls. But no, she was in earshot of the hammer. If he started banging away, she'd come investigating, he was sure—she'd proven her curiosity already. So what to do?

He jolted. Was he really hiding from Callie? How ridiculous. Why should he let some slip of a girl make him change his plans? If she saw him, she saw him—he'd deal with it when it happened. He wrapped his fingers around the handle of the bucket and set off for the water.

One eye on Callie and one on the ocean, he reached the sandy beach and stumbled over an exposed root. The metal bucket banged against his knee and he held his breath, waiting for—

"Hello, Dr. Winters!"

The elements of joy and welcome in her voice sent his traitorous heart into stuttering off-beats of pleasure.

"What brings you here today?"

How should he answer? He wouldn't share his secret hideaway with her, would he? He hoisted the bucket. "Getting some water."

Her brows dipped. "You came all the way to the beach for water?"

"Yes. I…" He wished he was more imaginative. "…wanted salt water."

"Oh." She shielded her eyes with one graceful hand and began swinging her feet—bare, he noted—back and forth. "What for?"

He searched his mind for something plausible, but before he could come up with anything, she released a startled squawk. She scrambled for a hand hold, found none, and rolled off the back side of the log.

"Callie!" He dropped the bucket and took off running. He reached the log and leaped, sailing over the way he'd sailed over hurdles in college track. He landed and dropped to his knees in the sand beside her. "Are you—" Fear swept away like a feather on the wind and amusement replaced it.

She lay on her back with her legs straight up against the trunk, her arms over her stomach and her eyes squinched tight. Her body quaked in silent laughter.

He shook his head, chuckling. He stood and held out his hand. "Here, clumsy, let me help you up."

With an audible giggle, she grasped his offered hand with both of hers and allowed him to pull her to her feet. "Thanks." She brushed the seat of her trim-fitting tan slacks, straightened her sleeveless blouse, and shook some remnants of dried moss from her hair. Then she grinned at him. "Dr. Winters, you really know how to sweep a girl off her feet."

"Oh, no." He held up both hands as if under arrest. "Don't blame me. If you're going to sit on a slippery surface, you need to keep your feet still." He pinned her with a serious look. "Did you hurt yourself?"

She shrugged. "Nothing dented but my pride." She scrambled back up where she'd been before, facing the ocean with her feet dangling. He swallowed a smile. She didn't swing her feet.

He walked around the end of the log. Catching the heels of his hands on the top, he boosted himself up backwards, then he turned and propped his left foot on the log. He wrapped his arm around his upraised knee to steady himself. From this position, he could admire her sweet profile. "So what are you doing out here?"

"Thinking." She turned her head and met his gaze. "I owe you a thank you."

"For helping you up just now?"

She shook her head.

"Then for getting you out of trouble with Miss Torkelson when you spewed like an angry volcano?"

Her cheeks twitched. "No, not for that, either."

"Then what?"

"For making me evaluate myself."

He dropped his chin a bit, peering at her with lowered brows.

She nodded. "You heard me correctly. I've been doing a lot of thinking about myself and my belief system since we started our little…, well, challenge, for lack of a better word. As I've tried to prove God's existence to you, I've rediscovered the truth of it myself, as well, which is good."

Holden released a short *hmmph*. "I thought you already had yourself thoroughly convinced. Why do you need to prove anything to yourself?"

"Oh, I'm not proving anything to myself. I know I'm right. I'm just reminding myself how I know I'm right."

He shook his head. "You lost me."

Callie turned and lifted her bare feet onto the log. She leaned against a sturdy branch that angled upward behind her and braced her hands at her sides. "You see, my parents believed in God, and their relationship with Him seemed so natural, it was easy for me to see it as real. God lived in the house with us—He was referred to and spoken to as easily as we spoke to one another. So my knowledge of God was established early in my life." She paused and scanned the area before fixing her gaze on him again. "But lately, because of you, I've been asking myself how I know it's true. How I know the Bible isn't just stories, as you keep trying to tell me. And everywhere I look, I see evidence that the Bible is real and is written to prove God's existence to us."

Holden considered arguing with her, but the serenity in her expression silenced him.

"For instance, in Psalms, there's a verse that says God's thoughts of us outnumber the grains of sand. I look at this beach"—her gaze shifted to the shoreline—"and I think, there's no way to count the grains of sand. That's how often God thinks of me. When I look at it that way, I get this feeling, deep in my soul…" She rested her hand on her chest and pulled in a slow breath. "The feeling fills me. It brings me to my own personal conclusions." She swung her legs to the front, facing the ocean once more.

She was waiting for him to ask, and he didn't want to ask, but for some reason he said, "And what conclusions have you drawn?"

Callie kept her gaze outward, but by the way her lips tipped upward, he knew he'd played directly into her hand. Even so, the thought didn't rankle as much as it once might have.

"It comes down to faith, Dr. Winters. You either have it or you don't." Finally she looked at him, and she patted the smooth surface of the log. "Take this, for instance. Someone who had never been to this island, but who had studied it minutely and knew every natural detail of what should and shouldn't be here, would never place something like this on the beach. It's too unlikely. Whatever this was, it's not the type of tree to grow here naturally. And Oahu is miles away from any continent that would have this type of tree growing on it naturally. How could something like this arrive on the beach of a Hawaiian island? They would say, 'Impossible! Outside of the realm of possibility!' Right?"

He had to agree with her reasoning so far, so he nodded.

Her face lit. "See? That's faith. We're sitting on something outside of the realm of human reasoning. I know it's here because I've fallen off of it twice, yet it doesn't make sense for it to be here." She tipped her head, and her eyes brightened with unshed tears. "Dr. Winters, you are a man of science. You must experience something before you will believe it. Faith is completely backward to that—you must believe it before you can fully experience it. And try as I might, I can't make that happen for you. You'll have to find it for yourself."

She'd been fervent in her presentation, but there was one thing she had neglected to explain, and that was the presence of so much pain and suffering. As a doctor he'd seen more than his fair share. As a man he'd personally encountered it. Believing something in order to experience it? He'd believed once, but now he didn't want to meet face-to-face with the God who'd allowed his wife and son to die before their lives had barely begun. But how to make this innocent, idealistic young woman see the truth without sharing his deepest hurts?

"Dr. Winters?"

He gave a start and nearly slipped sideways off the log. He righted himself and then playfully shook a finger at her, deliberately lightening the mood. "You did that on purpose."

She gave him an innocent look. "If I had meant to knock you off, I would have succeeded—just as I'll eventually succeed in proving to you that God is real."

He rolled his eyes. She was nothing if not persistent. He hopped down and started for his discarded bucket. But within three yards distance, loneliness slapped him as firmly as one of the roaring ocean waves might. He hesitated. Could he trust her? He slowly turned around. Green eyes connected with blue eyes, and all concerns whisked away.

"Miss Myers, would you like to see something?"

"Sure." She slid from the log and bent over, momentarily

disappearing from view. When she straightened she was holding a pair of white cotton tennis shoes. She grinned. "I love to feel the sand between my toes, but I know better than to run all across the beach barefoot." She aimed the bottom of her right foot at him. "See? No cuts." Still grinning, she plunked down on the sand and pulled on her shoes.

He couldn't take his eyes off of her. She was all woman, yet as carefree as a child. He'd never met anyone like her. How he wished—

She stood, looking at him expectantly. To cover his disconcerting thoughts, he drew on sternness. "If I show this to you, you have to keep it a secret." She drew an X on her chest with her finger. He swallowed a chortle. "And you have to help me."

"Help you?" She fell in step beside him as if she'd already agreed.

"I have a mighty mess to clean up, and since you've had so much experience of late with cleaning, I suspect you're the right person for the job."

She came to a halt and her mouth dropped, then she broke into a mighty grin. "Oh, you—you're impossible!" She shook her fist at him, about as threatening as a gnat.

He held up one finger. "You said you'd never call me impossible again."

To his delight, she planted her fists on her hips and glowered at him. He laughed and took off running. She pounded behind him, her gleeful laughter rolling with the waves. His heart was lighter than it had been in years, and today—just today—he would savor it.

13

Callie thought her chest might burst. She followed Holden on a narrow, winding path leading up the mountain. When he finally came to a stop, she collapsed on the mossy ground beneath sheltering kukui nut trees.

"Whew! When you asked if I wanted to see something, I didn't know you meant the top of the world."

He laughed, his eyes crinkling attractively at the corners. He didn't seem winded at all, and Callie marveled at his physical stamina. Apparently he'd made this climb numerous times before.

"How far up are we, anyway?" She stood and looked back toward the beach. From this vantage point, the stretch of sand appeared much broader, and the ocean seemed to roll into eternity. She located the log, which seemed no larger than a cigar, and an uneasy feeling struck. How many times had Holden watched her from this point? "It…" She gulped. "It's a wonderful view."

"I did not bring you to see the view, although I'm sure you will enjoy it. I'm also sure you'll give credit for the scenery to your God…again…but spare me the sermon, hmm? I've heard that one before."

She looked over her shoulder at him and pursed her lips. His words inspired ire, the teasing glint shining in his blue eyes erased her indignation. She shrugged. "All right, Dr. Winters, I'll not regale you with my opinion of Who is responsible for this incredible beauty, but that doesn't mean I won't talk about Him at all. So be forewarned." She shot him a mischievous grin.

Holden rolled his eyes and flipped his hands outward in a gesture of *Why me?* Then she spun on her heel and grimaced at the most ramshackle dwelling she'd ever seen. "May I assume if I'm not here to look at the view, I'm here to look at this hovel?"

He grinned. "This is it. My secret hide-away. At least, it will remain my secret hide-away if you are trustworthy." He gave her a sideways glance as if not certain she could be trusted.

She nodded. "Oh, yes, your secret is safe with me."

He examined her for a moment, his eyes narrowed into speculative slits, and then he grinned again. "Okay, Miss Myers, come on in and see my humble home-away-from-home."

He ushered her in, and she crossed to the center of the very dusty floor and turned a slow circle. Other than a rusty, wood-burning stove in the center, there were no furnishings. The walls looked like twigs woven together with vines, but the outside had been covered with thatch. The only light filtered through the door. The heavy covering of trees and undergrowth outside the hut blocked much of the sun.

"This place needs windows." She crinkled her nose. "Of course, if it was really bright in here, you'd see exactly how filthy it is."

Holden burst into laughter.

She gave him a puzzled look. "What's so funny?"

"You just said, almost verbatim, what I was thinking before I went down to the beach for water." His eyes sparkled with his grin.

"Really?" She couldn't help smiling, too.

He nodded.

She glanced around the small space again. "They say great minds think alike, but I would never have thought it possible with the two of us."

"That the two of us have great minds?"

She loved the witty side he showed far too infrequently. "Of course not, silly. That we would agree on something for a change. We're always arguing."

He raised one brow. "We wouldn't if you weren't so hard-headed."

"Me?" When he started to laugh, she joined in. "You are a caution, Dr. Winters. I'll have to be on guard constantly around you."

He braced one hand on the stove and heaved a sigh. "You said you'd help me, right? This place definitely needs help. Suggestions on where to begin?"

Callie nodded. "Yes. First of all, since we're not at the hospital, would you please call me Callie? And, with your permission, I'd like to call you..." She'd thought of him as Holden for weeks, but it suddenly it seemed too intimate to use his given name. Flustered, she lowered her gaze and she noticed something.

His shirt was missing a button.

The middle button.

The same button she had pulled from the shirt of her mysterious rescuer. She pointed, her finger quivering. "Your button."

He glanced down at himself and grimaced. "Yes, I know.

I lost it. That's why I don't wear this shirt anymore except for really dirty jobs. When the button tore off, part of the fabric tore, too, see?"

So he was the man who'd come to her aid. It had been him from the beginning, not Micah. The mystery was solved. So why was her heart beating so erratically? She folded her palms against her pounding chest and forced herself to meet his blue-eyed gaze.

He tipped his head, his gaze quizzical. "Does this shirt offend you? I realize it isn't proper to wear a shirt with a button missing, but this isn't exactly a proper setting."

Callie swallowed. "No, it isn't that. It's…" She licked her lips. "Holden, you didn't lose the button. I—I pulled it off."

He drew back, a half smile curving his lips. "What?"

"I tore it off, down on the beach, when you helped me up. I was still dizzy after hitting my head, and I must have grabbed onto your shirt too tightly, because I tore it off." He had such a strange expression on his face. Was she mistaken? "Was it you who helped me that day? When you had soot on your face to keep the mosquitoes at bay?"

He cupped his fist and placed it against his lips as if trying to hold something in. After a tense moment, he broke out with raucous laughter. Two birds darted from the bush outside the door. He doubled over, holding his stomach, and she couldn't help wondering if he'd suddenly gone mad. Should she run down the hill and summon help? As she took a hesitant step toward the door, he straightened, coughed into his fist, shook his head, coughed again, and then grinned at her.

"Callie, I apologize for my outburst. But if you could have seen your face. You were so serious, I couldn't help myself." He chortled, slapped his thigh, and shook his head again, obviously trying to gain control of his hilarity. "Now I must confess… I wasn't battling mosquitoes at all that day. I made it up because I couldn't admit what I had done."

She lifted her shoulders in a slow shrug. "What had you done?"

He pointed to the stove. "I wanted to see if the stove was still usable. I had taken apart the joints of the pipe, and I tried to look through the section that leads out of the roof. Something blocked it, so I banged my fist on it."

His words painted a picture in her head, and understanding dawned. She started to grin before he finished the story.

"The soot blocking the pipe ended up all over my face and this shirt." He chuckled. "It was one of the more foolish moves I've made in my lifetime."

Imagining his surprise when the soot exploded from the pipe, Callie couldn't hold back her laughter. An unladylike snort left her throat, and then she roared almost as uninhibitedly as he had. She regained control, and she aimed a wobbly smile at him. "Oh, my, Holden, I'm so glad to know that you're human."

"Do you mean you've doubted it?"

"Occasionally." His grin let her know he hadn't taken offense. She added, "You're so... serious. I like this side of you." His expression softened, changing from humor to...something else. Something she feared exploring. She swallowed again and side-stepped to the doorway, where the scented breeze filled her senses. "May I ask you a question?"

He didn't shift his penetrating gaze. "Certainly."

"Why do you have *MH* scratched on your button?"

His dark brows came down. "M.H.?"

"Yes. When I looked at the button, I noticed letters scratched on it—*MH*. So I thought..." Suddenly she was embarrassed to tell him what she thought.

He sauntered toward her, and she instinctively moved aside. He left the hut and returned a few moments later with a small twig. While she watched, puzzled, he sat on his haunches in front of her and carved *MH* on the dirt floor with the twig. "This is what you saw on the button?"

She peered past his shoulder and nodded.

He rose, took her by the hand, and drew her to the opposite side of the markings. "Now look. What do you see?"

She released a soft gasp. The letters upside-down were *HW*. "Holden Winters. I never realized…" She tilted her head and her gaze collided with the incredible blue eyes that had captured her heart the moment she'd seen them. Dizziness struck, and she couldn't blame it on a knock on the head. This man…

Flustered, she turned her back on him and stared out the door. "Why on earth did you scratch your initials onto your button?"

He moved into her pathway and leaned against the doorjamb. "As I recall, I was on the Pineapple Express, headed into Honolulu. I took out my pocketknife to clean my nails—something to keep me awake—and out of boredom I carved my initials on the button. It was a thoughtless gesture. I never imagined it would have any other meaning."

"It certainly gave me a mystery to solve." She stared at the foliage beyond his muscular frame. "You were unrecognizable under all that soot, so I was looking for a doctor with blue eyes and the initials *MH*."

"And when you met Micah Hatcher"—he leaned sideways, putting himself in her line of vision—"you thought he was the one who helped you up."

She folded her arms over her chest. "Yes, even though his voice didn't sound right, I thought it must be him. Everything else fit—blue eyes, a doctor, the right initials…" And her heart had tried to tell her otherwise every time she was with Micah.

"Is that why you've been spending so much time with him lately?"

She finally looked into his face. "I've been spending time with him because he's asked me to spend time with him." She frowned. "And it hasn't been *that much*."

He shrugged. "Okay." He pushed himself off the doorjamb. "Are you hungry?"

She gawked at him. "Hungry?"

He stepped past her and reached for a gunny sack attached to a rafter. "All I have is cheese and crackers, but that should give you energy so you'll be able to do a better job of cleaning."

The teasing smile was in his eyes again. She could not resist his playful side. She clomped to the center of the hut and sat on her bottom. "All right, Dr. Winters, I'll eat your food and help with cleaning. But only because I feel badly about ruining your shirt."

He sat in front of her and placed the bag between them. "Fair enough. But today it's Holden, and the soot ruined the shirt first."

She smiled. While she munched, she absently dug her finger in the fine dirt that coated the floor, tracing the letters *M* and *H* in every direction while berating herself for not having had the sense to look at the button in another way. Suddenly her fingertip encountered something hard. She shoved the last bit of cheese into her mouth and shifted onto her knees.

He shot her a puzzled look. "What are you doing?"

She rubbed with both palms, scrubbing away a patch of dust, and then she released a cry of elation. "Rock! This shack is built on a slab of rock."

Holden grabbed a little broom and brushed back and forth on the spot she'd cleared. He stirred up quite a bit of dust, forcing her to retreat a few feet, but as soon as he stopped swishing the broom, she hurried back.

She reverently placed both hands on the rough gray stone. "Solid rock. No wonder it's still standing. Built on the side of a mountain, and as ramshackle as it looks, it should have fallen down years ago. But it has a good, solid foundation, so it still stands."

She bounced her gazed to Holden. "If this shack had been built down by the water, on the sand, do you suppose it would still be here?"

He huffed. "Of course not. It's too unstable there."

"That's right." Callie couldn't hold back a smile. "A wise man builds his house on a rock. Rain and floods and wind can't destroy a house built on a rock. But those same rainstorms and floods and wind will knock flat a house built on the sand." She touched his firm forearm. "It's like that with people, too. People who put their faith in God are like this house—standing on the Rock. When things are tough, they have a good foundation to keep them upright. But people who refuse to acknowledge Him are the ones building on sinking sand. When the hard times come, they collapse."

Holden stood and moved to the doorway. "I thought we agreed you wouldn't deliver any sermons today."

"About the scenery." She rose and followed him. "I didn't say a word about the scenery."

He took in a deep breath through his nose and then released it slowly. "Yes, well then, I suppose you kept your word." He'd reverted to his formal, clipped speech with no trace of humor in evidence.

Disappointment swelled in her chest. She hadn't meant to trample his good mood. She placed her fingers on his elbow. "Holden, I—"

He jerked from her touch and eased past her to the sack, which lay crumpled on the floor next to the patch of exposed rock. "You know, Miss Myers, I've been up here for quite awhile today. I believe I'm ready to head to the base. I assume you borrowed Miss Eldredge's car. I'll see you safely to it. Shall we go?"

Callie sighed. So she was Miss Myers again. Her heart heavy, she preceded him out of the shack, waited while he secured the door, and then followed him down the hill. He didn't speak the entire distance down the mountain, and even though going downhill was easier than climbing up, the journey seemed much more laborious. Because she carried a burden of guilt. She'd driven him away.

They reached Lydia's car, and Holden opened the door for her. As she slid behind the wheel, she took his hand. His gaze dropped to their hands, then lifted to her face. She offered a quavering smile. "Thank you for a pleasant afternoon, Dr. Winters. I enjoyed the picnic and the view from your shack. I promise I won't let anyone know it's there."

He nodded, the gesture curt. "I trust you, Miss Myers. Thank you for your willingness to assist in cleaning."

"If you'd like—"

"That's fine. I'm sure I'll manage." He extracted his hand and closed her car door. He backed away from the car and lifted his hand in a brief good-bye. As he'd done the first time he put her in this auto, he turned and jogged up the beach without a backward glance.

Callie sat, blinking away tears. She'd found her mystery man, and she'd lost her mystery man. She rested her forehead on the steering wheel. *God, please help me. I think I'm falling in love with a man who cares nothing for You...*

14

Instead of returning to the base, Holden jogged along the sandy beach. He was seething inside, and although he wanted to direct that anger on Callie, whose words had stirred this indignation, why bother? She hadn't deliberately set out to anger him. She was only being...Callie.

His lope developed into a one-person race. He pushed himself to the limit of his endurance, trying to outrun the feelings Callie's words had conjured. His feet sunk deeply in the soft sand. *Sinking sand*, she'd said. Well, the sand was supporting him pretty well for this run. He gave his derisive thoughts free reign, even coughing a raspy laugh as he considered telling her she should give up her career as a nurse and become a minister instead, she was so good at preaching. Every conversation with her, she preached at him. The silliest things stirred a sermon—the sun, a washed-up log, a slab of rock...

Solid rock... *People who refuse to acknowledge Him are the ones building on sinking sand. When the hard times come, they collapse.* Ha! Falling on sand would hurt a lot less than falling on solid rock. He'd stood on her Rock, and that fall was painful. It stung yet. She didn't have a clue what she was talking about. Silly, childish woman—obviously without an inkling how things worked in the real world. Living in the hills of Arkansas must have shielded her to the point of ignorance.

He picked up his pace even more, gritting his teeth and driving himself relentlessly. Sand flew as he raced. His arms pumped. The salt air cut into his eyes and made them water. The muscles in his legs burned, his chest felt ready to burst, and still he ran. Until a sharp cramp in his side stole his breath and sent him into a clumsy half gallop, holding his ribs where the pain repeatedly stabbed. His chest heaved as he gulped air. His feet, against his will, slowed to a walk. And then, finally, he came to a stumbling halt, leaning forward at the waist, his hands on his knees, panting. His dry throat ached. He needed a drink, but he'd left his water jug back at the hut.

He hung there for several minutes, regaining his strength. Then slowly he straightened, and he turned to face the ocean— the vast, endless ocean that Callie insisted had been created by a loving God who upheld those who turned to Him. *When the hard times come, they collapse...* He raised his eyes to the cerulean sky overhead. "Where are You? Are You so far away You can't see? If You care so much, why do the hard times come at all? Why did You let them die? Our lives had just begun!"

His tight throat ached, but he shook his fist at the silent sky. "You're a farce if You're truly up there! Your thoughts of us as numerous as the grains of sand? Bah." He kicked at the beach, sending a flurry of sand particles into the foamy water washing toward his feet. "That's what I think of You and Your thoughts. That—and that!" He kicked again and again, and suddenly the ineffectiveness of what he was doing struck him. Did he think he could kick the entire beach into the ocean? It would only wash up again with the ever-present force of the tide.

Exhausted, he dropped to his knees, pressing his palms into the sand until his hands were buried shallowly. A mighty wave rushed at him, wetting his knees and carrying away the covering of sand from his hands as it rolled back out to sea.

Callie's words the night they dined in Haleiwa came back to haunt him: *"Deep down you know there's a Higher Being, but for some reason you've decided to fight against Him. And that in itself is proof of His existence because you don't fight a nothing."*

Who did he think he was talking to out here? What was he fighting? Oh, how he wished he could understand why Lorna and Timothy had been taken and he'd been left behind. He knew why he hadn't been with them that night. He slammed his fists against the sand, willing away the memory.

How he longed to find the comfort and peace that Callie exhibited. After what he had lost—after what he had done— it was impossible. "It's like trying to hold back the tide." He spoke aloud without thinking, completely defeated.

Overhead, sea birds flew, calling to one another. Up in the mountains, trees whispered with the touch of the breeze. Across the beach and across Holden's unresisting knees, the ocean continued its relentless journey.

He remained there on his knees—in a position of submission—for nearly an hour. Not until the sun was a brilliant orange ball hovering at the far edge of the sea did he finally get to his feet. He brushed as much sand as possible from his soaked pants, trudged to Micah's Coupe, and drove himself to the base.

Holden parked the vehicle in front of Micah's bungalow, leaving the keys in the ignition as was customary. His leg muscles ached from the punishing run, and the salt water had stiffened his pants as they dried. At least he didn't have to go far. He then scuffed to his own residence half a block's distance farther on.

When he reached the gate that led to his small yard, his eyes spotted something on the frame of the porch door—what seemed to be a small, white flag. He strode stiffly up the walkway for a closer look. A piece of writing paper, folded in half, had been tucked between the screen door and the doorjamb. He gave a quick, furtive glance both up and down the street, but saw no one. Hesitantly he plucked the paper from its moorings.

On the outside flap, his name was written in a neat, slanting script. He stepped inside the porch and pushed the button to light the small electric lantern beside the front door. Only then did he open the paper. Inside, in the same neat writing, he found a brief note.

> *Dear Dr. Winters (Holden),*
> *Thank you for sharing your island hide-away with me, as well as the lovely picnic lunch. I would very much appreciate the opportunity to return the favor. Please join me at 7:00 this coming Saturday evening at our log. All picnic necessities will be provided. If you are unable to attend, please leave a note in my message box at the nurses' station, but I truly hope you will allow me the chance to repay your kindness.*
> *Sincerely, Calliope Myers*

He folded it back the way he'd found it and entered his bungalow. He sank down onto the sofa, still holding the folded note in his fingers. A picnic. At "our log." "Our log," as if it held some sort of special meaning. Well, maybe it did. His life had been in a complete uproar ever since he'd seen her dancing with limitless joy on the log that day back in late February. An uproar of ups and downs and longings and aggravations. He leaned his head back and closed his eyes, sighing deeply. And now she wanted to subject him to more of the same, was even offering a somewhat formal invitation to subject him to more of the same.

He rose with some difficulty—he really needed to change out of these stiff pants—and crossed to the desk in the corner of the living room. Seating himself, he opened the drawer and found a pen. Some more scrounging turned up a yellow pad of lined paper. He slapped the pad onto the desk. He riffled the edges of the paper, thinking, debating, weighing his options. Then he took up his pen.

Dear Miss Myers...

CALLIE

Micah had intimated there was a reason why Holden held himself aloof from everyone, and Callie was determined to uncover the mystery. What a man of contradictions he was, one minute smiling and laughing, the next morose and stern. She never knew where she stood. And why she wanted a standing with him remained the biggest puzzle of all, yet she couldn't deny her sincere desire to win him over.

Christian caring. That's why Micah had gone after Lydia. Christian caring was at the center of her feelings for Holden. At least, that's what she told herself as she hurried to the hospital a full hour before her shift was scheduled to begin. She had to uncover what kept him from opening up to others if she wanted to help him. Micah wouldn't tell her. Neither would Holden. But she knew where to look.

Miss Torkelson had inadvertently pointed her to the hospital staff personnel files one evening when Callie had asked where to put away some paperwork. Surprisingly, the file cabinet wasn't locked so it should be a simple matter to find Holden's file and search it for answers.

What had Holden thought of the invitation she stuck in the doorframe of his porch yesterday? Would he accept and come to her picnic? Or would he refuse? Either way, she needed to know what she was fighting so she could be armed and ready to tackle his problem head on.

She entered the hospital and made her way up the corridor to the administrative offices. Her palms began to sweat, and she went jittery under her skin. She encountered Becky and Roxanne, the two nurses on duty, and nodded a reply to their greetings but hurried on, afraid to speak in case her voice emerged as shaky as her insides felt. She reached the office where the file cabinets were housed. The door's window was dark, which meant no one was inside. She sent a quick glance up and down the hallway to ascertain she wasn't being observed, then darted inside.

Callie closed the door and leaned against it, her heart thudding with adrenaline. She would make a lousy spy. When her pulse returned to normal, she scuttled to the row of file cabinets across the room and opened the top drawer of the middle cabinet. The creaking metal made her cringe, and she shot a glance over her shoulder at the door, listening for footsteps. Only silence. She blew out a breath of relief and returned her attention to the files.

Muted light filtered past the blinds shielding the room's single window, and she squinted at the names printed on tabs. Everything was neatly alphabetized, letting her locate the file marked *Winters, Dr. Holden (Capt.)* with ease. She carried it to the window and opened it. Holding the pages toward the faint light, she scanned the official-looking documents while keeping an ear tuned to the door. She came to page marked "Personal," and her heart thudded in both eagerness and trepidation as she began to read.

Name: Winters, Holden Frederick
D.O.B.: 1910 Jan. 10
Religious affiliation: Protestant
Marital status: Widower
Child/ren: One (boy child, deceased)

She'd read enough. She closed the file and hugged it to her chest. He'd been married and he'd had a child, but both his wife and son were dead. What had happened? How had they died? How long ago had he lost them? Questions that would remain unanswered unless Holden chose to share his sadness with her.

Sympathy struck with such force, tears stung her eyes. Little wonder his behavior was erratic. He was lost in mourning. How well she understood. How many years had it taken her to accept the death of her parents? Although she'd been young, she remembered days of overwhelming sorrow and others laden with anger. But Aunties Viv and Vi had been there to help her through the pain, to encourage her to lean on her Father in Heaven. Who lent support to Holden? The night they met, Holden had mentioned several older sisters. Was he close to them? Or had he shut them out of his life the way he pushed everyone else away?

The word "protestant" under *religious affiliation* encouraged her. A true atheist or agnostic would have put "none." Perhaps he wasn't as unbelieving as he pretended to be. Somewhere underneath all of his angry bitterness was a man who had once possessed a relationship with God, but his fellowship had been disturbed. If he'd once believed, his soul must ache for the lost fellowship. So how to convince him of that truth?

Callie slid the file back where she'd found it and slowly slid the drawer into place. As it clicked shut, the office door swung open and someone pushed the light button. She gasped and spun toward the door, certain Miss Torkelson or—worse!—Holden had caught her snooping. But it was only Roxanne.

Roxanne crossed to the desk and placed a report on its clean surface. "Hi, what are you doing in here?"

"Um…" Callie shrugged, her conscience pricking. "Just some filing."

Roxanne's fine brows came down. "In the dark?"

Callie forced a light laugh. "There was enough light from the window for me to see." At least that was the truth. She edged to the door. "But I'm all done, so I guess I'll head out."

Roxanne followed her. "Okay. Have a good evening."

"I will. Thanks." Callie turned for the front doors, eager to find a solitary spot and reflect on what she'd discovered in Holden's file.

"By the way, Callie," Roxanne called from behind her, "there's something in your message box."

Hope rose in Callie's breast. She reversed her steps and hurried to the cubbies. As Roxanne had said, a folded square of white paper waited in her box. Whoever left it hadn't put her name on the outside, so it couldn't have come from Miss Torkelson, who always scrawled the recipient's last name on missives. She removed it, her fingers trembling, and half walked, half trotted outside.

She wove between bushes to a bench tucked beneath a plumeria tree. She longed to peek yet was afraid to peek. If the note was from Holden, and he'd agreed to meet her, how would she face him now that she knew his secret heartache? She perched on the bench, closed her eyes for a moment and prayed for courage, then slowly unfolded the paper. Her pulse leapt when Holden's bold script came into view.

> *Dear Miss Myers,*
> *I thank you for your kind invitation. It is unnecessary to repay me in any way for the simple lunch. Your offer of assistance was payment enough. However, if you are willing to provide a picnic lunch, I am willing to "meet you halfway," as they say, and accept your invitation.*
> *Please allow me to call for you with Micah's Coupe at 5:30 PM on Friday, and I will provide transport to "our log" for the picnic. It is the least I can do to thank you for your kindness.*
> *Sincerely, Dr. Holden Winters*

When she encountered the words in quotations—*"our log"*—her heart set up such a clamor she feared it might jump from her chest. She read the entire message twice, trying to read between the lines for any hidden messages. But she found none. She refolded the note and held it against her front as she looked skyward. Knowing that others could wander by and hear her if she spoke aloud, she prayed silently, keeping the conversation a private one between herself and her Father God.

God, my heart aches for Holden. I know You understand his loss, too, because You watched Your Son die. Please help me help him reach out to You. I can't heal his heart, Lord, but You can. Please help me find a way to lead him to Your healing hands...

15

CALLIE

Micah's familiar Coupe with Holden behind the wheel rumbled up the street exactly at 5:30. Callie scooped up the basket containing ham sandwiches, fruit, and a quart jar of sweetened tea—simple fare, but more substantial than the cheese and crackers he'd fed her—and moved to the edge of the walkway.

The vehicle stopped, and he left the engine running as he stepped out. "Hello."

Such a common word. Why did it have such a decidedly uncommon effect on her heart rate? "Hello." She remained frozen for a moment, uncertain how to proceed. Then the weight of the basket captured her attention, and she hoisted it slightly. "Put this in the back for me?"

He took the basket from her, swung it over the front seat and placed it safely in the back. He pointed. "I grabbed a blanket so we can sit on the beach. Is that all right?"

She should have thought of a blanket. She nodded. "It's perfectly all right."

"Good." He opened the passenger door. "Hop in."

With a self-conscious giggle, she complied, and he closed her in. She gripped her hands in her lap and waited while he strode around the front of the vehicle.

He slid behind the wheel and angled a look at her. Only then did he finally smile. "Ready?"

She nodded, managing a small smile of her own. This had been her idea. Now she needed to relax and enjoy herself. Yet she couldn't find her tongue, so they drove in silence through the Kolekole Pass and parked at the end of the road that led to the beach.

Holden carried the blanket and the basket. Callie's hands were kept busy holding her skirt. She'd worn her favorite sundress, the white cotton with a full skirt, and the breeze did its best to whip the fabric around her knees. They reached the log, and Holden handed her the basket. Then he snapped the blanket. I took three tries, battling the stiff breeze, before it landed flat. Then he quickly knelt at one side and held out his hands for the basket.

She handed it to him then sat across from him, tucking her legs to the side. He placed the basket between them, and she opened it. She pulled out the paper wrapped sandwiches and paused, cringing. "I didn't bring plates."

"So you *can* talk."

She drew back and gawked at him. To her surprise, teasing glinted in his eyes. Her face flooded with heat, but she laughed. She was being silly, allowing the secret she'd uncovered to dictate her actions. He was still the man to whom she had written the note, still the man she intended to convince of God's reality. And now that she knew the reason he kept himself detached, she knew how to begin. But first she needed to draw on her former spunk and determination. Then everything would fall into place.

"I'm sorry." She shrugged, wrinkling her nose. "I've never

invited a man on a picnic before, and I guess I'm a little uncertain."

"Well, don't be." The warmth in his voice put her at ease. "Let's unwind and enjoy the view. What kind of sandwiches did you bring?"

They chatted companionably while they consumed their sandwiches and the assortment of tropical fruits. Callie hadn't brought glasses, so they drank directly from the jar. There was a certain intimacy in sharing the container of tea, and Callie's stomach trembled as she passed it to him for another drink.

When the food was gone, Holden leaned on one elbow, stretched out his legs and crossed his ankles, and turned a serious look on her. "This has been pleasant, but I'm quite certain you have an ulterior motive for inviting me here this evening."

Callie smoothed her skirt across her knees, an unnecessary gesture. She wished he wasn't always so candid, but he had offered a perfect lead-in. "I suppose by now my motives are a bit obvious, aren't they?"

He raised one eyebrow. "I'm in for another sermon, right?"

She frowned. "I don't preach at you."

He laughed. "That is a matter of opinion, my dear Callie, and in my opinion, you regularly preach at me." He shifted slightly and pinned her with a smirk. "So what's the topic for this evening?"

She saw the glint of humor in his eyes, but she wasn't in a teasing mood. The topic was too serious. His very soul depended on the outcome. "You challenged me to prove that God truly exists, and I think it's time I met the challenge."

"So how do you think you're going to prove that God exists?" He kept his relaxed pose, but his muscles tensed.

"Why are you so convinced He doesn't?" She dared to crack the door for him to reveal a bit of his hurt.

"That's easy I've seen the proof. Death. Destruction. The loss of innocence." He fired the words with as much force as bullets from a rifle. "If God exists, why is there so much unhappiness in the world? I thought He's supposed to be a God of love."

"He is." Callie placed her hands on her knees and leaned toward him slightly. "Just because sad things happen doesn't mean God isn't there."

"Oh, yeah?" His tone turned bitter. He rolled onto his hip and squared off with her, his face a mere twelve inches from hers. "Then explain this one, Miss Joyful. Three months before I came here, I operated on a six-year-old girl—a baby!—who had been beaten by her drunken uncle. Where was your God when that tiny girl was brutally attacked by the person put in charge of her care?"

Callie fought the gorge that threatened to fill her throat. She willed the vivid image to clear from her mind. Another image entered. "I believe He was in Heaven, weeping."

He snorted and shifted back to his original position, but he kept his scowl angled towards her. "He would have done more good to have been on earth, protecting little Sylvia. He should have kept it from happening in the first place."

Callie edged forward an inch on her knees. "But don't you see He couldn't? Because if He did, we would be nothing more than puppets dancing at the end of a string. He gives us free choice, Holden. He lets us choose His way or evil's way." Her voice broke and she battled tears. "I don't know why some men choose the evil things they do, but I do know that when evil occurs, God provides a way out. But someone, somewhere, was too selfish to do what was needed that night to prevent evil from having its way."

His face drained of color, and he turned sharply away. The muscles in his jaw clenched, but she didn't believe it was anger he was fighting. He seemed to be fighting for control of something deeper than anger.

"Holden?"

His entire body jolted, and he looked at her as if he'd never seen her before. A flush of red crept across his cheeks and fury flared in his blue eyes. He swung his hand, as if knocking over a stack of blocks. "Enough of this. You believe your way, and I'll believe mine, and we'll just have to leave it at that."

Callie shook her head, sorrow weighting her. "I can't do that, Holden. God could have sent me anywhere with the Red Cross, but He brought me here. There has to be a reason, and I've come to believe the reason is you. Whether you're ready to admit it or not, you need God in your life, and I can't leave you floundering without Him."

He blasted a snide laugh. "Why, Miss Myers, do I need God?"

"To fill the void that the loss of your family left. To heal the pain of missing them."

He sat up. The veins in his neck stood at attention and his cheeks flew bright banners of fury. She'd crossed a line, and for a moment she feared he might even strike her, so palpable was his rage. But he kept his clenched fists firmly applied to the ground. "How do you know about my family? Did Micah—"

"No, Micah didn't say anything. I..." She gulped. "I snooped."

His eyes narrowed. "You what?"

Admitting the truth could get her into serious trouble, but she wouldn't lie to him. "I peeked at your personnel file." His jaw muscles clenched. She swallowed. "I know I shouldn't have, but I had to find out what had created such a scornfulness toward God. I understand now. It grew from your pain and loss. But, Holden, God can take the pain away, if you let Him."

He turned his back on her, folded his arms around his upraised knees, and stared across the ocean. "What would you know about pain and loss, Calliope Myers? You're still a baby, a little girl with a mommy and daddy who obviously love you. Don't sit there and preach to me about how God takes away pain."

Callie's heart stung from his unfair accusations. She dropped her head and prayed for the strength to share what she had to in order to make him see the truth. When she'd summoned her courage she emulated his pose and directed her words to the rolling waves. "You're right, my daddy and mama loved me. I always knew it. We didn't have a lot of money, so my parents couldn't buy me presents, but we always did something for birthdays. Maybe make taffy, or take a day off from chores." She lifted one shoulder in a hint of a shrug. "Something special."

She sensed a movement, and she glanced out of the corners of her eyes. Holden had turned his head and was gazing at her intently although scowl lines still marred his handsome face.

"The summer of my seventh birthday, Daddy and Mama planned a picnic. Not just any picnic—a water picnic." A small smile of remembrance tugged at the corners of her lips. "Daddy borrowed a rowboat from one of our neighbors, and Mama packed sandwiches. Mama's homemade bread spread with butter and sprinkled with white sugar, my favorite kind. Daddy said we'd row out to the middle of Little Muddy Creek and eat our picnic there, then do some fishing. I was so excited. I'd never fished from a boat before, although I'd thrown in a line from the shore lots of times with Daddy."

She sighed, looking up at the pale bits of light beginning to dot the darkening sky, and she pictured the day in her mind. "It was a sunshiny day, with a breeze that kept it from being too hot. Kind of like today. On the way to Little Muddy,

Mama and I picked a whole cluster of wild aster and black-eyed Susans, and we sang as we walked along. The maples were so full and green, and with the sun shining behind them, Daddy said the leaves were almost as pretty as Mama's green eyes. Such a perfect day for a picnic."

She closed her eyes, letting her memories carry her backward. "We got in the rowboat, and Daddy warned me about sitting still as a mouse so I wouldn't get dunked. I snuggled close to Mama. I felt so safe. Daddy rowed us out to the middle. I remember his muscles bulging like cords in his arms as he pulled against the oars, and I thought I had the strongest daddy in the world.

"It was so peaceful there. Birds were singing—Mama whistled back to them just to be silly—and we saw otters splashing along the far bank. The sun reflecting on the water looked like diamonds." She licked her lips, eyes still closed. "Mama had just opened the basket and handed me a sandwich when"—her throat tightened—"something changed. The birds stopped their songs, the otters peeked upstream and then disappeared under the water. We heard this strange rushing noise, like a heavy rain. But the sky was clear."

Her brow remained furrowed, her chest beginning to heave the way it had then as events fell into place. "Daddy got this look of panic on his face—I'll never forget that look—and he grabbed up the oars and started rowing as hard as he could. He told Mama and me to hold on, and Mama grabbed me so tight. I dropped my sandwich and started to cry. I was scared, and I could tell they were, too, but I couldn't understand what was going on. Mama was soothing me, and Daddy was rowing, and then this huge rush of water and timbers came down and…and picked up our boat and dumped us out."

A hand clamped on her wrist. Callie opened her eyes. Holden sat near, staring at her. Silently pleading with her. But she'd started, and she had to finish. She ignored the fingers biting into her wrist and continued.

"Daddy went flying one way, and Mama and me another. We were in the water, and it was a wild thing, trying to push us under. It tore me away from Mama, and I screamed. I got my mouth and nose full, and I fought to get to the surface where I could breathe. Then Daddy had me. I still don't know how, but he grabbed me and kept my head above water. He swam against the awful current to the shore and threw me out of harm's way. I was crying and spluttering and I wanted him to stay and hold me. But he said, 'Stay here, angel-darlin', I've got to get your mama.' And he went right back into the roaring stream. I stayed there, just like he said, until night fell. I stayed there until the next morning when our neighbor came looking for his boat and found me instead. And—"

"Callie, don't." Holden's nostrils flared. He squeezed her wrist so tightly it hurt.

She shook her head. "They found Mama and Daddy the next day. My aunts—Daddy's sisters, Vivian and Viola—took me home with them afterwards. And they've been wonderful guardians, but I still miss Mama and Daddy."

She removed her wrist from Holden's grasp and offered her hand. He intertwined his fingers with hers. She viewed him through a watery haze, but even so she saw tears glistening in the corner of his eyes. "For a long time I blamed myself, because it was my birthday and I was the reason we were out there." Holden shook his head, his eyes glimmering, and she nodded, understanding the silent message. "I know. I know that now. Someone farther upstream had tried to dam the river and reroute it to irrigate his cornfields. The current was too strong and it broke through the dam. That's what came rushing at us. We just happened to be in the way. It wasn't anybody's fault. It just… happened."

Holden dropped his head. One tear rolled down his honed cheek.

Callie wiped away the moisture with her palm. "I understand loss, Holden. And pain. Losing Mama and Daddy that way… I thought my heart was broken and it would never mend. But because my parents loved God, I have the assurance of where they are right now, and I know I will see them again. I also have the assurance that I'm loved by my aunts. Those assurances helped mend my heart."

"It was so unfair…" He muttered the word, his head hanging low.

Callie tugged at his hand and waited until he had lifted his face so she could see his dear, beautiful blue eyes. "No one is promised fairness in life, Holden. People are imperfect and make imperfect choices. Sometimes those choices affect others, too. But if there's only one thing I know without a doubt." Tears welled and spilled over. "God is there, and He cares. He wants to lift us up out of our unhappiness and put our feet on sturdy ground." She pulled away and reached into the basket. At the bottom she located her Bible. She held it out to Holden.

"All the proof you need is right here. Take it. Read it. See for yourself."

He recoiled as if afraid of being stung. "I told you I don't read fiction."

"And I told you it isn't fiction." When he still wouldn't reach for it, she sighed and laid the Bible in her lap. She opened it, taking care as she turned the thin pages. "May I read a verse to you?" At his suspicious expression she held up one finger. "Just one verse. It won't hurt a bit."

He nodded, but his jaw was clenched tightly again, and he turned his face away. Inwardly she smiled. He sure was a stubborn one. But God could soften the hardest of hearts. She placed her finger under the verse she'd chosen and read. "'He lifted me out of the slimy pit, out of the mud and mire; He set my feet on a rock and gave me a firm place to stand.'" She pinned his profile with her steady gaze, waiting for him to face her. "That's from Psalms, and that's what God did for me. Almost literally. I have a firm place to stand, Holden, which is why I can face life's unfairnesses and unhappinesses and move forward. You're stuck. You're stuck in that mud and mire of bitterness, and you'll never be happy there. But if you look up and ask, He'll pull you free of that."

He didn't respond—didn't even look at her.

After a couple of minutes she sighed. "Okay for now, Holden Winters. Don't let it be said that I was too forward. My aunts have tried to teach me to mind my manners. But rest assured I'm not finished with this subject. I might have lost this battle, but I'm not conceding in the war."

Without warning, he burst out laughing.

She fought temptation to sock him a good one on the arm. "What is so funny?"

"Imagining you on the front lines of battle, wearing your white sundress and no shoes, with your hair all wild around your face and your green eyes daring them to raise their rifles…" He grinned. "You'd have them all just rolling over and playing dead."

Miffed at him for not taking her seriously, she folded her arms over her chest. "I don't know how I could have that effect on the Germans when I don't even have that effect on you."

His expression changed. The fire in his eyes lost the teasing glint, and something else glittered there. Something foreign to Callie. She held her breath, wondering what he was thinking. And then slowly, so slowly she thought she might be imagining it, he angled his torso toward her, his head tipping slightly as he drew near. Almost before she knew what was happening, his lips settled on hers. An intense rush of feeling swept over her, seeming to lift her from the sandy beach and hold her suspended on a cloud.

She leaned into the kiss, leaned into the wonderful feelings the kiss summoned, but when his arms closed around her, pulling her fully into an embrace, she pressed her palms against his chest and pushed while twisting her face away.

"Don't." She commanded herself as much as him.

"Why?" His face was so close she saw her own reflection in the depths of his eyes.

She leaned back, needed distance between them. "Because I can't become romantically involved with you. I—"

He put up his hand. "Don't tell me. Let me guess. It's because of my lack of *Christian convictions*."

How could he make something so beautiful sound like dirty words? Her ire flared. "Yes, as a matter of fact, that's exactly it. The Bible warns against becoming unequally yoked with unbelievers, and God never gives a warning without a good reason."

Holden rolled his eyes. "I'm not trying to become yoked with you, I'm just trying to kiss you." He leaned in again, his expression persuasive. "Come on, Callie, what's wrong with stealing a few kisses? Don't tell me you've never kissed someone for the sheer enjoyment of kissing."

She swung her gaze sharply away. Heat seared her cheeks, and she wished she could burrow under the sand and hide.

His hand snaked out and caught her chin between his thumb and forefinger. He tugged, making her look at him. His eyes narrowed in disbelief. "You've never kissed anyone before?"

Anger replaced the embarrassment and she smacked his hand away. "Before I came here I was hardly allowed to *look* at a man, let alone spend time alone with one. When was I supposed to be doing all of this kissing?"

She expected him to laugh at her, but instead his gaze softened. His gaze wandered from her eyes to her lips, then they seemed to follow the pathway of her jaw to her hair. While his tender gaze swept across her, she experienced the same sweet lifting in her chest she'd had when his lips had touched hers. Anger swept away, replaced by strange yearnings and tuggings within her soul. What was he doing to her?

He lifted his hand, and although she had time to pull away, she remained still until his hand settled softly at the back of her head. He smoothed her hair, the touch sending tingles down her spine, and then his hand slipped around until he'd cupped her jaw. She was tempted to tip her head to increase the pressure of his palm against her cheek, but her heart was already beating so rapidly she wasn't sure she could move.

"My sweet, innocent Callie, am I frightening you?"

She shook her head, unable to speak.

"But I can feel your pulse. It's racing."

Her eyes must be as round as the moon overhead, and she tried unsuccessfully to control her breathing. She wasn't frightened, she was... She didn't know what she was. Never having had this feeling before, she wanted it to end and wanted it to last forever, all at the same time.

"H-Holden?" She tried in that one word to convey all of the questions roaring through her confused mind.

"Callie?" His fingers moving lightly back and forth below her ear.

"Please..."

"Please what?" His tone was tender, but his expression developed a hint of hardness. "Please touch me? Please don't touch me? Do you even know what you want, Calliope Myers?"

Yes, she did. God forgive her, she knew what she wanted.

But she couldn't have it. Not now, not with this man. "I—" She couldn't find the words to adequately express what she felt without giving him the wrong impression.

Holden finally smiled. A bittersweet smile. No teeth, just an upturning of lips in a smile that didn't quite reach his eyes. His hand dropped from her jaw. "Okay. No more questions. But let me try to give some answers. You want me to believe the way you do—that God is there, and that He cares. Well, I believed it once, and look where it got me. I'm a widower who also lost his only child, a doctor who has seen too much suffering. I can't go back to that faith, Callie. It simply isn't in me anymore."

"But don't you understand?" Callie clasped her hands beneath her chin. "It *is* in you. If it was there once, it's still there. You've just buried it far below the surface. You've lost your fellowship, Holden, but to regain the relationship all you have to do is ask."

"Why can't you understand that I don't want to ask?" He let his head drop back, closed his eyes, and drew a great breath which he blew out with puffed cheeks. They sat in tense silence for long seconds before he suddenly bounced to his knees. "You want to help me, want to be my friend. I can accept that. I can even appreciate it. The problem is, Callie, that a simple friendship between the two of us will never work. There's too much fire. It's either going to roar out of control, or fizzle and be nothing."

He started gathering up the discarded pieces of waxed paper. "Do you ever wonder why you get so mad at me? That's passion. You're so beautiful when you're flaring, because passion bursts from your eyes." He threw the wad of paper into the basket, snatched up another one, and flung it in even harder.

He paused and looked her full in the face. "Even though

I fought it, I'm discovering I want it all—the fun, the teasing, the romance… I didn't want to open myself up to someone again, but you have a way of growing on a person. I may not want your God, but I do want you. You've brought a sparkle to my life that's been missing for a long, long time. But it really isn't my choice now. It's yours."

Callie's heart fell. No matter how much she wanted the roaring fire with Holden, she couldn't have it. Not while he adamantly refused to acknowledge God as his creator, and not when she knew there was no future for her here. Tears welled in her eyes, and he must have seen them, because he dropped his gaze and stood, scooping up the basket as he went.

"Let's go."

Callie stood and followed him to the Coupe. She spoke not a word on the drive back to Schofield. She said nothing when he politely walked her to her door. And she made no sound as she dressed in her night clothes and slipped between the sheets of her bed. But once her face hit the pillow, she erupted into sobs that shook her frame and threatened to tear her in two. Why did doing the right thing have to hurt so much?

16

Holden stopped the Coupe in front of Micah's bungalow, twisted the key in the ignition, then sat, his head
bent forward. He'd been unfair to Callie. He shouldn't have
dumped the burden of responsibility for their relationship in
her lap. Relationship... Did they even have one? What could
he call the up-and-down, hills-and-valleys association they
shared? So opposite the structured, predictable courtship he'd
enjoyed with Lorna. But then, Lorna and Callie were nothing
alike, either, except for that unquenchable faith.

Ah, yes, Lorna had been as firmly rooted as Callie when
it came to belief in a Higher Being. In fact, their first date
had been a church social with her father and stepmother.
Her father was thrilled to have Holden pay attention to his
daughter, and he'd encouraged their relationship to blossom,
a surprise considering the difference in their social status. In
retrospect, his father-in-law's interest in him was probably due
to his course of study. Mr. Ballard was a lawyer, accustomed to
living well, and he wanted nothing less for his child. The title
Doctor had won the elder Ballard. He'd expected Holden to

provide well for Lorna.

And Holden had. He began working full-time on the staff of the University of Chicago Hospital as soon as he completed his residency. Within the first year of their marriage, he purchased a beautiful home in one of Chicago's finest housing districts. Together he and Lorna filled the stately two-story house with new furnishings, gorgeous paintings, and all of the trappings that bespoke wealth and influence. He worked six days a week to make sure Lorna had everything she'd been accustomed to, and on the seventh day he relaxed—usually while Lorna attended church services without him.

But as their social prominence increased, Lorna grew distant. Holden rested his forehead on the steering wheel. Never one to complain and too proper to nag, Lorna asked Holden to slow down, to spend more time with her, to attend church with her. But there wasn't time. He was building his practice, accumulating his wealth. They'd have time for relaxing together and going to church later, when they were well established. His relationship with Lorna began to feel as tenuous as his relationship with God.

But then she discovered they were expecting a baby. The joy of that special day rose in Holden's memory, and he sat up and folded his arms over his chest as tightly as he'd held his wife when she shared the news of their impending parenthood. He'd promised, between kisses, that as soon as the baby came, he would slow down and be the family man she wanted. He'd kept the promise for the most part, until two staff doctors told him about a special event. The "King of Swing," Benny Goodman, was scheduled to perform at the Congress Hotel with his clarinet quintet in January. Tickets were scarce, but with the right connections, they could be found. The hospital administrator had a fistful of tickets which he was willing to distribute to those he believed had earned the privilege. It was an elite event, and Holden was determined to take Lorna and Timmy. In order to be included in the chosen few, he had to show his supervisor that he was dedicated to the hospital. Because of that, he'd been at the hospital instead of home with Lorna and Timmy at the time they'd needed him most.

His hands clamped painfully around his own forearms. He wanted to forget that night. Had tried so diligently to forget that night. Yet the memory persisted, the sequence of events imprinted into his mind much like an epitaph etched on stone...

Lorna's call to the hospital. *"Please be home early tonight, darling. I want to light the candles on the tree to show Timmy."*

His response. *"But, sweetheart, I'm trying to put in the extra time to earn us that weekend trip, remember?"*

Her reluctant agreement. *"All right, but not too late, please?"*

His stretch in the break room, laughing with a co-worker until well after eleven.

His drive home, spotting the smoke, his heart racing in fear.

His attempt to break past the firemen and go into his house which was fully engulfed in flames. The fire chief's sorrowful face as he explained, *"It must have started with the Christmas tree. It was so close to the base of the stairs, it trapped them on the second floor. They probably died of smoke inhalation."*

His overwhelming burden of guilt for placing the massive tree near the parlor window where those passing by would see its grandeur and be impressed. He had created a death trap for his family...

A light snapped on to his left, and Holden gave a start. He looked toward the source—Micah's porch light—and the silhouette of his friend behind the screened door. How long had he been sitting in the automobile? At least the light had sent his unhappy musings into the far recesses of his mind. He pulled himself out of the vehicle and trudged up the sidewalk.

The screen door popped open, bringing Micah's features out of shadow, and Holden held out the car keys. Micah snagged them, smiling, but then he frowned. "You okay, buddy?"

Holden aimed his gaze at his feet and shook his head. A hand clamped on his shoulder. He looked into his friend's concerned face.

"Come on in. Talk to me."

Ordinarily Holden would refuse such an invitation, but his reminiscing had left him lonely and heartsore. He didn't want to be alone. So he followed Micah into the living room and sat in the middle of the couch.

Micah plopped into a chair across from Holden. "So what's going on?"

What should he say? Talking was something his sisters did. Endlessly. Lorna had always wanted to talk everything out, too. And that Callie—once she got going, she could talk the hind legs off a mule. But Holden wasn't sure how to proceed in unburdening himself, so he sat in silence while Micah waited, chin in hand, gaze narrowed and thoughtful.

Finally Micah sighed. "Is this about Callie?"

Holden bit the inside of his cheek. Micah had confessed to feeling deeply for Callie. How would he react if Holden admitted he wanted her? Would he alienate the one friend he had? "Maybe, seeing how you're so taken with her, talking to you isn't a good idea."

Micah released a short, mirthless snort of laughter. "Listen, Holden, Callie's already told me she sees me as a brother. She means it, too. Sure, I would be the luckiest guy on earth if it was different, but all she and I are going to have is a friendship. So you won't be stomping on my toes if you tell me that you've fallen in love with her."

"I'm not sure I have." Holden leaned forward and rested his elbows on his knees. "I know I don't want to."

"Of course you don't." Micah spoke as matter-of-factly as always. "You don't want to love anybody. But it's not much fun being all alone, is it, buddy?"

Holden shook his head. "Callie says God sent her to Oahu because of me." He gave a derisive huff. "As if He'd care enough to do that." Sweat beaded across his upper lip as he remembered something else Callie had said—that God provided a means to prevent evil from having its way, that He wept when evil reigned triumphant, but it was always man's choice. Those words cut Holden to the very core of his soul. The night of the fire came back in rush. Had God wept over Holden's choice that night?

Micah crossed the floor and sat beside Holden. He curled his hand on Holden's shoulder. "I know I haven't been as vocal as Callie when it comes to sharing my faith. In fact, I'd let it slide too much before she came here. But her fiery exuberance has reignited my own flame. I want you to know that I've been praying for you."

Holden straightened, looking directly in Micah's face. He couldn't imagine the fun-loving Micah doing something as serious as praying.

Micah dropped his hand to his lap and laughed a bit self-consciously. "Yeah. Sounds kind of out-of-kilter, doesn't it? But it's true." He leaned back and crossed his legs, his face serious. "After Callie told me there wasn't any hope for us to have a relationship beyond friendship, I got to thinking how, even though it hurt me, I'd be okay. I'd be okay because I'm not dependin' on Callie to make me happy."

Micah reached back to a table behind the sofa and picked up a familiar Book. It wasn't dust-covered, like the last time

Holden had glimpsed it on Micah's desk. Maybe Micah had been making some changes in his personal life. Micah fingered through the thin pages the same way Callie had earlier.

"'Find rest, O my soul, in God alone; my hope comes from Him.'" He looked at Holden and pointed to the verse he'd read. "I have hope, even though I set it aside for awhile. If Callie isn't meant for me, there's something else even better waiting. But what do you have, Holden? You're one of the most unhappy people I've ever met. You put your whole happiness in buildin' a life for you, Lorna, and your baby, and then when they were gone, you had nothing. Now you're tempted to make Callie the key to your happiness. It won't work. As wonderful as Callie is, she'll only provide a surface happiness. You need somethin' deeper. You need the hope that comes from the God of miracles."

Holden flinched. Micah's statement, spoken kindly with a hint of his familiar southern twang, created a bruise on his heart. "I will not place my hope in the God who let my family die."

"Holden, listen—"

"No. You listen." Holden slammed his fist into his open palm with each word. "God—let—my—family—die!" He pressed the heels of his hands against the cushioned seat of the sofa, trying to gain control of his temper. "I prayed—I begged—for Him to bring them out alive. God of miracles? What a joke. I chose to become a doctor because I wanted to make a positive impact. I've seen it over and over again, people with illnesses or injuries whose recovery was out of my control, but I'd been taught that God was in control and He could save. But over and over people died. And then it was my family—my wife, my son…" His voice broke. He shook his head. "I won't put myself in the hands of that God again, Micah. I won't."

Micah closed his Bible and hung his head. "Then there's nothing more I can do for you, buddy."

Holden shot out of seat and paced across the room, his hands balled into fists. "So you're telling me it's all useless."

"Absolutely not." Micah countered Holden's fury with an unflustered countenance that angered Holden even further. "I'm tellin' you that no one else can change things for you—not me, not Callie. It has to be you. It's your own choice."

There was that word again. "Choice." Holden spat. "We have no choice. We make our choices, but nothing goes as planned. Whatever happens, happens—we're at the mercy of the winds."

Micah rose. "No, Holden, the world is at the mercy of the winds, but if you have God in your heart, then He's at the helm. But you have to give Him control. You have to look for His guidance. He won't force it on you—it has to be something you choose." His voice softened to a near whisper. "Holden, you became a doctor for all the right reasons. But you've told me before how you spent your days. I think you lost track of attending to need and got lost in attaining wants. When your focus changed, your heart changed. And things fell apart." He sighed. "You have to open up your fists and let go of the reins. Give them over to God and let him work a change in your heart."

Holden pressed the heels of his fists against his forehead. Micah and Callie made it sound so easy, but it wasn't. He'd thought he chose correctly—providing a good living for his family with a career that could make a difference in the lives of many people. But where had those choices gotten him? Here, on this island where his doctor's skills were scarcely needed. Here, where he was alone in his little bungalow. Here, on his own. Alone.

You're stuck in the mud and mire of bitterness... Callie's words taunted him. *Stuck… Stuck…* He tensed, his stiff legs holding him captive in the middle of Micah's living room floor. Then, intentionally, he lifted his right foot and stepped forward. One step. And he raised his face to the ceiling, smiling in grim satisfaction. He was exactly where he wanted to be—in control. *See, God? I can move anytime I want to. I'm not stuck.*

He turned and met Micah's gaze. The sorrowful expression on his friend's face caused his surety to waver momentarily, but then he hardened his heart once more. He clapped Micah on the shoulder, twisting his lips into the semblance of a grin. "Listen, I know you mean well, but I'm fine. Sure, I get lonely sometimes. Who doesn't? I suffered a little bout of that tonight, but it doesn't mean I'm hopeless, right? Ten more months and I'll be done here, free to move on and make a new start. And who knows? Maybe Callie will *choose*"—he emphasized the word, quirking one side of his lips upward in a sardonic grin—"to make that new start with me. I left it up to her."

Micah's eyebrows shot up. "You asked her to make a new start with you?"

Holden shrugged, assuming a devil-may-care attitude. "Not in those words, but the message was comparable. She knows what I want. I told her to let me know."

Micah whistled through his teeth. "Whew, buddy. You're setting yourself up for a fall."

Holden turned a hard look in Micah's direction. "Meaning?"

"Meaning Callie won't choose to follow you. She's already made her choice to follow God. She's put Him at the helm of her life."

Holden snorted. "It's a female's prerogative to change her mind, remember? You can't determine what Callie will do."

Micah shook his head, then opened his mouth as if to say something. He must have thought better of it, though, because he closed his jaw. He threw his hands outward in a gesture of futility, but his eyes were sympathetic.

Holden laughed—a harsh, mirthless sound. "As you stated earlier, Micah, there's nothing you can do for me." He turned to leave.

"I said there's nothing more I can do for you…than pray."

Unexplainably, the words sent a chill down Holden's spine. He drew his anger like a cloak around himself. "Save your breath, Micah. Nobody's listening. I should know." He stomped out the door, down the steps, and across the walkway that led to his own bungalow. But when he'd shut himself inside the quiet room, he allowed his chin to drop against his chest sadly. In all likelihood, Micah was right. Callie wouldn't choose him over her God.

Well, so be it.

He thrust out his chin, marched to his bedroom, and began changing out of his clothes with stiff, jerky motions. Who needed her? Always spouting verses from her book of fairy tales, sticking her nose where it didn't belong. Some wife she'd make. She couldn't even remember to wear her shoes. Would she impress the society elites of Chicago?

His hands stilled, holding the shirt he'd removed, picturing Callie's sweet face turned toward him with compassion as she fervently expressed her beliefs. He wadded up the shirt and threw it viciously into his laundry basket, drawing on anger to keep from giving in to the memory of her pleading eyes.

He dug in his dresser for clean pajamas, muttering to the quiet, empty room. "I've gotten along fine these past years on my own. So I get lonely now and then. It's nothing I can't handle. I don't need anyone." So why had he told Callie he wanted her? What had he been thinking to open himself up that way? It must have been her sad story pulling him off-balance and jerking the blanket of logic out from under his feet. But he was back on familiar footing now.

He crossed to the window, popped it open, and propped his hands on the window sill. Wind tossed the tree branches. "*When that wind touches you, you're experiencing the reality of an awesome God, whether you choose to acknowledge Him or not.*" Callie's words from the evening in Haleiwa played in his memory. What had he told Micah? Something about wind… Ah, yes, that they were at the mercy of the wind. Did that mean he was at the mercy of God?

He tromped to the bed and threw back the covers. Flopping onto the mattress, he folded his hands behind his head, elbows splayed outward, and stared at the ceiling. His thoughts continued with a will of their own.

God's mercy is compassion… That's what he'd been taught to believe. His mother read about the mercy of God in chapter one of I Peter, something about mercy giving people living hope through the resurrection of Jesus Christ. He scowled, pressing his memory to recall the rest. There had been an admonition to rejoice in the grief of trials because it would make your faith more fully known to others and, in so doing, bring glory to Jesus.

He released a snort. Callie must have read the passage and swallowed it whole, because she hadn't abandoned her faith in spite of her trials. A longing to be as calm of spirit as Callie seemed to be rolled through him. She'd suffered, too. She'd lost as much as he had. Yet rather than wallowing in bitterness, she'd emerged strong and joyful and at peace. He brought down his hands and laid them across his chest, pressing hard against the hollowness he felt there.

Micah had said he was setting himself up for a fall, waiting for Callie to make her *choice*. He didn't need another fall. Before she had an opportunity to decline his offer, he'd let her know he'd changed his mind. A moment of weakness had caused him to open his heart to her, but he was back in control of himself now.

He reached down and yanked the sheet across his hips, then settled against his pillows, shifting a bit to get comfortable. He lay still, staring at the dark ceiling, eyes wide open. The decision was made. Shouldn't he have a sense of satisfaction? Instead, the emptiness in his chest seemed to expand to his gut and ache with a craving he didn't know how to fill.

"Callie Myers, I rue the day I lifted you from that sandy beach..."

"He lifted me from the mud and mire, and gave me a firm place to stand..."

Holden hardened his heart against her sweetly uttered words.

"He lifted me from the mud and mire..."

Hardened his heart against Callie.

"...And gave me a firm place to stand..."

Hardened his heart against God. And he ignored the aching emptiness in his middle that felt as real as the echoing silence of his empty, lonely room.

17

Callie opened her eyes after offering her breakfast prayers and spotted Holden moving purposefully in her direction through the mess hall. Her heart leapt into her throat and her pulse immediately doubled in speed. She had spent a very difficult night, wrestling with her feelings for this man, asking God to give her the courage to do what must be done. She'd found her peace with the situation, but her feelings couldn't be turned off quite so easily.

"Miss Myers." Holden stood formally across the table from her, his hands clasped behind his back. He'd combed his hair away from his forehead, bringing prominence to those sapphire eyes that Callie found so hard to resist.

She allowed her lips to tip upward at his proper greeting. "Why don't you sit down, Holden. And please don't be stuffy with me—we've moved beyond that, don't you think?"

His shoulders twitched and a slight coloring mottled his neck. For a moment he hovered, appearing shame-faced, and then he pulled out a chair and seated himself across from her. He leaned his forearms on the table. "Callie, we need to talk."

"About last night," she guessed, and he nodded. "Then may I go first?" He set his jaw, and for a moment she thought he would refuse. But then he gave another brusque jerk of his chin which signified reluctant agreement.

"Holden, I've been thinking about what you said last night." She kept her voice whisper-level to provide a modicum of privacy. "You said a relationship between us is up to me, and—"

"I was wrong." He drew a breath so deep it expanded his chest, then blew it out. "A relationship should be a mutual decision, and I'd like to retract what I said in haste yesterday evening."

Callie didn't remove her gaze from his, but she pressed herself to the metal backrest of her chair, withdrawing as far as possible from him.By now she should expect to be thrown from the saddle just as she'd found her seat, but he still managed to take her by surprise. "Okay…"

"Please don't take it personally." She grimaced at his impersonal tone. "You are a very attractive young lady with many positive attributes. But you see, my future is uncertain. I am contemplating seeking a different career choice when my tour of duty here is completed, and as a result I have no security to offer you. Consequently, it is in your best interests to—"

"*My* best interests?" Callie pushed her plate aside and braced her arms on the table. "Don't try to be self-sacrificing, Holden Winters. I know what you're doing here. You're running scared."

"I beg your pardon." He set his lips in a grim line.

She released a brief huff of laughter. "This is what you do. When your emotions are on the line, you pull out that blanket of formality and wrap it around yourself so tightly you cut off your feelings. At least for awhile. You do this every time you start to get close to me."

"I do not wrap—"

"Yes, you do!" She nearly hissed the words. "But you know what, Holden? It's all right. You see, I'm not looking for a long-term relationship, either. I'm not on some husband hunt. My purpose in being here is to learn as much as I can about nursing so when I go home I can use it to help my own community."

"That's very noble, I'm sure, but—"

"I also believe that God wants me to be a witness for Him while I'm here, to help you find your way back to Him. You aren't making it easy, but then God never said doing His will would be easy, only that it was my responsibility, and somehow He'll give me the strength to stand up to you and your everlasting gloominess that sometimes makes me wish I could pinch your nose off."

She stood, leaning across the table so her nose was only inches from his. "Whatever your purpose is in being here is something you have to decide on your own, but while you're running away from me, you might consider something. You can get away from me, but you can't get away from God. He's everywhere. And He wants you back. And if it isn't me who manages to get through your thick skull, someone else will come along to do the same thing. So you might as well stop your back pedaling and just look to the heavens and make your peace with Him. It'll save all of us a lot of time and aggravation!" And she snatched up her untouched tray and marched away, her nose in the air.

HOLDEN

Holden slumped back in his chair. What a little fireball she could be! Her red hair was no ruse. But how incredibly cute she was in her fury. She wanted to pinch his nose off? His lips twitched with humor, then he quickly squelched the reaction. The conversation hadn't gone as he'd planned, but the end result was the same.

He propped one elbow on the table and rested his chin in his hand. Much as he hated to admit it, Callie had been right about one thing. He needed to figure out his purpose in being here. Not only that, he needed a purpose for living. He was no longer a husband or father. He wasn't planning to continue with the calling he'd had since childhood to be a doctor. If the things that had defined his identity in the past were forever gone, did he even have a purpose?

CALLIE

Callie stormed out of the mess hall, nearly colliding headlong with two uniformed soldiers going in. They whistled and backed off, holding up their hands in mock surrender, but she pushed by them without uttering an apology. Tears threatened, and she was determined to get off somewhere by herself before the impending gale struck. She would not humiliate herself by bawling publicly.

A gentle mist began to fall, and she picked up her pace, trotting the final distance to the base library. It would be dry there, and she would be able to find a quiet corner where she could examine her frustration and shed the tears that were pressing behind her eyelids. She preferred going to her apartment, but she couldn't. Lydia would be there. Her roommate's sour countenance would only add to her angst. When would Lydia get over her doldrums? At one time, Lydia might have been a good confidant, but not anymore. She was barely a roommate, seldom even speaking to Callie. Callie had sent up countless prayers for Lydia and for their friendship to be restored, but so far God hadn't granted her request.

She stepped through the doors of the library and wove between tables to the last row of shelves, to a tiny circular table shoved in the farthest corner. She seated herself with her back to the room, put her head in her hands, and allowed the angry tears to flow. Why did she allow him to affect her this way? She'd gotten so mad at him again. Her aunts had always cautioned her to control her temper—if she spouted with temper when she was little, they made her sit down and write James 1:26 until she'd filled a page both front and back. She knew she should keep a rein on her tongue lest she prove herself to be a poor example of God's patient love. She thought she'd learned to control her temper with their guidance. Until she'd met Holden. Oh, how he provoked her.

She swept away the childish tears rolling relentlessly down her hot cheeks. Reaching below the collar of her dress, she pulled out a string which she'd hung around her neck this morning. She dangled the string in front of her eyes, watching the button she'd pulled from Holden's shirt front spin and swing. She'd placed the button around her neck, to hang next to her heart, as a reminder to pray for him—and to love him with God's love. But he made it so hard.

What had Holden told her was the reason for her anger? Passion. Aunties Viv and Vi had warned her that men could become passionate, and when they did she should immediately walk away from them. She was sure her aunts saw passion as a bad thing. But Holden had said she was most beautiful when she was flaring with passion. So was passion good, or was it bad? And what difference did it make when she'd decided she could not enter into a relationship with Dr. Holden Winters?

Lowering her head to her hands, she turned her thoughts into prayer. *God, I thought we had this all worked out. I came to Schofield to practice my nursing so I'd be more prepared to be of help to the people of Shyler's Point. But there have been so few opportunities to nurse that I have too much time on my hands. I didn't come here to fall in love, so why did it happen? And why with Holden? If You wanted me to love someone, why couldn't it have been Micah, who is dedicated to You and is easy to get along with instead of pig-headed and irritating?"*

Her lower lip trembled, and homesickness for her aunts and her uncomplicated life in Shyler's Point struck hard. *I just want to go home, Lord.* She laid her head on her crossed arms on the tabletop and allowed herself a few more minutes of self-pity. When her tears were spent, she raised her head, swished away the last few vestiges of tears, and set her jaw. So she'd fallen in love with Holden Winters. Well, if something could be fallen into, then it could be climbed out of. She'd have to find a way out, that was all. She'd always been determined. Aunties Vi and Viv often berated her for being headstrong, but that personality trait could serve her well. She dropped the button under her bodice again and placed her hand over her heart.

Last night, God had given her peace in the midst of her emotional storm concerning Holden. Apparently peace only lasted when she was distanced from him. Their paths would inevitably cross—Schofield was only so big, and they worked in the same hospital. So God would have to guard her heart. And her tongue. With her hand over the button, which pressed into her skin, she closed her eyes again and whispered, "Help me love Him with *Your* love instead of mine. Please, Father…"

18

CALLIE

"Miss Nurse! Miss Nurse!"

A Hawaiian couple scurried up the main corridor of the hospital. Callie raced around the counter to meet them. The man cradled a small boy while the woman waved a stem bearing fragile yellow flowers. The mother's wide eyes were red from weeping. Callie briefly wondered why the stick had been brought into the hospital, but she was more concerned about the child—he was still, seemingly not even breathing, and her pulse immediately quickened.

Callie pointed to the first room in the hallway and gestured for the man to place the child on the examination table. She pressed her fingers to the vein on the child's neck. His heart rate was frighteningly low.

Betsy stopped in the doorway. "Callie, what's going on?"

"Get Dr. Winters. Tell him it's an emergency." The patter of feet let Callie know help would come soon. She lifted the child's shirt. His stomach was covered with inflamed red patches. She'd never seen a rash like it before. Her brow furrowed in concern. This baby was very ill.

The parents hovered near the bed, watching Callie closely. The man patted his wife's shoulder, and the woman clamped a fist against her mouth. She still clutched the flowered twig.

"Son chew on plant." The man pointed to the stick. "Be very sick. Spit much up. He go sleep, not wake. We bring here."

"You did the right thing." Callie glanced again at the flowered twig. The yellow flowers looked very much like the red one Micah had plucked and placed behind her ear—oleander, he'd called it. She turned her attention back to the baby. Her mind reviewed everything she had been taught about resuscitation should the child stop breathing completely, but she prayed that she wouldn't be required to use the knowledge.

Holden burst into the room, a stethoscope swinging across his chest. Betsy was on his heels, but she remained in the doorway, out of the way. Callie moved to the other side of the bed. "They said their little boy chewed on a plant, then became ill."

Holden glanced up, and he sucked in a sharp breath when his gaze fell on the twig the distraught mother waved like a flag of surrender. "Oleander. Very poisonous." He used the stethoscope, listened intently, and scowled. "His heart rate is barely above thirty. Much too low." He turned to the father. "How old is your son?"

"He… seven month." The man held up his fingers to show the number.

"And how long ago did he ingest the plant?"

The man looked puzzled. He scratched his head and shared a confused look with his wife. "I not know this—ingest."

"Chew." Holden took the twig and held it close to his own mouth, making biting motions. "When did he chew on the plant?"

Understanding dawned across the man's brown face. "Oh!

Morning time. Many hour."

Holden's forehead creased into a series of worry lines as he tossed the twig with its wilted flower into the waste can. "Hours..." He his hand lightly on the child's rash-covered stomach, his expression tender. "Miss Myers?" He spoke so softly, she had to lean close to hear him. "Now would be a good time to speak to that God of miracles you're so sure of. This little boy is going to need all the prayers he can get." He spun toward a cabinet in the corner of the room, opened it with a small key from his pocket, and withdrew a brown bottle and eye dropper.

Callie put her hands gently on the baby's head and began praying silently as she watched Holden fill the eye dropper with liquid from the bottle—Syrup of Ipecac.

Holden returned to the table. "Hold his head for me. I hope he will swallow—we've got to get him to vomit as much as possible."

"The father said he spit up already."

"That's good. He needed to bring some of that up. But we're going to have to make him vomit until all signs of the oleander are gone."

Callie raised the baby's head. His little mouth fell open, and Holden emptied the contents of the eye dropper into his throat. Miraculously the muscles in the child's throat convulsed, accepting the liquid.

"Roll him onto his side and prop pillows behind him to keep him that way—we won't want him choking on his own vomit." Without averting his attention from the child, he spoke to Betsy who still stood silently in the doorway. "Miss Barnes, I know we've got the antidote for oleander in the pharmaceutical cabinet in my office. Green bottle—third shelf, I believe, on the right." He held out a key which Betsy took as he finished his instructions. "It will have nerioside or oleandroside printed on the label. Retrieve it quickly, please. Time is of the utmost." Betsy shot off.

Holden turned his attention to the couple, who still huddled together in the corner, and offered them an encouraging smile. "We'll do everything we can for your little boy. What is his name?"

"Kimokeo. We call Tim."

Holden blanched, and he swallowed before seeming to force the smile back on his lips. "Tim… A good name." He turned to Callie, and in his sapphire eyes she read sadness. "Miss Myers, could you find two chairs for Tim's parents? This may be a long wait…"

Callie left as Betsy hurried in, carrying the bottle Holden had requested. By the time she returned, the baby had vomited, and Holden was tenderly cleaning his face. Apparently he and Betsy had already administered the antidote, because the bottle was on a table in the corner alongside a small syringe.

The mother stood beside the exam table stroking the baby's fine, dark hair and singing softly. Even though Callie couldn't understand the language, she was reasonably sure the mother was singing a lullaby, and her chest tightened as she prayed again for the sick child.

Callie offered the father the metal folding chairs, and he took them, giving Callie a grateful smile. But even though he invited the mother to come and sit, she remained beside her baby.

Callie crossed to Holden. "Will the baby be all right?"

Holden shook his head, and Callie thought his eyes looked haunted. "I can't say yet. With oleander, the first twenty-four hours are critical. If he was an adult, then I'd say without doubt he would survive since we were able to treat him within the first hours of ingestion. But a child's system is much more fragile. Especially one so young as little Tim here…"

Callie thought about the flower Micah had tucked behind her ear—oleander, too. Her heart rate increased. She had put something poisonous in her hair, had fingered it repeatedly... just as the parents had fingered the twig. She touched Holden's arm. "Can you be poisoned by handling the flowers?"

He shook his head. "External contact with oleander is not a danger, only internal."

"So you have to chew on the plant for it to be harmful?" Callie filed away the information for future reference.

Holden gave her a sharp look. "You should have been briefed on the harmful plants on this island when you arrived. Someone was certainly remiss in their duties. I'll need to check into that." He ran a hand over his hair. "All right, Miss Myers, let's have a quick lesson on oleander. A few weeks before you arrived, several G.I.'s were brought in suffering from oleander poisoning. They hadn't ingested the plant. They had, however, used twigs from an oleander bush to spear some fish they'd caught, and then used the twigs to hold the fish over an open fire for cooking. The toxin from the plant was transferred to the fish, and thus to the men. It was a mild case, and all were treated successfully, but the key is they were treated. Left untreated, oleander poisoning can have dire results. In some cases, even death, particularly with children..."

His gaze returned to the small form on the bed. "When... Tim...begins showing signs of waking, we'll need to force bananas. The vomiting will disrupt his electrolyte balance, so we'll need to replace the lost potassium. Bananas will be easiest on his system. Can you find some, please?" He looked at her, giving her an opportunity to once again witness the pain in his eyes.

She set aside the professionalism that should be addressed while on duty and placed her hand on his arm. "Holden, I know you're worried about the baby, but there's something else. What is it?"

He lowered his head, and the muscles in his jaw tightened. "Kimokeo means Timothy. Timothy was also the name of my son."

Callie's heart skipped a beat. She gave his arm a squeeze she hoped conveyed sympathy.

"He was nearly seven months old when I lost him." Holden turned his gaze to the father, and Callie looked at the man, too. Uncertainty and fear showed in the father's round face. Holden sighed. "I don't want to be responsible for inflicting that kind of pain on this father."

Callie tugged at his arm. "Don't talk that way. Think positively, Holden. You're doing everything you can for this little Timothy."

Holden stepped away from her touch and crossed to the table where the baby lay, his little arms drooping limply in front of him. and his tiny chest barely rising with shallow breaths. He looked up and met her gaze. "I can only hope it will be enough."

She scurried to the door. "I'll go see the cook and get some bananas so we'll have them when he begins to rouse."

Holden nodded, and Callie paused long enough to see him run his hand up and down Kimokeo's small back. All the way to the kitchen, she prayed. For the baby, for his parents, and for Holden. He and Kimokeo both needed healing.

A strange, wail awakened Callie. She lifted her head and grimaced as a pain shot through her neck. Why was she sprawled in a folding chair in one of the rooms at the hospital instead of lying comfortably in her bed? And what was that odd squalling? Then her bleary eyes focused on the tall bed which had been pushed into the corner of the room, and everything came back in a rush. The poisoned baby, the distraught parents, and Holden sharing a tiny piece of his heart with her. A movement to her right captured her attention.

Holden, disheveled and wearing a shadow of a beard, sat up straight from a chair at the foot of the railed bed. He rose and moved quickly, swinging around his stethoscope. He placed it against the crying baby's chest, and a smile broke over his face. He aimed it at Callie when she stepped next to his elbow. "Heart rate is one hundred ten!"

He lifted the little shirt and peeked at the child's tummy. The little boy squirmed, continuing to cry, and pushed irritably at Holden's hands, but Holden completed his examination. "Sh, now, little one. Let Dr. Holden take a peek." When he'd finished, he gave Callie another beaming smile. "Rash is abating, too. We're out of danger, Callie."

"Oh, thank the Lord."

She'd barely uttered the words when she found herself snatched close to Holden's chest in a hug. He just as quickly set her aside, took two steps away from her, and turned his back. He fiddled with his collar for a few seconds, and when he turned around his professional posture was in place.

"Miss Myers, would you please go to the next room and waken little Tim's parents? I'm sure they'll be pleased to see his improvement."

"Of course." She found it difficult to walk. Her legs seemed wobbly, the shock from the unexpected embrace still leaving her unsteady. She awakened the parents and led them to Kimokeo's room.

The mother cuddled and kissed her baby, but he continued to wail. She looked questioningly at Holden. "I feed?"

Holden nodded. "Yes, I think it would be all right."

When she began opening her blouse front, Holden

ushered Callie out the door. "Let's give them some privacy."

In the hallway, the father approached them, his eyes shining with gratitude. He shook Holden's hand and beamed a white-toothed smile. "Thank very much for help." He pumped Holden's hand, his eyes glittering with unshed tears. "You good doctor. Good man."

Holden smiled. "You're welcome. Now take care of that boy. Don't let him munch on garden plants again."

The father's face contorted. "Munch?"

Holden pretended to chew on his own finger. "Munch. Bite."

The father's mouth opened in horror. "Oh, no! No munch again on plant! We watch! No more!"

"Good." Holden patted the father's shoulder, smiling warmly. The man hurried into the baby's room, and Holden turned to Callie. The smile faded. "I'm going to keep Tim one more night as a precaution—to make sure he suffers no further ill effects. Would you please fill out the medications report on what was given to Kimokeo last night?"

"Certainly." She stifled a yawn. "And then may I be dismissed long enough to go to my apartment and clean up? I'm due back on duty in two hours."

"No, you're not. You're dismissed for the day."

"Oh, but—"

"Miss Myers, kindly do not argue with a superior." Holden folded his arms over his chest in a stubborn stance. "You were here all night. I'm within my rights to release you for the day, to sleep. Please go, relax—you've earned it."

Callie covered another yawn. "Well, I probably would be useless, as tired as I am. But what about you? You didn't get any more sleep than I did."

"I became accustomed to long nights with little sleep during my years in Chicago. Last night was nothing compared to some of the nights I put in there."

Another little glimpse into his past. Callie had learned more from Holden in the past twelve hours than in the previous four months combined. She would have dearly loved to ask questions, to delve deeper, but her eyelids were heavy, and his expression didn't invite exploration. So she gave a sleepy nod. "Very well, Dr. Winters. I will gratefully take this morning off to sleep, but I'll be back this afternoon."

He smirked. "Of course you will be. You never give in, do you, Miss Myers?"

Did she see approval in his eyes? She was too tired to pursue it. Drawing on the last bit of spunk she possessed, she lifted her chin. "Nope. And you'd be wise to remember it." She marched to the nurses' station, quickly completed the necessary forms to document the medications dispensed to their tiny patient, and then headed for her apartment and the promise of a nice, long nap.

19

CALLIE

Callie entered her small apartment. Lydia's bed was rumpled and unmade, but Lydia wasn't in it. She scanned the space. Although Lydia had changed in many ways, she hadn't set aside her practice of tidying her side of the room before leaving for the day. Trepidation sent tingles along her extremities. Something more serious than hurt feelings or resentment must be plaguing Lydia.

The bathroom door opened, and Callie jumped. "Oh, Lydia. You startled me. I didn't realize you were here." Lydia's red-rimmed eyes and wan pallor raised Callie's concern. She darted forward and guided her friend to the bed. Lydia sank down and put her head in her hands.

Callie sat beside her, wringing her hands. "I've heard you crying during the night, and you seem so angry. Or depressed." She touched the back of her hand to Lydia's forehead. Her skin was clammy, not hot with fever, but still Callie worried. "Are you coming down with the cat fever?"

Lydia released a sigh. "No, I'm not sick, but I don't think I will be able to fulfill my year of duty."

Callie took Lydia's limp hand. "Tell me what's wrong. Whatever it is, we'll fix it. Okay?"

Lydia laughed, a humorless laugh that made Callie's heart ache. "Oh, naïve Callie, there is not a 'fix' for every problem."

"We won't know until we try."

Lydia finally raised her head. Hopelessness reflected in her sad eyes. "You can't help with this. It's useless."

"Nothing is useless. Lydia, please tell me what's wrong. Is it something I did?" Her mind wandered back to her conversation with Micah. Micah said he and Lydia had a terrible argument that night in Honolulu. Callie swallowed hard. "Did—did Micah do something to upset you?"

"No, no one did anything. At least, no one you know..." She jumped up and moved away. "As I said, there's nothing you can do. But somehow, I have to get home."

Callie broke out in a cold sweat. Lydia sounded as if she was discussing someone's imminent demise. "Have you talked to Miss Torkelson?"

"No, not yet, but I need to. I—I just haven't known how to approach her."

Callie sighed. "She isn't easy to approach. Would you like me to go with you?"

Lydia shook her head, her hair slipping across her forehead. She pushed the errant strands back into place. "No, I'll handle it on my own." She moved to the window and stared silently outward. Callie thought she'd never seen a more dejected sight.

Fear rolled in Callie's stomach. She gripped handfuls of Lydia's rumpled sheets. "Lydia? Please tell me you will be all right."

Lydia faced Callie, and a hint of determination brightened her eyes. "I've been thinking about it, and I believe once I'm home I'll be better. It's being here, so far away, and not knowing..." She bit down on her lower lip for a moment. Then she nodded. "Yes, once I'm home, I'll be better."

A lump filled Callie's throat. She hadn't realized how much she had depended on Lydia's presence until faced with the prospect of losing it. "When will you go?"

"As soon as it can be arranged. I can't wait much longer. I'll speak to Miss Torkelson this evening." Lydia released another long sigh. "Before I go, I need to apologize to you. I've been hateful. I'm not angry with you—it's something else entirely—but I've used you as my battering ram."

Callie hurried across the room and wrapped Lydia in a hug. "I forgive you. But I wish you'd tell me what the problem is so I could at least pray about it."

Lydia released a short laugh and stepped free of Callie's embrace. "You and your prayers... If prayers could make this go away, I'd tell you everything, but not even praying will change this." She sighed deeply, her gaze wandering to the view outside the window. "I wish it could be different. I wish *I* could be different—more like you. You're almost perfect."

"Oh, I'm not perfect." Callie cringed. "I've done many foolish things."

"Nothing like I've done." She turned a wistful look on Callie. "I look at how Micah and even Holden look at you, and I'm so green with envy... You have some inner something that appeals to people. I..." She hung her head. "I'm just an empty shell."

Callie took hold of Lydia's shoulders and gave her a slight shake. "Lydia, you're far from just an empty shell. You're a beautiful person, inside and out, and you have a precious soul that is worth more than I can measure." Regret struck with such force, her knees buckled. She sagged against the wall, her hand over her mouth. In all of her months at Oahu, she had never sat down and discussed Christianity with Lydia.

She'd been so busy chasing after Holden, trying to convince him of God's reality, she'd completely neglected a person who desperately needed a Savior. "Oh, Lydia, I made such a horrible mistake…"

Skepticism furrowing Lydia's brow. "You? What kind of mistake could you make that would be so horrible?"

"The worst kind." Callie groaned. "I've been so caught up in my own pursuits, I ignored your spiritual needs. I should have spent more time sharing God's love with you." Tears sprang into her eyes. Maybe if she had taken time to talk to Lydia about forming a relationship with God, this mysterious trouble could have been avoided. "I'm so sorry. Please forgive me."

A sad facsimile of a smile graced Lydia's face. "Foolish Callie, as if you need *words* to share God's love. I've seen it everyday in just the way you are. I've watched you pore over your Bible, listened as you whispered in prayer, heard your arguments to Holden… You've shared God with me every day since we got on that ship together to make the journey to Oahu." Lydia dropped her head for a moment, then raised her gaze to look Callie squarely in the eyes. "I should never have accused you of being holier-than-thou. It was my own guilt speaking. I felt so…imperfect…and needy. I tried to make you feel bad to make myself feel better." She sighed. "It didn't work. I've been miserable."

Callie's heart ached with the unnamed pain Lydia was carrying. She wished she could take it away, but she knew she didn't have the ability. However, she knew Who did. "Lydia, as I've tried to tell Holden, God understands our secret heartaches. He wants to heal us of every pain. He's there waiting for you, too, if you will just reach out to Him."

Lydia's throat convulsed, and she blinked against tears. "I want to, Callie, but how can God forgive me and heal me when I make so many mistakes? Especially when those mistakes hurt others, too?"

Callie led her to the bed, and they sat side by side. "In the city of Jerusalem, terrible things were happening—idol worship, and all kinds of evil activities. But God told Solomon that if His people would seek His face, would humble themselves and pray, then He would forgive them and heal their land. The same promise applies to you right now. You feel sad and unworthy because you made some unwise choices. But God loves you no matter what you've done. He's ready to forgive you and bring you to a place of joy. All you have to do is ask."

Lydia sat with her hand in Callie's, her face puckered. "I appreciate what you've said, but I need to think about it. All right?"

Although Callie wanted to press Lydia, she sensed her friend's heart was fragile. She would pray and allow the Holy Spirit to finish the work they had begun. "I understand. Once you're back in California, will you write to me and let me know how you are doing?"

Lydia shrugged and turned away again. "It might be better if you forget you ever knew me."

Callie yanked on Lydia's hand. "I could never forget you!"

Lydia met Callie's gaze again. Tears glistened in her eyes. "You said God forgives when we say we're sorry. Do you suppose God can help people forgive, too?"

"Of course He can. Nothing is impossible for God."

Lydia shook her head slowly, blowing out a long breath. "Oh, Callie, I certainly hope you're right. Because I'm going to have to do some real work to make things right when I get home…"

The message was cryptic, and Callie longed to know what Lydia needed to work out. But she wouldn't force Lydia into sharing her heartache. Holden had told her she didn't need to know everything, and he was right. God knew what the problem was, and God had a solution in mind. Callie squeezed Lydia's hand. "I will lift you up in prayer, and I will stand beside you."

Lydia threw her arms around Callie and held tight. "You're one of the best friends I've ever had. Thank you for being here for me."

"You're welcome." She rubbed Lydia's tense back, closed her eyes, and began petitioning her Father to guide Lydia through this situation, to bring her peace, and make her whole.

20

L ydia left on the Pineapple Express for Honolulu on the morning of Callie's twenty-fourth birthday. Although Callie never learned how they came about—Lydia didn't volunteer to share her conversation with Miss Torkelson, and Callie didn't push—arrangements had been made for Lydia to travel back to California on the *S.S. Wilson* and her parents would meet her at the San Francisco Bay harbor. Both girls were in tears before the good-byes were over, but Callie knew that Lydia wasn't going alone.

Last night, in the midst of packing, Lydia shared that she had invited Jesus to live in her heart. Callie had seen the proof of it shining in Lydia's tear-swollen eyes, and her heart rejoiced. Becoming a Christian wouldn't remove Lydia's problem, but now she would have access to the strength she'd need to battle the situation and emerge triumphant.

None of the other nurses came to see Lydia off, but she shouldn't have been surprised. They hadn't forged close relationships with the others. However, Micah came to bid Lydia good-bye and good luck. Callie suspected his presence was more to offer support than to express any real affection for Lydia. That saddened Callie, too. Lydia still genuinely liked Micah.

After the train chugged down the track, leaving behind the acrid odor of coal, Callie turned to Micah and shed a few tears on his sturdy, dependable shoulder. When she finished, he offered her a handkerchief, which she gratefully if not a little self-consciously used. Finally she sighed, still stuffy from all of the tears. "It'll seem strange to be in the apartment alone tonight."

Micah crossed his arms. "The best cure for an achin' heart is busy hands. You're not on duty until three, but how about comin' to the hospital and helpin' me?"

"With what?"

"Refillin' jars with cotton balls and countin' tongue depressors—you know, real important stuff." He waggled his eyebrows and grinned.

When he pulled out that southern twang and let his eyes twinkle, he was difficult to resist. "You're not going to let me go off and pout, are you?"

"Nope." He put his hand on her back and steered her in the direction of the hospital. "No poutin' allowed today."

She trotted along unresistingly. "I'll go on only one condition."

"What's that?"

"Quit twangin'. It makes me smile, and I don't feel like smiling right now."

He threw back his head and guffawed at the blue sky.

She stopped and glared at him. "Micah, I'm not kidding. I am not in a smiling mood. I'll help you so I can stay busy, but don't try to make me to smile. I'm entitled to a day of mourning. I'm really going to miss Lydia."

All humor disappeared from his expression. "Okay, Miss Myers, I promise not to twang. And not to tease. And not to entice you to smile lest you lose that stern countenance that is so unbecoming."

"Good."

"But it's going to be very difficult."

She narrowed her gaze. "Try."

He nodded. "Okay."

They walked in silence past the bushes of oleander and tall stalks of hibiscus. Some of the hibiscus blooms were as large as dinner plates, and Callie's heart perked up a bit at the beauty of the gently rippled, pink petals. They reached the door of the hospital, and Micah opened it, allowing Callie to step through. They encountered Holden, who stood behind the nurses' station counter glancing at some papers attached to a brown clipboard.

He lowered the clipboard and checked his watch. "Good morning, Miss Myers. I don't see you on the duty roster until three this afternoon. You're quite early."

Callie shrugged. "I know. I'm going to help Micah count cotton balls."

Holden raised his eyebrows. "Count cotton balls?"

Micah cleared his throat. "Well, no, we're goin' to count tongue depressors, but as for cotton balls—"

Holden put up a hand. "Never mind. I'd probably be happier with less knowledge at this point." He turned a penetrating look on Micah. "I assume you know where the cotton balls are located?"

"Are they where we discussed they would be?"

"Yes, I believe you'll find them in the prearranged location."

"Good. Will you be offering your assistance in the counting of cotton balls later?"

"In all likelihood, yes. As supervisor of cotton balls I'll need to satisfy myself that proper procedure is being followed."

Callie looked back and forth, following the odd

conversation. Holden maintained a straight face, but Micah's cheeks and neck were mottled, as if he were ready to burst with something. The topic was certainly not cotton balls. Obviously they were sending some sort of secret signal to one another, but it was so muddled she couldn't figure it out.

"Very well." Micah placed his hand on the small of Callie's back and gave her a gentle nudge that set her feet into motion. "I'll escort Miss Myers to the cotton balls. Will you join us for your supervisory visit in a few minutes?"

Holden nodded. He boomed out, louder than she'd ever heard him speak, "Good day, Miss Myers. Happy counting."

Callie sent Holden a puzzled look over her shoulder as Micah herded her along. Holden's lips quirked up in a teasing smile, and he waved at her. Micah guided her around the corner before she could return the gesture.

Micah stopped her in front of one of the hospital rooms. Callie frowned. The supplies were kept in a storage room at the rear of the building, not in a room meant to house patients. She frowned at Micah. "Why are we here? And don't tell me it's to count cotton balls."

Grinning, Micah threw the door open. A shower of cotton balls flew toward her, and several voices chorused, "Happy birthday, Callie!"

Callie slapped her palms onto her cheeks, gaping. Micah propelled her into the room. Cotton balls rained like confetti, and Callie laughed as the soft puffs fell around her. Every nurse, including Miss Torkelson, was there, and Miss Torkelson was wearing the first smile Callie had seen on her pudding face.

Toilet paper streamers dangled from the ceiling, and a banner bearing HAPPY BIRTHDAY spelled out with brightly painted tongue depressors was tacked onto the back wall. Still laughing, she pointed to the banner. "Will I have to count how many tongue depressors it took to make that thing?"

Micah waggled his brows and grinned.

Callie turned to the group, who'd finally stopped pelting her with puffs of cotton, and drew near, all smiling. "How did you know it was my birthday?" She hadn't told a soul.

Miss Torkelson stepped free of the small group. Two cotton balls clung to her short, curly gray hair. "Dr. Winters informed us. He thought you might need a distraction with Lydia leaving."

Callie's mouth fell open. Holden had arranged this? As if by magic, Holden entered the doorway, wearing a smug look. Her heart lifted and began caroming wildly. She extended her hands to him, and after only a moment of hesitation, he took them. "You really planned all this?"

He gave a nonchalant shrug, but satisfaction and something she believed was akin to understanding shone in his eyes. "I know how difficult anniversaries can be. I thought perhaps a diversion was in order."

Tears pricked her eyes. "But how did you know that today was my birthday?" She drew back, releasing a soft gasp. "Did you snoop in my files?"

Humor crinkled his eyes. "No, Lydia spilled the beans. When she realized her leave-taking would correspond with your birthday, she was concerned that you would spend the day sitting alone. So she cued Micah and me." His thumbs gently pressed against her knuckles. "I hope we haven't put you in an uncomfortable position."

Callie shook her head. "It's good for me to be busy today. Thank you, Holden." Their eyes locked, and her lungs seemed to forget how to draw air. Just as she thought she might melt from the tenderness in his gaze, the others began chanting, "Speech! Speech!" She was forced to relinquish Holden's hands and face the smiling nurses.

She held her hands outward. "I don't know what to say.

I've never had a real birthday party before, so you've definitely given me a wonderful gift." She paused, raising her eyebrows in query. "And I hope there's a cake?"

Everyone in the room, including Miss Torkelson, burst into laughter. One of the nurses wheeled in a cart bearing a round, two-layer white cake circled with tiny, pastel-colored candles.

Holden lit the candles and then beckoned Callie near. "Make a wish."

Looking into his sapphire eyes made her long to ask for things she couldn't allow. But she closed her eyes for a few seconds, and a wish formed effortlessly in her heart. *I wish Holden would find his way back to his Creator.* She opened her eyes and expelled a mighty breath. Candles sputtered and died, and a cheer arose from the small circle of spectators.

The nurses clustered around and plucked candles from the cake. Miss Torkelson produced a huge knife, and everyone jumped back in mock horror, which earned another round of laughter. Micah held small plates, and Miss Torkelson served healthy slices of the cake to everyone. The other nurses perched in a row on the bare mattress of the bed, and Miss Torkelson settled her bulky frame on a folding chair near the bed. Holden escorted Callie to a chair in the center of the room, and he and Micah took chairs on either side of her.

She turned to Micah, a grin tugging at her lips. "You said you wouldn't do anything to try to make me smile."

"And you said you didn't feel like smilin'." He leaned forward and addressed Holden. "She told me she wasn't in the mood for smilin' today. I considered takin' her back to her apartment to sit in a corner and mope instead of bringin' her over here for her party."

Holden swallowed a bite. "I would have been tempted, too, if she was pulling one of her stubborn acts."

"Stubborn acts!" Callie squawked. Then she spotted the teasing glint in his eye. She shook her fork at him. "I'll have you know, Dr. Winters, that my stubbornness is no act. It's quite real."

"Oh, I'm very aware of that, Miss Myers." He smirked. "Of course, it's just one of your many charms."

"Yes," Micah put in from the other side. "There's also your penchant for blushin'…"

"Your startling temper…" added Holden.

"Your practice of quotin' scripture for every occasion…"

"Your amazing ability for tumbling off logs…"

"Not to mention your—"

Callie's gaze swung back and forth so quickly she felt dizzy. "Stop!" She didn't know whether to laugh or cry. "It's my birthday. You're supposed to be nice to me."

Holden pasted on an almost believable innocent expression. "Well, now, you started it."

She forced a frown, but underneath she quivered with suppressed laughter. "Then I'm finishing it."

"Okay." Micah sighed. "I guess that means I can't mention your—"

Callie threatened him with her crumb-laden fork.

He waggled his eyebrows at Holden. "I'll tell you later."

Holden smirked back. "I'll be waiting."

Callie rolled her eyes, but she couldn't hold back a smile. These two had certainly turned her sad day into a joyful one. The nurses approached her, and she rose, set her plate on her chair, and delivered hugs by turn.

"Happy birthday, Callie." Betsy patted Callie's shoulder. "If you get lonely by yourself, come see Ginger and me."

Roxanne nodded. "Trudy and I are always open for company, too."

"Especially if you're any good at checkers," Trudy said.

"Roxanne doesn't challenge me at all." Roxanne gave Trudy a nudge on the arm, but they both laughed.

Callie found herself battling happy tears. They were all being so nice. "Thank you."

Miss Torkelson stepped up and gave Callie a stiff hug and a brisk pat on the back. "Have a good rest of the day, Miss Myers." Her tone was brusque, but the lines around her eyes softened the command. In that moment, Callie genuinely liked the portly nurse.

"Thank you, Miss Torkelson." Her gaze swept over all of the nurses. "Thanks, everyone. This was a wonderful surprise."

The nurses left, and Callie waved goodbye, releasing a soft sigh of happiness. She sank back down on her chair. The she jolted—her cake!—and hopped back up again. She gaped at the empty chair seat. Where was her plate? Cringing, she reached behind her and explored.

"Ahem." Holden held up her plate, her half-eaten slice of cake intact. He gave her his one-eyebrow-raised look then turned to Micah. "What did I tell you? She would have sat right on it."

Grunting, Micah withdrew a fifty cent piece from his pocket and tossed to Holden. Holden caught it and slipped it into his own pocket. Micah pointed at Callie. "You just cost me fifty cents."

Callie gawked at Holden. "You bet him that I would sit on my cake?"

"Yes, I did. And I won."

She put her hands on her hips, struggling to maintain her stern countenance. "I would never have taken you for a betting man, Dr. Winters."

"I only bet when I'm certain I'll win." He placed her plate on the cart next to the cake. "And I'm betting you won't be able to keep a smile from your face for the remainder of the day."

The smile pulled hard, and Callie gave in to it. "You win that bet, too." Her gaze roved back and forth, touching both of the men with her grateful smile. "Thank you, both of you. You've truly made this a special day for me."

"You're welcome, darlin'." Micah stood and aimed his finger at her. "But remember we came in here to count tongue depressors and fill jars with cotton balls. You've still got a lot of work ahead of you." He swept his arm wide, indicating the scattering of white cotton puffs on the floor.

Callie's mouth fell open. "You mean, I have to clean this up?"

Both Holden and Micah exploded with laughter, and Callie's face flooded with heat. Holden bumped Micah with his elbow. "We can add gullible to her list of attributes."

Micah chuckled. "No, Miss Birthday Girl, the nurses on duty will straighten this room. You are free to go. But I am on duty. So…" He lifted her hand and kissed her knuckles. "I bid you a happy birthday, with many more to come."

Callie raised up on tiptoe and placed a quick kiss on his cheek. "Thank you again, Micah. You're a wonderful brother."

"Awwww." He pressed his toe against the tile floor in mock embarrassment. Then he gave her a broad wink, dropped his empty plate on the stack on the cart, and headed out the door.

Callie and Holden remained standing in the middle of the suddenly very quiet room. Callie's pulse sped as it always seemed to do when she found herself alone with him. To give herself something to do besides stare at him, she began rearranging the dirty plates on the cart.

"Do you—" His voice cracked. He cleared his throat. "Do you have any special plans for the rest of your day?"

Callie shrugged, not looking up. "No, not really. I'm on duty at three, or I'd probably drive to the beach."

"Drive?"

"Yes. Lydia wasn't able to arrange to have her Hudson shipped to California on such short notice, so she gave me use of it until November." She risked a glance in his direction.

He was rocking on his heels in a curious, nervous gesture. "That was kind of her."

"Yes."

Holden thrust his hands into his pockets. "So have you received any birthday greetings from home?"

Callie smiled, recalling the note written on one of her birthday postcards. "Mm-hm. And my Aunt Vi tattled on Aunt Viv—seems Mr. Shakely, a widower from town, has been calling on Aunt Vivian."

Holden's eyebrows rose. "Really?"

"Yes. But Aunt Viv hasn't said anything about it."

Holden nodded.

Silence fell. A lengthy one. The longer it grew, the more she fidgeted. How she wished she could reach a comfort level with this man and remain there. The constant yo-yoing left her unsettled. The plates were all stacked and there was nothing else to do. She turned toward Holden and shrugged. "Well…"

"Well…"

"I—I guess I'll go to my room and—"

"Miss Myers." Holden lowered his gaze momentarily, shook his head, and then met her eyes. "*Callie*, since you don't have plans, may I treat you to a birthday lunch?"

Her face flamed. Was he asking her on a date? "I… I…" She gulped. "Suppose so." If her foolish pulse would settle down, she wouldn't need to stutter.

"Given the time constraints, it will have to be at the mess hall." Regret colored his tone. "But there's something I would like to discuss with you, and I believe the sooner we have that conversation, the better."

Callie wrinkled her brow. "What is it?"

"I'll tell you all about it at lunch. That is…" He turned suddenly shy and boyish. "…if you're willing to join me."

Oh, yes, she was willing. Curiosity nearly overwhelmed her. "I'd enjoy meeting you for lunch."

"Very good." He reverted to his professional manner. "Then I shall meet you at the mess hall at, shall we say, one o'clock? That will give us time for the cake to settle."

Callie grinned. "Perfect."

He gave her another brisk nod then marched out the door. Callie crossed her palms on her chest. Her heartbeat pounded beneath her hands. Was he ready to recommit himself to his walk with God? Had He answered her birthday wish already?

21

HOLDEN

Holden waited for Callie's arrival and paced back and forth across the mess hall vestibule's tile floor. The smell of sauerkraut wafting from the kitchen made his stomach churn. Of all the things to serve on her birthday—wieners and sauerkraut. He sighed. It would have been nice to celebrate her birthday at a restaurant in Honolulu with candles on the table, orchids in a vase, and soft music in the background. A girl like Callie deserved something special. He'd do it, too, if he meant to woo her. But neither of them was interested in dating.

If the remotest possibility existed of either of them changing their minds on the dating issue, he wouldn't even consider making this offer. But he trusted Callie to remain professional, and he knew he could maintain a professional distance. After all, he'd been doing it since he lifted her from the sand when she'd sailed off the log on the beach all those months ago. Oh, he'd had his moments. He was human, after all. But common sense always prevailed. Eventually. He could hang onto his common sense for another half of a year and then be merrily on his way, none the worse for having encountered the irrepressible Miss Calliope Myers.

He frowned. Shouldn't she be here by now? Surely she hadn't stood him up. He glanced at his watch. Twelve fifty-five. Little wonder. He was ahead of schedule. No sense in staying in here, forced to smell sauerkraut. He'd wait outside where the air was fresh. He swung the door open, and discovered Callie on the other side. She wore her nursing uniform—the familiar knee-length tan dress covered with a tan and white striped pinafore. Such a simple costume, but somehow it suited her. She broke into a grin and stood primly before him, and a smile automatically tugged at his heart.

"Hello, Holden. Phew. It stinks in here. What is that?" Her bright expression remained intact.

Holden chuckled. He never knew what to expect from her. "Wieners and sauerkraut." He placed his hand on her back and guided her toward the chow line. "We can only hope they are also serving some sort of green vegetable or decent dessert to accompany that abomination to the taste buds."

Callie laughed lightly. "Now, Dr. Winters, sauerkraut is high in vitamins A and C, so it's good for you."

"And the redeeming features of the wieners would be…?" He raised his eyebrows like a querying professor.

She tapped her lips, her forehead puckered, then flipped her hands outward and shrugged. "They balance the sauerkraut's tang with saltiness?" He blasted a short guffaw, she grinned. "Well, I honestly don't know what's in a wiener. It is meat, isn't it?"

"I think perhaps that is a question best left unanswered." He handed her a tray, and they began moving through the line with Callie in the lead. She took the sauerkraut but left the wieners behind. He followed suit. They filled the remainder of their trays with creamed corn, canned peaches, and cornbread squares dripping with butter.

They turned from the chow line and moved to the dining area. It was late enough that most had already eaten and gone, so very few people were still in the mess hall. Even though privacy would be assured wherever they seated themselves, Holden gestured toward a corner at the far side of the room near the open windows. The fresh air took the edge off the heavy odor of pickled cabbage permeating the entire building.

He kept his hands in his lap while she offered a prayer for her food. She raised her head, and her eyes met his. His stomach began churning again, but this time it wasn't due to the odor of sauerkraut. How would she react to his proposition?

She scooped up a small portion of creamed corn with her fork, the motions graceful. "So, what did you want to talk with me about?"

Her bright-eyed expression of curiosity enticed Holden into scooting his chair closer and leaning toward her. "Nursing."

Callie's brows came down, and he could swear she looked disappointed. She tipped her head to the side. "Nursing?"

"Do you still intend to return to Shyler's Point and offer yourself as the medical care-giver for the community?"

"Yes."

"Then I would like to make a suggestion." He set his untouched tray aside and rested his elbows on the edge of the table. "Remember little Kimokeo—Tim? The baby who was poisoned?"

"Of course I do." She stabbed into the sauerkraut. "I'm so relieved he survived."

As was Holden. "I've been thinking about your questions that day. You weren't adequately prepared to care for a person in that situation." She opened her mouth to speak, and he sensed a defensive rejoinder. He waved his hand. "It wasn't your fault. Someone else should have briefed all of the nurses about oleander since oleander poisoning is rather common here. But it led me to another thought—you're taking on a challenge for which you are ill-prepared."

Callie plunked her fork down on the table and leaned back, crossing her arms. The stubborn scowl Holden knew well marred her features. "Are you going to tell me that I can't serve my friends and family as a nurse?"

"Absolutely not."

She dropped her arms. "But you just said I wasn't prepared for it."

"Yes, at this point, with the training you've received from the Red Cross, you are not prepared for it." He held up one finger to stop any further protests. "However, I have concocted a plan for you to receive more comprehensive training." He paused. "That is, if you're interested."

Callie bit down on the corner of her lower lip as she seemed to consider his words. He could almost see the wheels turning in her head, so serious was her expression, and he stayed silent to let her think. Finally she sighed. "I am interested in more training, but the reason I chose the Red Cross training is because my aunts don't have the money to send me to nursing school."

"Well…" Holden stroked his chin. "I am speaking of schooling, but this particular training will not cost you anything more than your time."

Uncertainty creased her brow. "A school that doesn't charge for classes? What school is that?"

Holden sat up and held his hands wide. "Holden Winters' School of Medicine."

Callie shook her head. "Are you playing a joke on me? If so, I—"

"No joke, Callie." He propped his elbows back on the table, bringing his face close to hers again. "Granted, it isn't an official college of medicine. You certainly won't be given any kind of degree. But I believe I could impart enough knowledge for you to be quite competent in meeting most basic needs in your community."

Her green eyes widened. "But why would you be willing to do that? You don't even know the people in Shyler's Point."

"No, but I do know you, and I would like to help you reach your goal."

Callie pinned him with her frank, steady appraisal. "Please understand I'm not trying to offend you, but how I can I be sure you'll follow through on this offer? After all, you've said things before"—her cheeks splashed with pink—"and then changed your mind."

Her statement stung. Mostly because it was so true. He squared his shoulders and met her gaze. "I won't change my mind. If you're willing to learn, I'll teach you." At least some good would then come of his years of training.

She took a deep breath through her nose, then blew it out with her lower lip stuck out. Her fine bangs lifted and flopped down. "Holden, this is a very generous offer, and I deeply appreciate you offering your time and knowledge to teach me."

He scowled. Was he about to be turned down?

"I'd like to think about it, pray about it, and decide what would be best."

He cleared his throat. He hadn't planned to start today, but he had at least hoped for some enthusiasm. "That seems fair. But don't wait too long to decide. There's much to learn, and we're on borrowed time. My tour of duty is nearing its end. I'll be leaving Schofield in early February."

"You're leaving, too?" Dismay colored her tone and expression.

"Yes. I only signed up for a two-year tour of duty, and it is nearing its end."

Tears suddenly formed in the corners of her eyes, making the green irises shine even more brightly. "I don't like to think of you leaving, too. Especially today, with Lydia just leaving…" One tear spilled over and ran quickly down her cheek. She brushed it away with an impatient swipe of her hand. Her bereft appearance tugged once more at his heartstrings in ways he couldn't understand.

"My leave-taking won't be for another five months." He hoped his assurance would quell the tears for good.

"Five months…" She looked past his shoulder for a moment, then sighed and settled her gaze on him once more. "When you're done here, will you go back to Chicago?"

"Probably not." His chest tightened. "There's nothing there for me anymore."

"There's the hospital."

But he shook his head. "No, I won't return to the hospital."

"Then what?"

Holden frowned. "I don't know. But whatever I do, it won't be related to medicine."

Callie's eyebrows shot upward. "But, Holden, you're such a wonderful doctor!"

He released one short snort of laughter. "And how would you know that?"

"I've seen you in action. With little Tim, and with that soldier who needed stitches, and even with me. Why don't you want to continue with medicine?" She seemed so genuinely concerned, Holden found himself wishing he could confide in her. But what purpose would that serve?

"It really doesn't matter."

"It's because of your family, isn't it?" Her question, so gently uttered, sent a stab of pain into his heart. "Holden, you can't throw away your talents because somebody died. How will that change anything?"

Holden gritted his teeth. He would not argue with a slip of a girl who held too firmly to fanciful ideas of a perfect world. "Miss Myers, you are moving into areas where you are not welcome. I am willing to share my medical knowledge with you to better equip you for the goal you have set for yourself. Think about it and let me know what you decide. You know where to find me." He started to stand.

"Wait!"

Slowly he settled back in his chair.

"I want to do it."

She hadn't given herself time to think. Or pray. "Are you sure?"

She nodded. "I'm sure. The people of Shyler's Point need the best care I can give. You can help me be a better caregiver. I want to do it." Then her serious expression relaxed into a smile that sent Holden's heart bouncing. "I want to be the first student to attend Holden Winters' School of Medicine."

He chuckled, shaking his head at her bright eyes, trying to control his rapid heartbeat. "I'm quite certain you will be at the head of the class."

She laughed, a joy-filled expression. Then she sobered and reached for his hand. "Thank you, Holden."

The simple touch sent a quiver of awareness up his arm, and he very gently withdrew from her grasp. "Don't thank me yet. I can be a pretty hard taskmaster."

She smirked at him, her eyes shining impishly beneath the tousled mop of auburn curls. "That's because you're bossy and grumpy."

He laughed. He couldn't help it. Ah, yes, teaching her would be a pleasure. But he'd have to be very cautious. All he wanted to give Miss Callie Myers was the benefit of his medical knowledge, not his heart.

CALLIE

Callie sat on a chair behind the tall counter of the nurses' station and made a list of all the things she wanted to learn from Holden. She chewed the pencil eraser thoughtfully between writing the entries as her mind sorted through the various maladies that were common in her small town: fevers, influenza, insect bites, occasional snake bites, broken bones, cuts and contusions... What an incredible offer Holden had made! She could scarcely believe that he was willing to share his wealth of knowledge and experience! Providence had definitely smiled on her.

At first, when he'd suggested teaching her, she had wavered. Not because she didn't trust him to be a good teacher. She didn't trust herself to be able to stay within the role of student to teacher. When she considered spending more time with him, almost certainly alone, her pulse raced, her hands got moist, and her throat went dry. Was it wise to spend time alone with Holden when he created such havoc on her emotions? Yet what better way to become the best nurse she could be?

She'd also been hoping for more opportunities to have one-on-one time with Holden. Surely in their lessons she would be able to interject her beliefs and eventually guide him back to his Heavenly Father. When one considered the two very positive aspects of accepting Holden's wonderfully generous proposition, there was no other option but to say yes.

But she would need to be careful.

She added *coughs* to her list. If they had their sessions here in the hospital, there would always be other nurses around, as well as Miss Torkelson and Micah. With so many chaperones nearby, she would be able to keep her focus on the book learning instead of Holden's intriguing sapphire blue eyes and that single freckle dotting the left side of his nose and the slight cowlick where his dark hair parted… She pressed the pencil so hard against the paper as she wrote *rashes*, the lead broke. Releasing a grunt of displeasure, she rose to scavenge for a pen knife to sharpen the point. When she stood, Holden seemed to materialize in front of the counter.

"Oh! There you are."

His smile created a fan of creases on the outer edges of his eyes, which served to call attention to the unique color of his irises. Staring into those eyes, she nearly lost herself, and she gave herself a little shake. He was talking. She needed to listen.

"If we got an early start tomorrow, we could take Lydia's Hudson to the beach and have your first lesson at the log. It's a shame to stay cooped up when it's so pleasant outside. What do you think?"

She blinked rapidly. What did she think? She thought his relaxed, eager expression was the most handsome thing her eyes had ever seen. She thought being alone with him would only provide a distraction from her studies. She thought she needed to stop staring at him like a brainless scarecrow and answer his question. And she thought she better tell him no.

"That sounds wonderful. Shall I be ready at eight?"

His smile sent her blood pounding in her temples. "Eight would be perfect. I'll pack a picnic basket so we won't miss lunch. I will see you tomorrow morning, Miss Myers." He glanced at her list, then gave her an approving wink. "Good thinking. Bring that with you, and we'll see what we can get covered, hmm?"

She nodded, and he pushed off from the counter and turned to leave. As he headed down the hallway that led to the outside doors, she found herself appraising his broad shoulders. She swallowed hard. He was as good-looking going as he was coming… She jerked her gaze to the list. Should she add *lovesickness?* Before these sessions were over, she'd definitely need a cure…

22

CALLIE

"All right, let's review." Holden placed the clipboard in his lap and covered the bold scribbles with both hands. "A worried mother brings her child to you because the child has a rash. What do you do?"

Callie scooped up a handful of warm sand and let it drift between her fingers as she considered the question. "First of all, I look at the rash, and I answer questions for myself. What part of the body is affected? Is the rash only in one location, or in several places on the body? Is it flat, raised, or blistery? Does the child look unwell in addition to having a rash?"

Holden nodded. "Good. Then…?"

"Then I ask questions of the parent. Has the child eaten something unusual? Does the rash itch? Has the child run a fever or had an upset tummy recently?"

"Excellent!"

Holden's approval made Callie's heart soar. She smiled and tucked a breeze-tossed strand of hair behind her ear. "Thank you."

"Now, let's assume the rash is located only on the child's

legs, specifically in the ankle area. It is raised and bumpy, and it itches. What do you suggest?"

Callie chewed her lip. "Well, in that case, I would presume the child was having an allergic reaction to some sort of plant growth. To keep the rash from itching, I would advise applying a baking soda paste as needed. Also, I'd tell the mother to leave the rash area uncovered as much as possible so it can dry out and have the child avoid going barefoot through tall grass and weeds in the future."

Holden smiled, nodding. "Good, Miss Myers. That's exactly what I would have recommended." He tipped his head to the side, his brow creasing. After eight weeks of lessons, she'd become quite familiar with his thoughtful pose, and she waited patiently, a smile hovering on her lips. At last he straightened, his brow smoothed, and he leaned forward slightly. "This time the patient is…"

They went through three more projected scenarios involving different types of rashes, each requiring a different treatment. Callie offered a treatment plan and Holden gave his approval or offered additional suggestions. Most of the time, Callie was correct, and her confidence in herself increased as her knowledge base broadened.

"And—" He inhaled deeply with the word, his signal that he'd reached the most crucial question. "—when do you not treat the rash itself, but send the patient to a medical doctor immediately?"

"If the rash is not centrally located—meaning, if it covers most of the body—or if it resembles tiny bruises, or if it is accompanied by fever that has lasted more than two days, then I send the patient to a doctor. That type of rash could mean rubella, measles, or meningitis."

Holden gave Callie's hand a squeeze. "Very good. You've obviously been paying close attention. I'm proud of you."

His praise made her feel as if she floated three feet off the ground. She leaned against the warm log and stretched out her legs. Over the past two months, they had worked their way a little more than halfway down Callie's list. Holden had a list of his own, and he'd promised to put together a kit of items that would be helpful to her when she returned to Shyler's Point. As often as possible, they held their lessons at the beach. She loved the relaxed setting, the crashing surf, and the call of seabirds. The limitless scope of turquoise ocean and azure sky never failed to thrill her senses, and she wished she could come every day. But the lessons had to be fitted between her nursing duties and Holden's responsibilities at the hospital.

Some weeks they managed four lessons, others only one. She counted off the weeks, knowing his time at Schofield was drawing short. The thought of never seeing him again made her chest ache. Despite her greatest efforts, she hadn't yet managed to "climb out" of love with Holden Winters.

She angled her chin in his direction. "Are we finished for today?"

He gave a nod, but he kept his face aimed toward the rolling surf. Callie admired the firm line of his jaw and the sweep of his dark hair. What was he thinking as he gazed outward? Although they'd had much more time together and she'd learned a great deal about Holden Winters the doctor, she still hadn't managed to learn everything she wanted to about the man. In many ways, he remained as much a mystery as he'd been when she was trying to decide if it was he who owned the button that still hung on a string around her neck.

Holden suddenly pointed out to the ocean. "Do you see a ship?"

Callie thought she spotted the gray shape of a large ship far in the distance. A feeling of dread pressed down on her. "Yes, I do. Do you suppose it's either German or Italian?"

"After the way our Navy threatened to torpedo any invading vessel? I sincerely hope not."

The underlying anger in his voice increased her angst. She gripped her hands in her lap and shifted to face him. "But the warning had to be given. They've proven they're up to no good when they move into U.S. waters."

"Yes, I'm aware of that." He sent a brief, impatient scowl in her direction. "But I wish to avoid further blood shed. I see no useful purpose in immediately attacking a ship only because it sails into an area of ocean claimed by a particular country."

Callie nibbled her lip. "I suppose if all they were doing is sailing, it wouldn't be a problem. But you know that if the ship belongs to either Germany or Italy, it isn't a pleasure ship."

Holden sighed. "I know all of that, Callie." Despite the seriousness of the topic, Callie felt her heart lift when he used her name. He rarely addressed her as Miss Myers anymore.

"Then why are you so concerned? We're only protecting ourselves."

Holden looked at her and shook his head, his expression unreadable. He cupped his broad hands over his upraised knees. "You make it sound so clinical. Do you realize that when a ship is torpedoed, there are people on board who die? At that point, it doesn't really matter if they are Americans, Germans, or Italians. They're all just…dead."

Instinctively, Callie placed her palm on the back of his hand. He didn't resist when she slipped her fingers between his, and he even rubbed his thumb back and forth on her little finger, offering a bit of himself to the contact. They watched in silence as the ship angled itself away from the island and disappeared over the horizon line. Only when the tips of the masts slipped out of sight did Holden relax again.

Wanting to lighten the mood, Callie gave his hand a brisk pat. "Would you like to walk up to the hut? I'm dressed for it."

She'd taken to wearing slim-fitting trousers and lightweight blouses when she wasn't on duty. With her tennis shoes in place over white cotton anklets, she was equipped for a hike up the mountain.

Holden bounced to his feet and offered her his hand. He pulled her to her feet then brushed off the seat of his trousers. "Shall we have our lunch up there, too?"

Callie smiled. "Perfect."

He scooped up the backpack he had purchased at the PX for their hiking excursions and slipped it on. Callie watched him, amazed how such simple movements—the plunging of strong arms through sturdy straps then grabbing those straps to give the backpack a settling bounce—were so arresting when performed by Holden. The weight of the backpack stretched his shirt taut against his chest and stomach, clearly outlining the muscular structure of his build. She turned her face quickly before her overt attention gave her thoughts away.

He set off across the beach. "Let's go."

She followed, pausing occasionally to examine a flowering plant or to look backward at the wonderful landscape stretching below them. She'd made this climb several times now, and her legs muscles no longer complained and cramped as they had the first few times they'd journeyed up the mountainside.

The hut's open doorway seeming to grin a greeting, and Holden quickened his pace. Then he suddenly halted, his torso angled forward. Callie nearly bumped her nose on the backpack before she realized he had stopped. "What is it?"

"Shh!"

She fell silent, and her heart skipped a beat. He stood so still and attentive, he might have been carved from stone. The gentle swish of palm fronds and the continued pound of the surf created their usual music, but Callie jumped when another sound intruded—an odd, off-beat bump-bump. It came from inside the hut.

Holden held out his arm in silent warning to stay back. He called, "Who's in there?"

The noise changed to scrambled scratching.

Holden slipped off the backpack and placed it noiselessly on the ground by her feet. He held up his palms and mouthed, *"Stay here."* Then he crept forward with stealthy steps. Callie's heart thudded in her ears as she watched Holden inch sideways along the wall of the hut, his face turned toward the opening. When he reached the edge of the doorway he paused, his entire frame tense. Then he sprang, twisting his body in midair and landing in the doorway, knees bent and arms upraised. "Yaaah!"

A wild thrashing erupted from the hut, and Callie clamped her hands over her mouth in fear. She expected Holden to come running, but instead he entered the hut. He called from inside, "Callie, it's okay. Come here. You'll never believe this."

She jumped over the backpack and darted to him. It took her eyes a moment to adjust to the dusky interior, but then her heart turned over in sympathy. "Oh, the poor thing!"

A bird—a large one with oddly webbed feet and white and black feathers—cowered in the corner with a tin can stuck on its head. The odd bumping must have been the creature walking into walls inside the hut.

Callie frowned at the creature. "Is it a seagull?"

Holden shook his head. "No, I think it's a goose. It'll either starve to death or badly hurt itself if we don't get that can off its head."

"Well, how difficult can it be to catch a blind goose?"

Holden shrugged. "I guess we'll find out."

He hunkered low and advanced on the bird. Somehow it must have sensed him approaching, because it flapped its wings and waddled toward him. Callie leaped into the doorway to keep the goose from escaping, and Holden chased the panicked bird around the confines of the hut. It scuttled in her direction and slammed against her legs. She released an involuntary shriek, and she must have scared the poor goose into flight. It struck Holden in the stomach. He fell backward, the goose flopping away from him. Feathers and dust filled the air, making it almost impossible to breathe.

Holden rolled to his feet, grabbed Callie by the arm, and pulled her out of the hut. "Whew!" He wiped his sweaty brow. "Too bad we don't speak Hawaiian. Maybe we could convince that thing we only want to help."

In spite of the frustration, Callie laughed. "What difference does language make? A goose isn't going to speak any human language."

He grinned sheepishly. "I suppose you're right. It was worth a try."

Callie cringed at the bumps echoing from the hut's interior. "Why do you suppose it stuck its head in a can?"

"Who knows? Maybe something smelled interesting. Maybe the shiny tin intrigued it. Maybe it was an accident. It can't talk, so—" Awe broke over his features. "Do you know what I think we have in there?"

"An example of where the expression 'silly goose' originated?"

Holden released a snort of laughter, but he shook his head. "No, I think it's a nene—the Hawaiian goose. I've been on this island close to two years, and this is the first one I've seen." He drew her to doorway and pointed at the goose, which had backed itself into a corner and huddled there, twisting its head left and right. "Look at its feet. See how they aren't completely webbed like you would expect for a duck or goose? I am certain those are the feet of a nene." He huffed. "Of course, it would have to make a house call and destroy my

241

little home-away-from-home."

The goose finally settled in as if nesting. Callie pointed. "It's still. Maybe it's finally worn out. Should we try again?"

"Yes, but this time no screaming. That thing really packs a wallop!" He rubbed his belly and grimaced. "Chasing it around didn't help at all. We only frightened it more. What we need is a plan…" He glanced around, his brow furrowed in thought, and then his face lit. He crossed to the backpack, removed the cloth tablecloth they used for their picnics, and held it up the way a matador held his cape.

"I'll throw this over the goose to keep it from escaping. When I pull the cloth away from its head, you yank off the can, and then I'll let it go. Okay?"

Callie gave him the A-OK sign.

Holden tiptoed to the doorway. He paused and frowned at her. "Remember, no screaming."

Callie put her hands on her hips and grinned at him. "You really are scared of that little goose, aren't you?"

"Don't be sassy. It wasn't your stomach that got smacked." He pointed at her. "No screaming."

She saluted. "Yes, sir!"

He gave her one more warning look before going back into a crouch, the tablecloth held at the ready, and sneaked across the dirt floor. Just as he raised the tablecloth, the goose lifted into flight. Blind, it flew straight into the square of cloth. Holden wrapped his arms around it and fell flat on his rear. A strangled, hollow honking echoed throughout the little hut. He seemed to wrestle with the tablecloth. "Help me!"

Callie dashed forward, scampering back and forth to stay with him as he rolled from side to side. "Holden, for heaven's sake, hold still and uncover its head!"

"I can't hold still if it won't! And I don't know where its head is right now!"

"Uncover something and find out!"

Holden rolled to his hands and knees, trapping the cloth-wrapped bird beneath him. Callie waited, ready to pounce the moment she saw the can. He pinned one side of the cloth to the ground with his knees, then carefully peeled back a section. Callie viewed the feathered hindquarters of a goose. He flopped the cloth into place and turned a weary look on Callie.

"You'll have to go behind me and uncover its head. Please hurry. I can't hold on to him much longer. I can't believe how strong this guy is."

The tablecloth seemed to have a life of its own, rolling and lifting like sheets hung in a stiff breeze. Callie's hands shook and she feared she might hyperventilate, but she crouched behind Holden and lifted the edge of the tablecloth. To her great relief, she spotted the glint of tin. She grasped the can between her palms and eased it free.

The goose shook its dark head and began honking riotously. With joy, fear, or fury? It shot out between Holden's legs. He fell flat on his stomach in the dirt, crushing the tablecloth beneath him, and Callie fell onto her backside trying to get out of the bird's path. The goose, now free, waddled at full speed out the front door with its wings flapping. The moment it cleared the hut, it lifted into the air, honking as if it would never stop.

Callie and Holden scrambled to their feet and rushed outside to watch it go. It cleared the surrounding bushes and landed several feet away, its honk ringing in their ears. Then, to their great pleasure, two more of the beautiful geese suddenly appeared with the first one, adding their noise, and together the three majestic birds vanished into the thick foliage. He slipped his arm around her waist and continued to stare at the spot where they'd disappeared, wonder in his expression.

She smoothed away the perspiration from her forehead. "That was hard work."

"'Let us not become weary in doing good, for at the proper time we will reap a harvest if we do not give up.'" He sighed. "That was quite a harvest, watching the gorgeous bird go free."

Callie leaned her head against his shoulder, feeling closer to him than she ever had before. They had shared something special in rescuing the goose together. Holden had given her a glimpse of his tender heart. A mental image of him posing with the tablecloth in hand, ready to pounce, flitted through her mind, and all at once the humor of the situation struck her. She erupted with giggles.

Holden released her and took a step away. "What's so funny?"

"If...if you could have seen yourself..." She choked out words between snorts of laughter. "...ready to pounce on that poor, unsuspecting goose." She raised her arms and imitated his sneaky stance. "Then on all fours, wrestling with the tablecloth..." She laughed so hard she lost her ability to speak.

Holden smirked at her. "What was I supposed to do? That was a strong bird."

"I couldn't tell there even was a bird." Callie gasped, holding her stomach as another round of giggles captured her. "It looked like you were fighting with a...a checkered ghost. Oh, it was the funniest thing I've ever seen!"

Holden crossed his arms and peered down his nose at her, but his eyes twinkled. "I'm so glad I could amuse you."

She waved her hands, fanning herself and trying to stifle her giggles, but it took awhile. Holden watched her, shaking his head. When at last she'd calmed, she released a lengthy sigh. "Oh, my, that was fun."

Holden rolled his eyes heavenward. "'Fun,' she says. Took ten years off my life, but she calls it fun." He grabbed up the backpack. "I don't know about you, but that battle gave me an appetite. Should we eat?"

She smoothed the tablecloth on the ground outside the hut. They sat and shared the simple lunch while continuing to rehash the events, spending equal time laughing and expressing wonder at what they'd witnessed.

Holden dropped the wrapper from his sandwich into the backpack, his expression turning somber. "Callie, may I ask you something?"

She wiped the crumbs from her lips and gave him her full attention. "Certainly."

"Why do you like the beach so much?" His forehead pinched. "Having lost your parents in a rush of water, it seems you'd be reluctant to spend time gazing at water."

Callie shrugged, wadding the sandwich wrapper in her hands. "I suppose because there are too many pleasant references to water in the Bible. Springs of living water, being led beside still waters… The ebb and flow of the ocean soothes me rather than disturbs me. I suppose it's a gift God gave me— the ability to enjoy cool water rushing across my feet without a moment of unhappy remembrance."

Holden nodded slowly, his mouth set in an uncertain frown.

She touched his knee. "Think how much enjoyment I would have sacrificed if I had developed a fear of the water. My happiest moments have been the ones on the beach." She swallowed and dared to add, "Many of them with you."

His tender gaze fixed on hers. After several long seconds of silent eye contact, he sighed. "I'm glad you're not afraid. I would have missed these times with you, too."

Before Callie could respond, someone down on the beach called their names.

"It's Micah." Holden stood and cupped his hands beside

his mouth. "We'll be right down!"

They stuffed the remainder of their picnic items into the backpack, and Holden shrugged the backpack into place. Callie followed him down the carved path to the beach. Micah was waiting at the break in the foliage. Worry showed in the grim set of his mouth.

Holden trotted the final few feet. "What's going on?"

Micah kept his gaze aimed at Callie. The moment she joined the men, he held out a telegram. "This came for you. It's from one of your aunts. I thought it might be important."

She broke out in a sweat. Telegrams were expensive. There must have been an emergency or her aunts would have sent a letter. "Do you know what it says?"

"No. I just thought it might be important."

Holding her lower lip between her teeth, Callie opened the yellow envelope and withdrew the simple telegram. She sensed Holden's and Micah's concerned gazes on her as she read the stilted message. When she'd finished, without a thought to the repercussions, she turned her face into the curve of Holden's neck and began to cry.

23

HOLDEN

"Callie?" Holden rubbed her back while he looked helplessly at Micah. He thought his own heart might break as she sobbed against his neck. "Callie, sweetheart, please don't cry. Tell me what's wrong."

Callie just shook her head as she burrowed, her arms wrapped tightly around Holden's torso, her shoulders heaving.

Micah stepped forward and patted her shoulder. "Hey, c'mon—whatever it is, it can't be that bad."

"Th-there's—" Callie stayed pressed against Holden's shirt front, which muffled her voice. "...nothing wrong. I'm just so happy!"

Holden and Micah exchanged surprised looks. Holden took her by the shoulders and pulled her away, peering into her face. "Did you just say you're happy?"

She lifted her tear-stained yet beaming face to look from one man to the other, and her emerald eyes shone bright with unshed tears. "Yes. It's about Aunt Vivian. She's getting married!"

Holden released a loud huff of annoyance. "You mean to

tell me you cry this hard when something *good* happens?"

She rubbed her fist below her nose, looking up at him in complete confusion. "Are you mad at me?"

Holden rolled his eyes, unable to answer that question. He turned to Micah. "Explain it to her, please."

Micah touched Callie's shoulder, and she turned her face toward him. "Callie, you scared us to death, falling apart like that. We thought something awful had happened!"

"Well, I'm sorry," she sputtered, sounding a bit defensive. "It just hit me, that's all. Aunt Vivian—she's been a spinster for all these years—and now there's someone who loves her and wants her to be his wife." Her chin quivered.

Holden shook a warning finger in her direction. "Don't you start crying again."

Callie sucked in her lower lip and blinked, keeping the tears from spilling down her cheeks. "I don't understand why you're mad."

The confused tone nearly unraveled Holden. His heart rate was still out of control. He had felt as if his innards turned inside-out when she wept against his neck. She'd frightened him half out of his wits, and now she was making him feel guilty. He took a deep breath to calm himself. "Callie, I'm not mad. But the next time you decide to throw yourself into my arms for a good cry, would you please tell me ahead of time what the tears are all about? If I know in advance they are happy tears, then I won't be worried."

Callie blinked a few more times, swept away the remaining moisture from her cheeks, then offered a one-shoulder shrug. "Okay." She smiled. "Would you like to hear my telegram?"

Holden and Micah chorused, "No."

Her mouth dropped open, and she presented her back, her arms crossed over her chest tightly. "Well!"

Holden looked at Micah, and Micah looked at Holden.

They both looked at the back of Callie's head. And without warning they both began laughing.

Callie spun around, glowering at them, but after a few moments she lost her icy expression and joined in. Micah gave her a congratulatory hug, and she read the telegram, shedding a few more tears as she did so.

Holden memorized the details of the day, knowing that when he left this place—and this woman—behind, he would want to draw on them to remind himself how it felt to be truly happy.

As October slipped into November, Holden was relieved that Callie had something positive on which to focus her attention. She seemed largely oblivious to the happenings in the world around her—happenings that would frighten Holden if he allowed himself to dwell on them—so intent was she on her own small corner of the world.

At supper one evening near Thanksgiving, she rested her chin in her hand and sighed. "I wish I could be there to see Aunt Vivian exchange marriage vows."

Holden swallowed a bite of meatloaf. "When is the wedding?"

"Right after Thanksgiving." Another morose sigh followed. Then she sat up, much like a gopher, and visibly brightened. "But do you want to see what I'm planning to do to my old room?"

Holden wiped his mouth with his napkin then nodded. He watched her slap her napkin down in the center of the table. She stuck her finger in ketchup and drew out a shaky floor plan.

"You see, the way the house is arranged," Callie explained

as she pointed to the napkin, "there is a door leading from the front porch right into my bedroom. Now, of course, I never used that door—in fact, I kept my dresser pressed against it to keep it from being used unexpectedly! But it's perfect if one needs a private outside entrance, which I do now for my medical practice."

He hid his smile at the words "medical practice." She was so serious, and she had no idea how cute she was in her earnestness.

"I'll just move my bedroom furniture into Aunt Vivian's bedroom. Then I'll hang a curtain down the middle of my old room so the front half can be used as a waiting area, and the back half—the part that leads to the rest of the house—will be the examination area. The room isn't terrible large, but it's certainly big enough to suit both needs." She smiled at him, her eyes shining. "God's just worked it all out for me, Holden! The outside door of the house that has never been used, Aunt Viv's unforeseen marriage, and even you!"

"Me?" Holden leaned back, raising an eyebrow high.

Callie threw her hands outward. "Of course! The lessons you offered. Everything is just falling neatly into place for me to open my own little clinic."

This intimated, of course, that he hadn't come up with the idea of teaching her himself. And, he acknowledged somewhat reluctantly as he sipped his coffee, perhaps she was right. Perhaps there was a Higher Force at work, setting things into place for people like Callie who certainly deserved good things to happen for them.

Holden supposed the people of Shyler's Point would be willing to bring their medical woes to Callie in the absence of a "real" doctor. In a way, he envied her. She was so sure of what she wanted, and he admired her willingness to work to make it all happen. He still wasn't sure where he would go or what he would do when he left Oahu, and that time was drawing near.

To have a hometown—a small, close-knit community—beckoning him home. He wondered if Callie knew how lucky she was.

CALLIE

Callie paid for the box of Christmas cards and turned from the counter at the PX. Her face broke into a smile as she found Micah standing behind her.

"Well, Micah!" she greeted cheerfully. After he dropped his small items on the counter, she gave him a quick hug. "Merry Christmas!"

He hugged her tight, smiling broadly. "You're a little early, aren't you? We've got three weeks yet."

She held up her box as they stepped away from the counter. "I'm in the holiday spirit. I'm going to address Christmas cards tomorrow afternoon after chapel."

"That sounds like fun. Are you sending one to me?"

She laughed at his teasing smirk. "Well, of course, silly. I wouldn't neglect you. And it will be fun to address one to my new *uncle*. That's a first for me."

"So Aunt Vivian is doing well?"

"Oh, yes, very well. Her last letter was brimming with happiness." Her spirits fell momentarily as she admitted, "I still regret not being able to attend her wedding, but I wouldn't have wanted her to wait. After all"—she shrugged, smiling—"she waited sixty-five years already!"

Micah laughed. "Well, I'm glad you're in the holiday spirit. Kind of hard for me to believe it's so close to Christmas. The weather is just too nice. I need snow to put me in the holiday mood."

"I suppose I could cover your bungalow with cotton balls," Callie suggested impishly.

He threw back his head and laughed again. "That's okay. We'll reserve cotton balls for birthday celebrations."

Callie sighed. "I miss the snow, too. I'm sure there's at least a foot of it on the ground at home. I love watching it come down—so calm and peaceful-looking. But this island has its own peacefulness, doesn't it? It's nice to know, with all of the storms brewing elsewhere in the world, we're still at peace."

A strange expression crossed Micah's face—not fear, exactly, but something that sent a shiver of awareness down Callie's spine. But as quickly as it appeared, it was wiped away, and Micah asked cheerfully, "Are you going to the theatre tonight?"

Callie set aside the strange feeling of dread. "Of course. I'm looking forward to it. I've heard that Abbott and Costello are very funny. Are you going?"

"Oh, I might…" He paused, waggling one eyebrow. "If you don't mind me horning in on you and Holden."

Callie felt color flood her cheeks, and she gave Micah a light thump on the arm with her card box as her heart began dancing crazily at the pairing of herself with Holden. "Don't start that, Micah. You know Holden and I are just friends."

He nodded seriously, but his eyes held a smile. "Whatever you say, Callie."

She thumped him again. "Please come. It is supposed to be a funny movie. You like to laugh."

Micah nodded slowly, his eyes suddenly far away. "Yes, I do like to laugh…" Callie got another one of those prickles, but then Micah seemed to startle, and he met her gaze again. "Well, I guess I'll meet you around seven at the theatre. Save me a seat, huh?"

"Sure." Callie headed for the door as Micah turned to the counter with his purchases in hand. She paused before leaving, looking back at Micah, puzzling over the strange reaction she'd had to some of his words. Then she shook her head. She was being silly. It was excitement over all of the good things that had happened lately—finishing the last item on her list of things to learn with Holden, Aunt Vivian's marriage, the prospect of opening her own little medical clinic, Christmas around the corner...

She stepped briskly down the sidewalk, planning her Christmas card recipient list. Even in December, the sky was clear, the weather pleasant. She loved the bright colors of the poinsettias that were in full bloom everywhere she looked. She took in a deep breath of the fresh-smelling air and she prayed inwardly, *Thank you, God, for all the glory You've created. Thank You for the gifts You've bestowed. Thank You for sending Your Son so that all can find peace in this world...*

24

CALLIE

Callie had just scooted up to the breakfast table when she heard the drone of airplane engines. Puzzled, she turned to Miss Torkelson. "Why are they practicing on a Sunday morning? They've never done that before."

Miss Torkelson's forehead crinkled into lines of query. She crossed to the window and peered out. She gasped. "Those aren't our planes!" She scurried to the table, fear pulsating from her tense frame. "There's a rising sun on the underside of the wings—it's the Japanese! Girls, quickly! We must get to the hospital!"

The Japanese? What were they doing here? The nurses jumped to their feet, chair legs squealing across the tile floor of the mess hall. Callie's breakfast tray tipped onto the floor with a noisy clatter, but she kicked it aside instead of picking it up. Trudy clasped her hand and they raced outside with the other nurses. Soldiers were running from every direction, all seemingly heading for the shed where ammunition was stored.

A rhythmic growl warned of more planes overhead.

255

Soldiers in the open courtyard fell flat on their faces in the grass. Callie instinctively ducked even as she realized the ridiculousness of such an action. Thunder crashed in the distance. Callie looked skyward, puzzled. Then she realized that it wasn't thunder, but an explosion. Holding her breath, she swung her gaze in the direction of the sound. After a tense moment, a mushrooming cloud of smoke blackened the sky in the south. The soldiers jumped up from their flattened positions. One shouted, "Let's get 'em!" They all took off again while the booms of more explosions assaulted the morning.

"Oh, dear Lord, protect us," Callie prayed aloud, staring wide-eyed at the mayhem around her.

"Come, girls!"

Callie obeyed Miss Torkelson's command automatically. The first admonition delivered by this portly nurse played in her memory—*"Someday there will be a time when your immediate action will mean the difference between life and death."* The fine hairs on Callie's neck prickled at the reality of those words.

The nurses clustered closely behind their head nurse with Callie bringing up the rear. They sprinted across the street separating the mess hall from the east barracks. Another pair of Japanese Zeroes buzzed by, the vibration from the engines tickling the soles of Callie's feet. The planes flew nearly one atop the other, the bottom one dipping low enough over the courtyard that Callie could see the goggled face of the pilot.

She froze, her hands stifling her cry of fear at the sight of the torpedoes mounted beneath the wings. Strong hands pulled her backward against the wall of the barracks where a second-floor balcony provided a modicum of protection. Her heart raced while a constant, simple prayer repeated itself in her mind, *Deliver me from evil… Deliver me from evil…* Once those planes were past, torpedoes intact, the women rushed as a group the remaining distance to the hospital.

Inside, Miss Torkelson placed a steadying hand against the wall and panted. When she had caught her breath, she began issuing swift instructions. "Roxanne, take my keys and open every medicine cabinet in the hospital. We will need extra beds. Callie and Betsy, gather up all the blankets you can find and begin making pallets along the walls in the hallway, but leave enough space for people to pass. Ginger, Trudy, begin placing bandages and antibacterial salve—first aid supplies, you know what they are!—on carts and wheel them into rooms. Roxanne, fill every basin you can find with water. We will be very busy if those Japanese fulfill their missions." Her face was white, her lips set in a thin line.

"Miss Torkelson?" Trudy's face drained of color as she clasped her hands against her ribcage. "Do you suppose they will bomb us, too?"

Miss Torkelson's many chins quivered as she shook her head. "They had their chance already, but they went on by. They're after the ships at Pearl. And probably the airplanes at Wheeler. We aren't enough here to bother with—they won't waste their ammunition on us." Her voice was firm and calm—just what the frightened nurses needed to send them into action.

Callie took Betsy's hand and the two ran through the hallways to supply closets, where they filled their arms with blankets and sheets. As they began their task of bed-making, Callie couldn't help remembering Holden had said an attack on Pearl Harbor was unlikely, but now it was happening. What if Miss Torkelson was wrong, too? They could all be killed.

With each explosion, Callie thought her heart would stop, but somehow it always started itself again and she continued working. The sounds of artillery—American fighters returning fire?—filled the air. Sirens began wailing, and Betsy turned a grim look on Callie.

"The ambulances are going now. It won't be long and we'll have wounded to care for."

Callie reached out her trembling hands, and Betsy took hold. Callie closed her eyes. "Lord, give us Your strength. We can do all things through Christ who strengthens us. Make us worthy of the task before us. Amen."

"Amen," Betsy squeezed Callie's hands and then let go. "Let's get more beds made."

Another half hour passed—a strained, trembling half hour of waiting, wondering if they, too, would be attacked—before the first half dozen stretchers arrived carrying pilots from Wheeler Base. Callie checked the tourniquet an ambulance driver had placed on the upper arm of one young pilot. The man's arm was missing from the elbow down. The sight of the jagged wound brought the bitter burn of bile to the back of her throat, and she swallowed hard against it, refusing to give way to the nausea. With his remaining hand, the pilot grabbed Callie's wrist with unbelievable strength and whispered hoarsely, "We was heading out to launch a counterattack when they hit us. Got caught in the crossfire. My name's Jimmy Phelps. Get word to my mama that I died proud."

"I'll get word to your mama that you're recovering nicely." Callie twisted her wrist free to take his hand. "You rest easy. A doctor will be with you soon." She gave him a morphine injection then took a moment to utter a brief prayer for him before turning to the mayhem behind her.

More than one of the men were missing limbs, they were all frightened, and some were in shock. Helplessness flooded her in light of their needs. Her Red Cross training had not prepared her for such intense human suffering. She took in a deep breath of fortification and reminded herself of her prayer—she could do all things through Christ who strengthened her. Determinedly she stepped next to Betsy to offer assistance.

Betsy's patient was more badly wounded than Jimmy Phelps, but he was just as anxious to talk. "Is there a radio here somewhere? Surely the President will declare plans for our retaliation!"

"All in good time." Callie cut away his filthy jumpsuit so they could treat the burns on his chest while Betsy injected a tranquilizer into his arm. She could scarcely believe this man had the ability to talk considering the severity of his injuries.

"We couldn't fight back—they took out our fighter planes at Wheeler. But two of our pilots made it up! Bet they'll do some damage to those blasted Japanese!" He coughed, his face contorting dreadfully. "Where's my buddy? His name is Terry. Need to find my buddy..."

His voice trailed off, the tranquilizer blessedly taking affect, and Callie and Betsy finished cleaning the deep burns that ran from his neck almost to his knees. Callie's prayer for this man was longer. She feared that the extent of his injuries would result in his death despite their diligent efforts.

More wounded arrived, and Callie deliberately focused on the pound of her own pulse as a way to ignore the frightening sounds outside the hospital walls. She moved from patient to patient, applying ointment and bandages, administering morphine. In spite of the chaos, a moment was spared with each man to smile encouragingly and touch his head or his hand—and to pray even if it was only a quickly uttered, "God help this man." God would recognize the sincerity of her heart and would hear her silent groanings.

Brief snatches of conversation captured her attention.

"...Lots of men killed at Hickam..."

"...They bombed the barracks at Hickam and Wheeler. Wonder why they didn't bomb Schofield..."

"…There must've been more than forty planes! They were coming and coming…"

"…How many ships were hit? Does anyone know?"

In response to that question, one man began sobbing, "Gone. They're all gone. They got 'em all…"

Was it only yesterday that Callie had commented on the calm of this island in the midst of storms elsewhere in the world? Now the calm was shattered. For her, it might never to be recaptured.

"We're going to set up a makeshift hospital at the mess hall for those who aren't as badly wounded." Micah's authoritative voice rose above the din, and Callie's head shot up. She'd never heard him use that tone before. His teasing Texas drawl was completely gone, replaced by a firm competence that gained immediate attention. "I need two nurses and two orderlies to come with me."

Miss Torkelson called out. "Miss Barnes! Miss Welker! Go with Dr. Hatcher!" Ginger and Roxanne immediately stopped what they were doing and rushed to Micah's side. He paused only for a moment to make eye contact with Callie, his expression grim. She gave him a tremulous smile and was gratified when the hard lines around his mouth softened for just a few seconds. Then he and the two nurses shot down the hallway, disappearing from view.

Callie turned her attention back to the pallet at her feet. She dropped to her knees and smoothed the writhing young man's hair. He looked no older than eighteen. "I know you're hurting. I'll help you with that…"

HOLDEN

On and on… During the first thirty hours following the attack, a steady stream of victims of Japan's carnage filled and overflowed the hospital. Just when Holden thought they'd surely gathered them all, another group arrived, the latest survivors from the naval battleship *Arizona*, all of them badly burned. Holden was nearly dead on his feet, as were all of the hospital staff. They hadn't been prepared for such an emergency, yet somehow they had to push beyond their abilities and meet the many needs.

Volunteers from Honolulu had taken over tedious tasks of cleaning, carrying stretchers, and transporting the dead to a room designated as a temporary morgue until the crisis had passed. A blackout was ordered on the island, so a handful of volunteers painted the hospital windows black. Holden appreciated their efforts. How would he care for the wounded if all lights were extinguished inside? Despite the unexpected assistance, there were so many more casualties than medical personnel, many men died of their wounds while waiting for care.

Several times during the frantic hours, Holden's path had collided with Callie's. Deep purple smudges made her normally sparkling green eyes appear sunken and her face was chalky white, yet her calm countenance remained. Not once did he hear her complain, her focus always fixed on the men who needed her. Her gentle hands were raw and chapped from the alcohol used to keep from spreading germs into open wounds. She spoke softly and soothingly as she cared for their injuries yet wasted no time, moving purposefully from man to man, yet never giving the impression of hurrying through a task—each injured soul was treated as if he were the only one in need. Nursing seemed as natural as breathing, and Holden's heart swelled in admiration for her tranquil bearing as much as her skill.

Blessedly, the Japanese bombers had apparently finished their duty and were gone for good. A few men bragged that not all of them had made it back to Japan alive. Holden shut off that kind of talk—death was death, as far he was concerned, and he would not celebrate the loss of any life. The fear of Japanese foot-soldiers remaining on the island, waiting to launch more surprise attacks, kept him from relaxing his guard even now.

The hospital staff received updates by short-wave radio, so they knew the occasional explosions were caused by their own weaponry or boilers. Fires continued to rage as oil from the ships fueled the inferno. Although the base was more than ten miles from the sites of attack, the smell of smoke permeated everything. It was that smell, even more than the putrid odor of burned flesh, that plagued Holden. He pinched his nostrils shut, willing the unpleasant odor away.

A frightened soldier clutched at his arm. "Doc, am I gonna die?"

He'd been asked that question many times already. As he had before, Holden made no promises, only answered with what he hoped was a reassuring squeeze to the man's shoulder. "I'll do everything in my power to save you." Feelings of incompetence dogged him as he treated the burned, battered bodies of what, only hours before, had been hale and hearty men.

He bent over the unconscious form of yet another of Japan's victims, and he noticed Callie farther down the hallway, holding the hand of man who shivered in shock. Her eyes were closed, her lips moving in obvious prayer, and a sigh heaved from his chest. What he wouldn't give to be able to tap into her Higher Power.

Ask.

He jolted. Had the voice been real? He looked around, seeking the speaker. Everyone was bustling as before—no one was speaking to him. Yet he knew he'd heard the simple instruction.

Ask. I'm here, as I've always been. Ask.

His hands began to shake, his breath coming in short bursts that made him fear he might hyperventilate. He whispered, "Who is it?" And one more time the still, gentle voice came. *Ask, and it shall be given to you; seek, and you shall find; knock, and it shall be opened to you...* Other pieces of his past—childhood remembrances and former conversations—winged their way through his mind. *God's thoughts of us are as countless as the grains of sand on the beach... You're stuck in the mud and mire... I can face life's difficulties because I have a firm place to stand... You may have misplaced your fellowship, but the relationship is there, waiting to be recaptured...*

For a few seconds the bustling activity seemed to still. Tears stung his eyes. His strength wavered as his footing on the sinking sand kept slipping, slipping, slipping until he was sure he would collapse from the effort of staying upright on his own. He wanted a firm place to stand. He couldn't go on one more minute without it.

He turned his glimmering eyes toward the ceiling—toward the gates of Heaven—and whispered raggedly, "God, if You're there, I'm asking. I need You back in my life."

The rush of peace that washed across his body nearly drove him to his knees. Joy filled his heart, a joy he hadn't known since he was a young boy. He felt as if he'd been transported to another plane. He looked around, surprised to find that he was still standing in a busy hallway full of gurneys and groaning wounded and frenetic activity. The awe—the unbelievable inner peace—overcame the horror around him.

He gathered it close, he drew on it, as he turned to his patient.

Holden was exhausted, footsore, taxed beyond the limits of human endurance. But he continued diligently, upright and strong, supported by a solid Rock.

CALLIE

For nearly four days the staff worked around the clock, ministering to the needs of the wounded. It broke Callie's heart to see the bodies of the dead stacked without a care. But the care had to be given to those still living. She hadn't known what exhaustion was prior to the attack. She hadn't realized how far a person could be pushed and still keep functioning on little food and less sleep. Yet she didn't feel sorry for herself. She'd been sent to this island to serve as a nurse, so she continued it to the best of her ability. In spare moments, she thanked God that Lydia had been spared this ordeal.

She turned toward yet another patient, a badly burned man wearing what was left of a navy uniform. He had been rescued from the belly of an overturned ship, although she couldn't remember which one. Her mind was too fuzzy for details. She knelt beside his pallet and took his hand. She asked his name as she waited for Betsy to bring a syringe of morphine.

"D-Dan." He pawed at her, his fingers too weak to take hold. "I—I'm gonna die, nurse. I know it. I'm scared..."

"Shhh..." Callie wouldn't lie and tell him his fear was unfounded. His wounds were horrible, and he'd lost so much blood. Death was imminent. She longed to smooth his forehead, but the raw flesh didn't bear touching. There was something she could do for him, though. "Do you know where you're going if you die, Dan?"

Almost imperceptibly his chin lifted and fell in a brief nod. "When—when I was a boy, I committed my life to Christ. B-but I've strayed…done wrong things…don't know if—if He'll take me now."

Callie took Dan's hand between hers. "God forgives the most heinous of sins—would even forgive the Japanese for inflicting such horror on innocent lives if they asked. If you know Him, Dan, talk to Him. He'll remember your voice. And He'll take you home."

Dan's eyes, filled with pain, focused blearily on hers. "Y-you think so?"

"I know it's so." Her head weighed heavy from exhaustion, but her voice was strong. "Talk to Him."

His burned forehead contorted in pain. Dan closed his eyes. "Forgive me, God. I—I've messed up. I'm sorry. T-take me back, p-please…"

Callie watched as his expression altered. The lines in his forehead smoothed, his face relaxed. His lips parted and his chest rose with the effort of drawing one sharp breath. Then the air released slowly, but no more was taken in. He was gone.

She dropped her head, battling tears. Very gently she placed his lifeless arms across his chest. She stopped one of the volunteers who was rushing by. "This man will need to be removed." The man nodded, signaled to another man, and the two of them carried Dan's limp body from the hallway.

Callie stood, but the muscles in her legs gave way. Two strong arms caught her and held her upright. She lifted her gaze and discovered she'd been rescued by Holden Winters. She offered what she knew was a sorry excuse for a smile, but it was all she had left. "Thank you."

"You're welcome, Miss Joyful." He hadn't released her yet. "Can you stand now?"

She nodded and proved it by stepping away a few inches.

Her heart pounded having him so near. His arms had felt so strong, had offered so much security. How she wished she could lean into his sturdy chest for the rest of her life. But there wasn't time for those kinds of thoughts now. She turned to head back down the hallway, back toward the men still waiting for care.

Holden caught her arm and stopped her. "Callie, we just got word that reinforcements are coming from the hospital in Honolulu. Go back to your room now and sleep."

He delivered orders, but in such a tender tone. His eyes were as gentle as she had ever seen them. Such tired eyes, with drooping eyelids, yet a light she'd never seen before shone in his sapphire eyes. She squinted at him, trying to decide if she was so tired she imagined things that weren't real.

Suddenly he grinned, the expression so incongruous to their surroundings. He brushed her cheek with his knuckles. "You're going cross-eyed."

Heat filled her face. "No, I'm not." Then she straightened as tall as she could, throwing back her aching shoulders into a belligerent pose. "And I'm not going to bed, either. Not as long as there's still work to be done."

Holden shook his head at her, his expression caring. "Callie, there will be work to be done for several days to come, and I'll make sure you're a part of it. I've seen you with the men. I know you want to be here. But, sweetheart, you'll make yourself ill if you don't get some rest, and then what good will you be?"

His kind tone and the use of the endearment nearly moved her to tears. She blinked rapidly, keeping them at bay. "But…" She was too tired to form an argument.

"My poor, tired Callie…" He took hold of her shoulders and drew her to his chest. He rocked her sightly, stroking her hair. The gentle pressure of his cheek resting on the top of her head comforted her.

Her arms hung limply at her sides. She didn't possess enough strength to return the embrace. She stood, relaxed, within the circle of his arms. She closed her eyes, reveling in the warmth and security of his enfoldment. Slowly consciousness slipped away, and a fleeting thought trickled through her mind.

I love you, Dr. Holden Winters...

25

Callie awakened slowly, drifting into consciousness as gently as a leaf wafting from a treetop. She stretched languorously, her eyes still closed, savoring the support of the mattress beneath her back and the softness of the sheet that covered her. The sun's warmth washed through the open window. Birds sang nearby, and her lips tipped upward at the sweet song as she continued to nestle in her warm nest.

Sunshine? Birds singing?

She sat bold upright, her eyes popping open. What time was it? She squinted at the clock, rubbed her eyes, then looked again. Almost ten thirty!

She sprang out of bed, raced for the bathroom, and jumped into the shower, still wearing her pajamas. She twisted the faucet knobs viciously, lifting her face to the icy jet of water that spewed from the showerhead. How could she have slept so long? She was due at the hospital at eight. Or was it three? Or was this her day off?

Her frenzied motions came to a halt. She stood in the now-warm water which soaked her pajamas, trying to remember what day of the week it was. Her memory returned in bits and pieces.

Planning to address Christmas cards, preparing for chapel, sitting down to breakfast, hearing planes overhead, caring for wounded—so many wounded... And finally Holden's arms around her as she drifted off to sleep. But her memories ended there. How had she gotten to her apartment and into bed? How long she had been sleeping?

She snapped off the water and reached for a towel, rubbing herself and her pajamas as dry as possible. She left her wet night clothes hanging over the edge of the bathtub and dressed in her nurse's uniform. She glanced at a jumbled pile of clothes lying on the floor at the end of the bed—her dress, nylons, and shoes she had worn on the Sunday of the attack. She couldn't even recall having taken them off. She felt as though she'd lost a part of herself, and she wouldn't be able to regain it until she had filled in the gaps.

Dressed, she trotted out of Grant Hall and headed for the hospital.

HOLDEN

Holden whispered, "Amen," then released the hand of the man on the bed. "Rest. We'll get that telegram sent off to your family immediately."

"Thanks, doc." The soldier's voice rasped out. "And thanks for the prayer. I feel better already."

Holden nodded, offered a smile, and stepped into the hallway. At the nurses' station, he gave Trudy instructions on where to send a telegram informing the soldier's family of his injuries. Trudy headed for the office housing the telegraph, and he turned, intending to proceed to the next room. But

Callie moving up the hallway in her determined gait—chin thrust forward with a stubborn tilt, arms pumping—stilled his progress.

Her damp hair lay in a charming disarray of curls around her face, and even from several feet away the green of her eyes shone startlingly clear. His heart lifted, and he smiled. "Good morning."

She came to a halt directly in his pathway. "The last thing I remember is you telling me to go to bed. But I don't know how I got there, or how long I slept, or—"

"Whoa, slow down." He chuckled. "You're like an out of control freight train."

Callie pursed her lips and crossed her arms. Her voice dropped to a harsh whisper. "Holden Winters, you're the last person I talked to before waking up an hour ago. My clothes were dumped at the foot of my bed and I was wearing my pajamas, but there's this gap—this hole in my memory— and I want to know what happened during the time I can't remember."

Understanding bloomed. Holden drew back, his mouth falling open. "You think I undressed you and put you to bed?"

Callie's face flooded with color and she glanced up and down the hallway. She turned back, her brow crinkling. "Did you?"

Holden straightened his spine. "No, I did not. I did assist you to your quarters—you were nearly asleep standing up— but when I left you, you were sitting on the edge of the bed, your chin on your chest, staring at your feet. I encouraged you to change into your pajamas and slip between the sheets. Apparently you followed my instructions…for a change."

Callie heaved a sigh. "So I dressed myself…" She stared off to the side for a moment, then gave a start. "When was that? And what is today?"

A grin tugged at his lips. "Feeling a bit like Rip Van Winkle, are you?"

Callie graced him with a smile. She lifted one shoulder in a self-conscious shrug. "I suppose I am."

Holden pointed at the calendar on the wall behind the nurses' station. "It's December thirteenth, Callie."

"December thirteenth. Almost a week…" She turned her gaze on him. "Have you slept at all? You look terrible."

He laughed. "Well, thank you very much. As a matter of fact, I've managed to sneak in a few hours, and I'm sure I'll catch up completely when the new doctors arrive."

"New doctors?"

Holden nodded. "Yes, more will be arriving late this week. They were scheduled for February, but with this attack, plans have changed. Micah and I will have assistance shortly, so we won't be overwhelmed with the volume of patients here now." He pushed away from the counter. "And speaking of patients, I need to be making rounds instead of filling in your missing gaps. It takes me a bit longer to see each patient when I take the time to pray with them, but I believe it's worth it."

Callie's green eyes appeared to double in size. "You—you're praying?"

Oh, how he loved the reaction to his casually-dropped bombshell. He smirked. "Don't look so astounded, Miss Myers. You said you were going to prove God's existence. Did you think you would fail?"

"But—but—"

He crossed his arms. "You're very persuasive, Callie." He set all humor aside. "Add to that the fiasco of the past week, my utter exhaustion, and the realization that I simply could not take one more step on my own." He pulled in a deep breath, reliving the wonderful moment when he stretched out his hand to his Father and the Father's hand reached back.

"He lifted me out of the mud and mire and gave me a firm place to stand. My feet are on solid rock again, where they belong. I'm no longer in the sinking sand."

Tears trailed down Callie's cheeks. "Oh, Holden..." Without warning, she embraced him. He returned the hug, inhaling the sweet scent of her hair. "When? How?"

Reluctantly he set her aside. "Callie, I really must return to rounds. But I will talk to you soon. Perhaps this evening? When you're off duty? It'll be late, but I'd like to drive out to our log, if you don't mind."

Callie nodded, her eyes still brimming.

"This evening." Then he followed his instincts, leaned forward, and bestowed one quick kiss on her surprised mouth. He gave a casual wave and headed to his patients, leaving her standing, speechless, in the middle of the hall.

Holden boosted Callie onto the log, then settled himself beside her. He placed his hand on her knee and dove into the subject he'd been waiting to share. "Callie, my joy is back. It's been gone for so many years, I'd almost forgotten what it felt like to have the 'peace that passeth all understanding.' It was so much a part of me when I was a boy, and I had it when I made the decision to practice medicine. The peace is how I knew I'd made the right choice."

Callie frowned. "Then how can you give it up, Holden? Medicine, I mean. You're so gifted! You can't just turn your back on that calling."

"I know that now." Holden shifted sideways, his knee brushing against hers. "And I'm not turning my back on medicine. This past week has proven to me I'm meant to be a doctor. Yes, I fought it. I fought my inability to save every person who came to me hurting and looking for a cure. But all I can do—all any of us can do, really—is our best, and then leave it in God's hands. I knew all of that as a boy, but I let ego and pride get in the way."

Under the starlight, Callie's face beamed. "I'm so glad you aren't giving up as a doctor. I can see you have a peace about it. I noticed it before I drifted off to sleep. A light. I saw it in your eyes, and I see it there now, too."

Holden swallowed. "I tried to pretend that I lost it when Lorna and Timmy died, but that really isn't true. It had been slipping away long before that. I was just pretending at happiness for many, many months before the fire."

"You lost your family in a fire?" Compassion colored her tone. She slipped her hand into his.

He linked fingers with her. "Yes. The smell of smoke brings back very unpleasant memories. This past week was difficult, with the constant essence hanging overhead. But getting past the memories has become much easier since I put it all in God's very capable hands." As he spoke, his fingers relaxed their hold on Callie's hand.

Her attentive gaze never wavered from his face. "What caused you to harden your heart, Holden?"

"Me." He cringed. "And my focus. I became determined to impress people—Lorna's father, the hospital administrators, even my own family who couldn't have cared less if I had no more than two dimes to rub together. The more determined I became to acquire the things of the world, the less important it became to be the man God had called me to be." He sighed. "Then, of course, when things didn't go the way I thought they should, I held God accountable for my poor choices."

"And what brought back your joy?"

His gaze roved across her dear features, and he couldn't help but smile at the familiar tousled hair and bright eyes.

"You—and your unwavering faith."

Tears immediately appeared in the corners of Callie's eyes, but the smile in them never faltered. "I'll see Lorna and Timmy again someday. Lorna had your faith, too, so I know where they are. I'd like to think that they've met your parents and have been rooting for me down here." He laughed softly, somewhat self-conscious of his whimsical admission. "Having that assurance takes the sting out of missing them."

"I'm so glad."

"I will always carry Lorna and Timmy here." Holden placed one hand against his chest. "They will forever be a part of me, just as the memory of your parents is very much a part of you. But I've been able to release the bitter sting of losing them. Your constant, shining example of joy in spite of pain has made me reach out for the same peace and contentedness. Thank you for being that example, Callie."

The two bright tears which had quivered on the fringes of her lashes now spilled downward in a crystal trail. Callie smiled through them, looking like a dew-washed flower in the moonlight. "I'm so glad your heart is happy again, but please don't give me the credit. I couldn't do it on my own. I have God's strong hands holding me up. Give Him the praise and glory."

Holden shook his head in wonder. "You're something else, you know that? I've never met anyone as unselfish and unspoiled as you are. It's little wonder..." He paused, gazing toward the distant horizon. Should he tell her? He shifted his gaze and found her waiting, her head tipped sweetly to the side, and he knew exactly what he was meant to do.

26

CALLIE

Callie didn't resist when Holden released her hand and tucked the strand of hair drifting across her cheek behind her ear. The simple touch raised a quiver of awareness from her head to her toes. His gaze nearly mesmerized her. She held her breath, afraid of divulging her secret feelings for this man.

"You'll be going back home soon, to Shyler's Point, won't you?"

She nodded, swallowing a sob. How would she be able to leave him?

"Shyler's Point… It's a small town, isn't it?"

His suddenly conversational tone confused her. "Yes. Very small, not even a thousand people."

"And you're still planning to provide medical care to the community?"

Again, Callie nodded. "I promised my aunts I'd come back. At least if I'm there, people will have someone to turn to in an emergency. I won't be able to do a lot, but thanks to your tutoring, and everything I've learned at the hospital here, I'll be better than nothing."

"You'll be far better than nothing." Holden gave her hand a light squeeze and then linked his hands in his lap, staring across the water. "You're a wonderful nurse, Callie, and people instinctively respond well to you. You were born to it."

His compliment warmed her. She ducked her head. "Thank you."

"Do you think the community would benefit from a full-time doctor?"

Callie jerked her gaze to his profile. "Of course it would. People have to drive clear to Little Rock right now for a doctor's care." She'd never forget overhearing Aunt Vivian tell two grieving women at her parents' funeral, "*Vincent was alive when they found him. If only we could have gotten him to a doctor on time...*" A doctor in Shyler's Point could mean the difference between life and death. "Do you know someone who's interested in beginning a small practice?"

He angled his body toward her, stretching out his hand to her once more. She placed her smaller hand in his, and his warm, strong fingers curl around hers. "I've been thinking of going there myself."

"You?" She shook her head in disbelief. "But why?"

He shrugged. "I need a new start. I need...to be needed. I've been praying about it, and I feel God is pointing me in that direction." He pulled back slightly but kept them connected with their loosely joined fingers. "So what do you think of my establishing a practice in Shyler's Point?"

How wonderful it would be to have a real doctor right in the town. Callie could hardly believe that such a dream might be a reality. But did he fully understand what he would be giving up? "Holden, you'll never have wealth and all of the other things most doctors gain if you come to Shyler's Point. There are no wealthy people there. Sometimes they'll ask to pay you in trade rather than cash. Are you sure you can live with that?"

Holden closed his eyes for a moment, his brow creasing. Callie chewed her lip. Was he rethinking his offer? Then he opened his eyes and sighed. "Callie, I have no desire to acquire things." His voice tightened with emotion. "I stood on the sidewalk outside my beautiful home and watched it burn to the ground. Not once did I consider the things that were burning—our opulent furniture, or the jewelry I'd given Lorna, or the accumulation of bric-a-brac that spoke of wealth and influence. All I wanted from that raging inferno was my wife and my son."

Callie squeezed his hand in what she hoped was a comforting gesture.

He sighed deeply. "No, things don't matter. Not at all. What matters is people. I became a doctor to help people, not to gain wealth. I lost sight of that for awhile, and I'm afraid my greed may have even cost me my family. But being here has reminded me of my original calling. I want to go where I'm needed, and I believe God is directing me to Arkansas." He paused. His forehead pinched into a scowl. "Unless you'd be opposed to my going there."

Opposed? Oh, no, she would dearly love to have him there. But how difficult it would be to have him so close, loving him as she did, and not being a part of his life. He had said once that he wanted her, but he'd never confessed to loving her. Would he even be able to love her the way she loved him? Tears welled again, and she turned her face aside.

He cupped her chin and pulled gently. "What is it, Callie?"

She stared into his eyes. What could she say? Could she be selfish enough to ask him to put aside his memories of his former life and open himself up to loving her? She lowered her gaze to her lap even while his hand still held her chin.

"Callie?"

She couldn't look at him. He'd read the hidden message of her heart, and if he knew he might rethink coming to Shyler's Point. Then the people she loved would continue without a doctor. She couldn't frighten him away with her foolish longings. She remained silent, her eyes averted.

"Callie, look at me."

Reluctantly she lifted her gaze and peered at him through a fringe of lashes. His serious expression held her captive more than the warm hand on her face. "You didn't answer my question. And I need an answer. Because part of the attraction of that little town in Arkansas is a certain joyful redhead who has turned my world upside-down and given me a reason to live again. I hoped that you felt the same way about me. But if not, then—"

Callie pushed his hand aside and scooted backward a few inches. "Holden, do you love me?"

His eyes flew wide, and he released a huff of laughter. "That's just one of the things I love about you—your straightforward honesty." His expression softened. "Oh, yes, Miss Calliope Myers, I do love you. I didn't think I would ever love again, not after losing Lorna. I didn't want to love you. I fought it as fiercely as I fought God's tug on my heart. But it's there, planted deep, and I can't uproot it no matter how hard I try. Nor do I want to anymore." He leaned forward, touching his forehead to hers, and his breath came out in a sigh. "I love you, Callie, from the very depth of my soul."

She held her breath, scarcely able to believe she'd heard him correctly. Unable to speak, she only stared into his eyes. They were so close she could see her own irises reflected in the sapphire depths of his. "Holden, I—"

He placed his finger against her lips. "Before you say anything, you need to know all of the reasons that I turned my back on God. And if it changes your opinion of me, then I will have to accept it." He sat up, but his gaze remained locked on hers. "The day of the fire—the day Lorna and Timmy died—I had chosen to stay at the hospital for an extra shift. I wasn't required to, but I wanted to. Lorna had called and asked me come home. She wanted to spend a quiet evening before Christmas, just us and Timmy. She needed me home to light the candles on the tree, but I put her off. I told her my extra time could earn us an overnight stay in the Congress Hotel where Benny Goodman was performing with a clarinet quintet. I convinced her how much Timmy would enjoy it— he so loved the phonograph, and he giggled with glee when Lorna danced him around the room—but the truth is, I was more interested in being able to brag about spending a weekend in the Congress, as well as being lauded as the most dedicated doctor on staff."

His face clouded, and he swallowed hard. "When I finally headed for home, and I saw the smoke from a distance, I began praying—don't let it be my house. Yet it was. I wanted to go in, to find my family, but the firemen held me back. So I stood on the sidewalk outside my flaming home while the heat seemed to sear right through me, praying, begging God to let my family come out alive. All those miracles in the Bible—Daniel saved from hungry lions, the three young men saved from the furnace, David facing Goliath and emerging victorious... God could save Lorna and Timmy. I knew He could! When He didn't, I decided He wasn't there."

Callie's heart ached for him. She clung to his hands, wishing she could take his hurt away.

"I tried to blame God, but mostly I blamed myself. If I had been there, maybe I could have gotten them out."

"And maybe you couldn't have." She took both of his hands. "Holden, finding blame solves nothing. You don't know what happened in that house that night. And one thing I've learned—focusing on what might have been only creates unhappiness. You've got to let it go."

He squeezed her hands. "I still don't understand why they were taken, why God said no to my prayer. Maybe I never will. But I'm finally able to accept it. I'm ready to move on." He leaned forward, his expression fervent. "And I don't love you as a replacement for Lorna. I love you for yourself. You need to know that, too."

Her chest expanded with joy at his profession of love. She knew how difficult it had been for him to overcome his loss of Lorna, and his words had touched her deeply. Her throat went tight with emotion and she lost the ability to speak.

"Callie, darling, the appropriate response is to reciprocate with a similar statement of devotion, or to inform me that the attraction is strictly one-sided."

There was his formal side again. He must be feeling pressured. She giggled self-consciously and found her voice. "I'd like to reciprocate."

Holden seemed to freeze as if in disbelief. Then his eyes widened and he broke into a huge smile. He erupted with laughter and threw his arms around her. His enthusiastic embrace rolled both of them off the back of the log. They lay on their sides in the dried grass with his arms still wrapped around her. His laughter rolled, and she laughed with him until her sides ached. The pounding surf continued on the other side of the log, competing with their raucous mirth, while the heavy moon shone directly overhead, illuminating the joyful expression on his face.

Their laughter finally faded, and Holden propped himself up on one elbow, toying with a strand of her hair. "What a relief. If I come to Shyler's Point, I'll need a good nurse."

Callie shifted to her bottom and folded her arms over her chest. "Is that why you proclaimed your love for me? You want a nurse?"

He rolled to his feet, pulling her up with him. Then, still holding her hands, he went down on one knee. He brushed his lips against her knuckles, and her heart fluttered like a butterfly taking wing. His eyes sparkled as he gazed intently into her face and spoke the words she never thought she would hear.

"No, my dear, spunky, sweet, silly Callie, I want you to be my wife." He paused, pressing his lips to the back of her hands again. "Calliope Myers, will you marry me?"

She closed her eyes, memorizing the blue-tinted shadows cast by moonlight, the pounding surf roaring in her ears, the strength of his fingers around her hand, the warmth of his lips against her knuckles, the scents of the island filling her nostrils, the blaze of fire in his precious eyes... When she opened her eyes, she found him watching, waiting, an expectant smile lighting his face.

Joy filled her, and she couldn't hold it inside. "Yes, Holden! Yes, yes, yes!"

He stood, sweeping her from her feet and into his arms in one smooth motion. He spun a happy circle, swinging her while she clung to his shoulders and laughed against his neck. The circle slowed, and his lips found hers. She buried her fingers in the thickness of his hair as his kisses ignited a fire inside of her she knew would never be fully quenched.

At last he set her down, keeping his arms looped loosely around her waist. She gazed at him, her arms around his neck, still amazed at the turn her life had taken so abruptly.

Every promise would be kept—to convince Holden of God's reality, to return to Shyler's Point, to marry a Godly man… Everything had fallen into place.

He kissed the end of her nose. "Happy?"

Callie's heart overflowed with gratitude. "Blissfully." She nestled her head against his chest, thrilled that such an action was hers whenever she chose.

"Is there someone I need to ask for your hand in marriage?"

How she wished her father were alive to grant that permission. But she had her aunts, and they would no doubt giggle like teenagers when meeting Holden for the first time. She smirked. "You'll have to convince Aunt Vivian and Aunt Viola that you will provide well for me and will be a Godly influence to our children."

"That doesn't sound too difficult."

"It might be harder than you think." She pulled back slightly and gave him a warning look. "They are very protective, and they love me very much, and they want what is best for me."

His gaze turned tender. "Then we already have something in common." His arms tightened across her back and he rested his head on top of her curls. "Ah, Callie, you've made me so happy. I thank God for bringing me here, to this place and to you."

She closed her eyes again, relishing the feel of his strong arms surrounding her, the steadying comfort of his heartbeat beneath his shirt. *His shirt…* Her eyes popped open and she leaned away, examining the shirt he was wearing. She burst into happy laughter. He wore the stained, awful shirt that was missing one button. She looked up to find him smirking at her. How many men would come dressed in a ragged, soot-stained shirt to deliver a marriage proposal? He couldn't have proven his love to her—or his conviction that people were more important than things—more clearly.

Callie catapulted into his arms. She snuggled against his chest, against the shirt with a gaping hole where a button should be, against the heart of the man God had given to her to love. And she smiled. They'd been plucked from the mud and mire and given a firm place to stand. How glorious to stand on that firm foundation together.

THE END

Acknowledgments

There are many people who contributed to the completion of this story:

Mom and Daddy, whose endless support is something I can always count on. Thank you for being willing to listen, console, or celebrate. You are always there when you're needed—I love you muchly!

Candy Kaline at the Hutchinson Public Library, who gathered information about the hospitals on the island of Oahu. Thanks for your kind and willing assistance. You are appreciated.

Fellow ACFW members—*Carrie, Fay, Gloria, Lisa, and Melody*—who shared their personal knowledge of Oahu. The details on flora and fauna, climate, landscape, and traditional names gave Sinking Sand the realistic details that helped it come to life in my imagination. Thank you.

Beverly and Jill, my first critique partners, your advice and suggestions were invaluable to me as I worked to follow the "rules" yet develop my own voice. Thank you for your patience, your support, and your prayers as the story took shape. You're a blessing!

The many "prayer warriors" who lift my writing ministry before the Father. You know who you are! There is no way to measure the gift of steadfast prayer support. Thank you, and may God bless you as richly as you have blessed me.

My beta readers—*Anastasia Crowley, Catherine DaCosta, Bobbi Graffunder, Lorie Heinrichs, and Joanna Pace*—who checked for typos and inconsistencies for nothing more than my appreciation. You definitely have it.

Finally, and most importantly, thanks be to **God** who planted the seed of desire to put words on paper, who watered the seed and brought it to fruit. In Your word You promise that He who began a good work will be faithful to complete it. Thank You for keeping Your promises. May any praise or glory be reflected directly back to You.

FULL-LENGTH NOVELS BY KIM VOGEL SAWYER

Bringing Maggie Home
Courting Miss Amsel
Echoes of Mercy
Fields of Grace
Grace and the Preacher
Guide Me Home
A Home in Drayton Valley
A Hopeful Heart
In Every Heartbeat
My Heart Remembers
My Soul Sings
A Promise for Spring
Room for Hope
Sinking Sand
Something Borrowed
Song of My Heart
Sweet Sanctuary
Through the Deep Waters
Waiting for Summer's Return
What Once Was Lost
When Hope Blossoms
Where the Heart Leads
Where Willows Grow
A Whisper of Peace

SERIES BY KIM VOGEL SAWYER

Est. 2013

CPSIA information can be obtained
at www.ICGtesting.com
Printed in the USA
LVHW02s1509240118
563843LV00012B/742/P